Books by R. J. Lee

GRAND SLAM MURDERS

PLAYING THE DEVIL

COLD READING MURDER

Published by Kensington Publishing Corp.

Cold Reading Murder

R. J. LEE

KENSINGTON
PUBLISHING CORP.

www.kensingtonbooks.com

KENSINGTON BOOKS are published by

Kensington Publishing Corp.
119 West 40th Street
New York, NY 10018

All Kensington titles, imprints, and distributed lines are available at special quantity discounts for bulk purchases for sales promotion, premiums, fund-raising, educational, or institutional use.

Special book excerpts or customized printings can also be created to fit specific needs. For details, write or phone the office of the Kensington Sales Manager: Kensington Publishing Corp., 119 West 40th Street, New York, NY 10018. Attn. Sales Department. Phone: 1-800-221-2647.

The K logo is a trademark of Kensington Publishing Corp.

ISBN-13: 978-1-4967-3148-7 (ebook)
ISBN-10: 1-4967-3148-4 (ebook)

ISBN-13: 978-1-4967-3147-0
ISBN-10: 1-4967-3147-6
First Kensington Trade Paperback Printing: March 2021

10 9 8 7 6 5 4 3 2 1

Printed in the United States of America

To my beloved Will

CHAPTER 1

She was married at last. It had finally happened just a little over an hour ago on a warm June afternoon in her childhood home perched atop the hill with the big pecan trees looming on either side. Wendy Lyons Winchester was now Wendy Winchester Rierson after a courtship of two years, plus a seven-month-long engagement that seemed like it would never end. Not that she hadn't enjoyed every minute of it, nor the attention and cavalcade of gifts that the higher-profile families of Rosalie, Mississippi, had lavished upon her.

Wendy's father, the sturdy Police Chief Bax Winchester, had spared no expense in giving his one and only daughter away, and she could not help but cherish the sparkle in his eyes as he had walked her down the makeshift aisle in the family parlor. Moments later, Wendy and Detective Ross Rierson had exchanged their original vows in front of a Presbyterian minister, and then the celebration had begun in earnest.

At the moment, Wendy was gazing fondly across the vast expanse of the air-conditioned reception tent that had been pitched out on the lawn to accommodate the extensive guest list. Her father and her new husband in their navy-blue, double-breasted dress uniforms were the objects of her affection; both men having a grand old time with their arms around each other's broad shoulders, while enjoying their liquor and exchanging what were likely ribald jokes of some kind. It was more of that special, police-work bonding that they always had going for them down at the station, and most of the other officers attending had joined up with them now and then and peeled off after they'd had their fill of that precinct camaraderie.

Meanwhile, the towering, three-tiered, Madagascar vanilla bean wedding cake had already been cut into manageable portions and much of it distributed to the crowd after the seated dinner of salmon for some and prime rib for others had come off without a hitch. It was now that time of the reception when the art of mixing drinks with sentimentality had entered the equation, and few were feeling any pain.

To add to the frivolity, another huge contingent of the guests had wandered with gusto into the separate dancing tent next door to step to the trendy rock beat of Mississippi's hottest new four-man group, Bishop Gunn, who would be headlining in October at Rosalie's popular Hot Air Balloon Festival. They were the current favorites of Ross and most of the younger officers who worked alongside him.

There was one of the round tables, however, consisting of five, eclectic-looking people who were doing neither much drinking nor any dancing at the moment. With her luxurious red hair piled high atop her head to crown her elegant bridal coiffure, Wendy finally turned away from the throng of officers and focused instead on her "bridge newbies," as she now referred to them.

Over the past seven months, Wendy's Rosalie Country Club Bridge Bunch had recovered from all the unfavorable publicity generated by the murder of the unscrupulous, insufferable Brent Ogle in the club's hot tub. Wisely, the decision had been made to remove it entirely to avoid lingering, morbid curiosity. The question, "Is that where it happened?" needed to be retired once and for all. As a result, the membership had grown steadily to the point where the original single bridge table had now expanded to six, with two dozen players in the fold. Furthermore, there was this one other table that could only be described as a work in progress.

Separately over that period of time, these five from widely disparate backgrounds had come to Wendy and asked if she might consider the possibility of teaching them the game of bridge. For different reasons, they all said they wanted to learn how to play and play well, but knew next to nothing about it, except that it was an extremely social game and that it might be easier to make friends that way in a Deep South, layered town like Rosalie.

In addition, four of them were newcomers to the city— ranging anywhere from a month or so to five months arrived upon the scene. The exception was Sarah Ann O'Rourke, who was a Rosalie native. Wendy still couldn't quite believe there was this much interest in learning bridge from scratch on the part of that many people within such a short time frame.

The paying job she held down—her nearly two-year stint as the *Rosalie Citizen*'s first full-time investigative reporter— was working out well for her. Her experienced female editor, Lyndell Slover, was pleased with the steady progress she was making in the quality of her work; as an interesting sidebar, her widowed father and Lyndell were also fully enjoying one another's company in every sense of the word on a regular basis.

Would Wendy's mentor also eventually become her mother, in a manner of speaking?

Stranger things had been known to happen, particularly with the social complexities that composed the Deep South.

Wendy had hardly rushed into the decision to teach, however. After all, she'd only been playing the game herself for about two of her twenty-seven years. Was she truly qualified to set others on the path to making successful contracts and winning 500 or 700 rubbers? It had not been all that long ago that she had been in training as a substitute for the much-revered but now very expired Rosalie Bridge Club with its legendary Gin Girls. Finally, Wendy had gathered up her courage and told those five that she would take them under her wing, and they had all seemed ecstatic at the prospect.

Wendy chose her words carefully as she approached their table, fearing she had been neglecting them just a little throughout the busiest afternoon of her life so far. "I sincerely hope you've all been having a wonderful time. I've had to make my manners to so many people here in Rosalie all day, or I would have chatted with you all long before now."

The widowed Charlotte Ruth—whose corny running joke about herself was that her name sounded like a dessert with a lisp—was the first of the five to speak up. "Don't worry about a thing, sweetie. It's just been a spectacular wedding and reception. I've had more than my share of salmon and cake and champagne, I can assure you. I'll have to go on my diet again tomorrow. When you reach my age, you have to watch every calorie, you know."

Wendy was as diplomatic as ever, a trait she had inherited from her late mother, Valerie—the talented acrylic artist and quintessential socialite. "I'm sure that's not true, Charlotte. That's a stunning lavender gown you have on, and you are wearing it to perfection."

"You're too kind," Charlotte said, adjusting her décolletage ever so slightly while tilting her chin upward to tighten the folds of her aging neck. She was clearly under no illusion about her late middle-aged appearance, but one never knew when or where interesting men might show up. Weddings, in fact, were notoriously good venues to meet them, and Charlotte had been more than grateful to receive her invitation from Wendy.

Vance Quimby spoke up next. "I've been getting some wonderful images and bits of dialogue all afternoon. Note-taking seems rude, so you have to shut your eyes and memorize all these joyous scenes and snippets so you won't forget them." If such a thing existed, there was indeed about Vance a suggestion of something "writer-ish," what with his carefully trimmed mustache, receding hairline, and glasses hanging off the end of his nose. "A genuine Rosalie wedding can't be beat for local color, and that's just what I need to bring this Great Southern Novel of mine to life. Thank you so much for including me in your plans today."

"Think nothing of it. We do go all out in this town," Wendy said, making a sweeping gesture that included the entire tent full of chattering people. "And I can assure you that my wedding wasn't even one of the especially big ones. Not by a Mississippi River mile."

Vance's expression indicated he clearly wasn't buying the observation. "I'd like to see a big one if this was an example of small. I've never seen so much attention to detail—all the lovely flowers, especially the gardenias, even the slightly bruised ones—and the elaborate decorations, like these little bits of gold and silver glitter on the tables. It seems nothing was overlooked. Writers like myself aren't worth a hoot unless we get all those fascinating details ironed out just right to bring our plots to life."

"You can thank Party Palooza for that," Wendy continued. "They planned everything, and if they couldn't come up with it themselves, they found somebody who'd work with them, such as Bluff City Caterers. If you ever need to throw a party of any kind while you're here in Rosalie doing your research, they're a one-stop shop, believe me. As a matter of fact, I can introduce you to Merrie and Rex Boudreaux before you leave today. I'm sure they'd be delighted to meet a new customer. They're party prodigies, believe me."

"That would be terrific, Wendy. A party might be just the ticket for me as a break from all this research I've been doing at the courthouse. That, and the thousands of questions I've been asking around town. I guess I've become the town's busiest busybody."

Wendy gave him a gracious smile and said, "This town has inspired many writers. Enjoy your research." But she still had three more of her newbies to fuss over.

Wearing a pink chiffon dress, which seemed more appropriate for a retro, junior-senior prom, Sarah Ann O'Rourke looked every inch the gangly, freckled-faced student who was entering her senior year at the local College of Rosalie. She was studying English because she said writing had always fascinated her, but had no idea what she was going to do with her degree after graduation. She had never actually sat down and written anything—short or long form.

"I just wanted to tell you that your wedding dress is so lovely. It just looks so feminine. And how do you pronounce that style—*emm-pire*?"

Wendy's response was light and carefree. "In France I believe they say *awmm-peer*."

"I would love to have one like yours when I get married. It looks so romantic and Old World."

Wendy moved to her side and gently patted her on the shoulder. "You should plan for it, then. You and your mother should get together whenever the time comes and make it happen. Have exactly what you want on your big day."

Sarah Ann's expression suddenly went sour, followed by silence, and Wendy sensed that the subject of the girl's mother, Dora O'Rourke—whom Wendy had met just once and found to be rather high maintenance—might be one to avoid further, so she signed off with another of her polite smiles.

Aurelia Spangler was seated in the next chair, perhaps the most intriguing of the five pupils whom Wendy would soon be teaching. Her dark eyes, olive skin, and tall frame imparted a sense of mystery to her, making it difficult to discern what her ethnicity might be. Eastern European, perhaps? Italian? Greek? Perhaps a mixture of those?

"I can't help but ask you if you have any predictions for my marriage," Wendy said with a great deal of playfulness. "Any cold readings you just happen to have on hand at the moment?"

Swathed in perhaps the most unconventional of all the outfits present at the wedding—her busy gown featured a myriad of neon-bright swirls running from bodice to hem—Aurelia shook her scarlet scarf-wrapped head slowly. "Not this second, but those will come in time. It's my intention to give every one of you at this table a free cold reading after we've had our first bridge lesson next week. That is, if you want one. Some people prefer not to know things."

"What an interesting idea," Wendy continued, surprised by the comment. "It's not everyone that can say they have a practicing psychic in their bridge club."

Aurelia fingered her shiny, metallic necklace, which caught the lights inside the tent now and then from every possible angle. It seemed as though its mission was to blind people—at least temporarily. "But I don't need a reading to predict how you and your husband will get along. From what I've seen so far, I'm sure you'll make it to wedded bliss without any outside help."

"Now that certainly doesn't need any interpretation," Wendy said, while some of the others around the table tittered. "And I thank you for the happy prediction."

"My pleasure, of course. But you haven't told us yet

where you're going on your honeymoon," Aurelia continued, waving her hand about as if it were a wand.

The enthusiasm level in Wendy's voice fell off just a bit. "As a matter of fact, we're postponing it until sometime this fall. That's the only time we could book this particular cruise to all of the Hawaiian Islands. We wanted to be sure and do it up right. We didn't just want to settle for Diamond Head, Pearl Harbor, and Waikiki Beach—the usual touristy spots, you know. Our cruise takes us to Maui and Kauai, as well as Hilo town on the Big Island. Ross says we're even going to climb right up to the edge of Mauna Kea to top it all off."

"Living on the edge. I've always abided by that, and I love it. It sounds like perfection," Aurelia said. "I wish I were going there. I've only been once, but the islands are so much more laid back than the Mainland. People are so much more in touch with their environment there."

"I haven't been there yet," said Milton Bagdad, the last of the five newbies making up the table. "I love traveling around, even if it's just from door to door."

"And in black tie, no less," Wendy added with a wink as she eyed the handsome young man with the irresistible dimples and mop of curly blond hair.

To be sure, he did cut quite a figure in his tux; but then, as Party Palooza's jack-of-all-trades, it was among his duties to deliver signing telegrams all over Rosalie and the vicinity.

Only when he was off the clock did he get to relax in shorts and sneakers in front of the TV like a regular guy, stretching his legs in his recliner while drinking beer and scrolling on his phone.

Wendy amused herself with the image of Milton ringing doorbells to deliver those delirious telegrams and briefly reflected once again on her table of newbies. She could not possibly have assembled a quirkier group of people if she had summoned them from consulting a Ouija board. They would likely be a challenge to teach, but they also might turn out to be a lot of fun, and she was banking on the latter to help her through it all.

Then she pointed once again to Vance Quimby. "You know what? Before I forget or get tied up with other people, why don't I take you over to meet Merrie and Rex Boudreaux right this second, and the three of you can get started talking about party planning? Milton, you could go with us, too, since you know some of the ropes."

"That I do."

Wendy glanced quickly around the table. "Do any of the rest of you want to come? They really are the best at what they do."

There were no takers among the others, however. "Now, don't any of you leave before we get back," Wendy told the rest. "I insist you three ladies take home a piece of wedding cake to put under your pillows for good luck and sweet, romantic dreams. That's how it's done here in Rosalie, you know."

Wendy thought Merrie and Rex Boudreaux just might be the cleverest couple of entrepreneurs in the world. Or at least in Rosalie. When it came to parties and receptions, they did it all. They could dress up as clowns, cartoon characters, historical figures, or famous actors. They worked wonders with makeup, balloons, party favors, and costumes to entertain children, and they weren't half bad playing corny speaking or singing parts, even though they sometimes fell back on lip-synching to recordings when discretion was the better part of valor.

When quiet, aristocratic elegance for adults was the goal, they pulled off that kind of celebration equally well, and their reputation had grown exponentially since they had come to Rosalie from the New Orleans French Quarter several years ago. The original Party Palooza was down there, too, and it was still being run by Rex's maiden aunt, Mathilde Boudreaux.

At one point, the short, graying, but thoroughly organized little dynamo had encouraged her nephew and his wife to branch out on their own. "I know it's not comfort food like fried chicken or catfish with hush puppies or anything close to that you'll be selling," she had told them together in a pep talk for the ages. "Instead, you'll be selling a different type of comfort that comes with celebrating the milestones of people's lives, and I've proven there's a huge market for it with both my parties and singing telegrams."

She had also done a substantial amount of research for them, suggesting that they move quickly into the vacuum left when Rosalie's loopy grand dame of party planners, Fayette Marie LaFonda, had retired and moved to Arizona with its dry warmth to try to give her eternal asthma the old heave-ho.

"She'd become the Queen of the Cough, as someone in Rosalie said," Mathilde had explained as a footnote.

Fayette Marie had also been socially reserved and all about letting people come to her with her many strings of pearls hanging down over her prominent bosom when they sought advice about their events; but Party Palooza had taken no prisoners with their aggressive advertising in the *Citizen* and on the local broadcast outlets. Thanks to Aunt Mathilde, they knew in advance that there were boatloads of money to be made in a storied old river port like Rosalie, and they had definitely been making the most of it.

At the other end of the tent, where the crowd was far more sparse, Wendy began introducing Vance Quimby to Rex Boudreaux first. "Rex is the brawn behind Party Palooza," she added as the two men shook hands vigorously.

Rex was undoubtedly a hulking specimen of a man, standing six foot five with a forehead that overhung his deep-set, dark eyes like a cliff. He towered over everyone, including nearly all of the many police officers milling around, and his booming voice was always an immediate attention-grabber, if not even somewhat startling at times. His impressive set of even white teeth and full head of dark hair rounded out his mesmerizing appearance. There was even about him a believable echo of the Classic Hollywood leading man. Had he missed his calling?

"We're always happy to meet new clients," Rex said, taking one of his cards out of his tuxedo pocket and handing it over to Vance. "As Wendy may have told you, if we can't stage your party idea, it simply can't be done."

Wendy continued her introductions, pointing to Merrie next, whose smile was as captivating as her husband's was. "And our Merrie here is the raving beauty to Rex's brawn."

Merrie waved her off but managed something close to a giggle. "You flatter me, Wendy." Then she extended a bejeweled hand to Vance, and the two exchanged pleasantries.

If anything, Wendy was reserved in her description. Merrie Boudreaux stood poised before the group in a breathtaking aqua gown—still a stunning woman in her early forties with a beauty mark beneath her right cheekbone and long, dark eyelashes that needed not a hint of mascara to dazzle. They set off the palest of blue eyes, complementing her ivory skin with its pleasing hint of a rosy blush. And then there was her voice—melodious, cultured, measured—it had a reassuring authority about it that drew customers in effortlessly. It seemed to be saying to them, "You can rely on my advice for a successful event. Trust me."

Merrie lost no time in pursuing Vance Quimby as the potential customer he was. "And just what type of party were you thinking of throwing?"

Vance shrugged his shoulders but was hardly at a loss for words. "I have to be honest with you and say that I'm not quite there yet. You see, I've been in Rosalie the last couple of months to do research for this Southern novel I want to write. Haven't even thought up a good title yet. And it won't be the Margaret Mitchell kind of thing, you understand. Something more contemporary, less predictable. No cotton fields back home or anything like that. I'm thinking of trying my hand at something mysterious and Gothic. Meanwhile, I've been getting the lay of the land regarding dialect, the food people eat around here, the pace they prefer—all the little details that make the difference to a writer and the believable universe he has to create. I know next to nothing about the South, you see, since I'm from Omaha, Nebraska. But I do know that you can't write what you don't know anything about—unless you do the research. So, here I am paying my dues. Wendy's even going to teach me some bridge so I can try to interact socially with some of you Rosalieans. Or at least that's the plan."

"What an interesting approach," Merrie said, and then turned to Wendy. "Well, I knew through the grapevine about your success with the Bridge Bunch out at the RCC, but I had no idea you were actually going to start teaching people, too. Maybe I'll even think about taking up the game myself—that is, if I can ever find the time with the breakneck schedule Rex and I keep."

"You'll never have the time for card games, honey," Rex said, shaking his head but maintaining a smile. "We have all we can handle. We're victims of our own success when it comes to leisure activities. I guess you could call us the party planners who never get to party themselves."

Then the kibitzing Milton Bagdad broke in. "They keep me plenty busy, too, Mr. Quimby. People can't seem to get enough of my singing telegrams. A few'll even use any old occasion or excuse for a return engagement for a relative or friend. I think everyone likes to collect the little miniature rag dolls in tuxes and top hats made out of cloth that I leave as a souvenir on every delivery. They're really so cute."

Merrie laughed brightly and pointed toward her husband. "They're the cutest little things ever. They were Rex's aunt Mathilde's idea a while back, and they've been a big winner for us. That, and Milton's professional singing voice. When our previous singer unexpectedly quit on us a few months ago, we didn't think we'd ever find someone who could do the job as well as he could. But our Milton here majored in theater arts down at LSU, and he took us up on this entry-level job. There could be more responsibility and money for him in the future, of course."

Milton closed one eye and managed a wry grin. "Hey, you gotta start somewhere. It's not exactly Broadway or even regional theater, but at least I get to sing and do a little Fred Astaire routine with my cane. I think the element of surprise is what really blows people's minds. I mean, no one ever expects a singing telegram to show up at their house or workplace."

"He's perfectly charming with his moves," Merrie said. "No one else could touch him during the auditions. It's no wonder we sometimes have a repeat customer or two. That's when you really know you're doing things right."

"Maybe one of these days I'll order one up for Ross down at the police station," Wendy added with a wink. "When he least expects it."

Bishop Gunn had played their last set, and the crowd had thinned out considerably in both tents. The event was essentially over, especially since there was no honeymoon getaway to stage with the traditional throwing of rice by a noisy, well-wishing crowd; nor any cans tied to the end of a bumper with tacky soap signs scribbled on the rear window for the bride and groom to endure as they sped away to their future.

Wendy and Ross had been joined at one of the round tables by her father and Lyndell Slover, who had disdained her usual crisp business suit for a romantic, flowing gown in a shade that could best be described as "close to champagne." She had never looked less like the no-nonsense editor she was and more like a woman in the midst of a promising relationship, particularly with the gardenia she had tucked behind her right ear. Billie Holiday could not have worn it better. Wendy had decided that she was fine with it all as long as it made her father happy. He had been a widower now for nearly a dozen long years of healing. Perhaps he really was ready to move on.

"I think it all went well, daughter a' mine," Bax told Wendy as he nursed one last glass of champagne. "Were you pleased with everything?"

"You know perfectly well I was, Daddy," she said while sitting next to Ross, holding his hand.

"You outdid yourself, Bax," Ross added. "And who knew you had such wild moves on the dance floor once your jacket came off?"

Lyndell threw her head back and laughed. "He gave me quite a workout, I'll tell you that."

"All your bridge pals seemed to have a good time, too," Bax said. "I'm not talking about your newbies. They seemed a tad bit nervous, if you ask me. I meant Miz Deedah and her son, Hollis."

Wendy nodded enthusiastically. Deedah and Hollis Hornesby were the other two RCC Bridge members besides herself left from that original table, and both had been anything but restrained while enjoying the afternoon. The director of the RCC had forsaken her usual caftan getup for a simple black gown that had done wonders for her ample figure, while resident acrylic artist Hollis had realized he could not show up for Wendy's wedding in one of his throwback, psychedelic '70s outfits and had actually rented a tux—navy blue with a red cummerbund. Of course, no ordinary tux would do. Never mind that it had given the humorous impression of swallowing up his tall, slender body whole. Both Deedah and Hollis had managed to find a variety of dancing partners and let off some steam while gyrating to the rock music.

"Wonder of wonders," Wendy told Bax out of the side of her mouth. "I finally saw Hollis eating something in public for the first time ever. It seems he couldn't resist a piece of my fantastic wedding cake."

"That was some righteous cake," Ross said. "I hope there's some left for us for later on."

Wendy gave him a playful nudge with her elbow. "Half the bottom tier. We can put it in the freezer to make it last longer. I predict you'll get tired of it soon enough. That much sugar isn't good for you."

Bax finished off his champagne and said, "By the way, who was that woman wearing the opera gloves and the tiara in her enormous hairdo? She spoke with a British accent. She's not really from the UK, is she? She didn't bother to introduce herself and shook my hand in the receiving line as if I was supposed to know who she was. So, do I actually know her?"

Wendy had to restrain her laughter. "No, you don't, Daddy. But you've heard of her. That was Miz Crystal Forrest of Old Concord Manor right here in Rosalie. And, no, she's originally from Al-*benn-y*, Georgia, as she's happy to pronounce correctly for everyone. It's so ironic that she spends so much time on that while simultaneously trying to pretend to everyone that she's seventh- or eighth-generation Rosalian. She just tries way too hard. But she isn't fooling anyone."

The recognition instantly spread across Bax's face. "Ah! The one you call the Queen of the Social Climbers. The wealthy widow who gives a party at the drop of a hat to impress people."

"The very same. Our wonderful Merleece works full-time

for her, cooking and cleaning, except for the one day she reserves to clean for us. What an angel she is."

That one day fell every Tuesday. In the mornings, Merleece Maxique cleaned for Wendy and Ross, and in the afternoons for Bax. Father and daughter had switched houses a month or so before the wedding—with Wendy and Ross moving into her childhood home on the hill and Bax taking up residence in the modest little bungalow out on Lower Kingston Road that he had helped Wendy buy as her college graduation present.

"Merleece looked perfectly lovely today, I thought," Wendy continued. "She was simple and elegant in that gold gown she was wearing, and those big gold earrings just set everything off perfectly. I'll bet it was some sort of African motif. She was positively regal. Miz Crystal could take a few tips from her when it comes to presenting your best face to the world. But can you imagine that—Miz Crystal taking fashion tips from her servant? Rosalie will fall off its two-hundred-foot bluffs into the Mississippi River before that ever happens."

"How is Miz Crystal as a bridge player out at the RCC?" Lyndell asked. "I understand she made a huge donation to make sure she got to play, but I don't want to sound like I'm gossiping."

Wendy's expression was friendly but skeptical. "It wasn't quite like that, though. The donation was to keep the RCC in the black after Brent Ogle was murdered. He'd made no provision in his will for the RCC, as it happens. But Miz Crystal would be a halfway decent player if she'd pay more attention to the cards. She's always pumping people for gossip so she can keep up with the latest. She frequently forgets what trumps are and annoys her partners. Her heart really isn't in the game. She's just there for appearances and fitting in."

"I hope you haven't bitten off more than you can chew

with teaching these bridge lessons," Lyndell continued. "It's not the easiest game in the world to learn. I tried taking lessons once a long time ago, and I lasted about a week. You either get it and love it, or throw your hands up and run screaming from the table from what I've seen and heard."

Wendy paused briefly before finding the right words. "We'll find out what they're all made of this time next week when I start from scratch. But I think my bottom line will be that I will let no man or woman play bridge before their time. They will not end up embarrassing themselves or me on my watch. I figure it'll take me about a month to make them presentable." She then crossed her fingers. "I'm not suspicious, but just about all card games have an element of luck. I may need a little of it myself before this is over."

CHAPTER 2

It had been Wendy's intention to begin bridge lessons in the great room at the Rosalie Country Club, where the six-table Bridge Bunch met every other Saturday afternoon, enjoying hors d'oeuvres along with juleps and other cocktails prepared by Carlos Galbis, the talented barkeep of long-standing. But Aurelia Spangler—dressed in an exotic outfit similar to the one she had worn to the wedding—paid her a visit at the *Citizen* a few days before the first lesson was to take place.

"You know I have this perfectly atmospheric old mansion that I'm renting and rattling around in on the High Bluff," Aurelia began, as the two of them settled into a small interview room away from the maze of gray cubicles in the newsroom.

"Ah, yes, Overview," Wendy said, her brain flooded with unforgettable memories from childhood forward. "We were all told as little bitty things that it was haunted. That the builder had had some terrible accident just before moving in back in 1896, when it was finally completed. Supposedly, he was on a final inspection tour. It's said his ghost wanders up and down the stairs still trying to finish that inspection. But then, I could swear every old Victorian in Rosalie has some sort of tragic or weird story connected to it. Just comes with the territory in this town. Have you tuned in to anything paranormal so far?"

Aurelia seemed suddenly guarded. "I don't know whether I should say anything, but . . . truthfully, I have. I was awakened one night by a strange noise out on the stairs. It was more like a muffled thud of some kind. Was a break-in in progress? So, I got my handgun, which I keep on the nightstand, and went out to the landing immediately, but there was no one there. Of course, my brain was working overtime at that point. Was it the sound in a dream I was having that woke me up, or was it real? Did it have something to do with the builder, J. Lindford Calmes? Is he up to unfinished business? Who knows? I may have a treasure trove of paranormal phenomena at my disposal. If so, it will be worth every penny I'll be spending renting Overview."

Fascinated, Wendy said, "What did you finally decide about the noise? Do you think you have a genuine poltergeist? They say they have them inside King's Tavern on Jefferson Street."

"The verdict's not in yet. It's only happened that once. But it got my attention, believe me."

"So it hasn't made you think twice about renting Overview at all? Some say it's cursed, you know."

Aurelia became most emphatic. "Not really. How could I as a practicing psychic resist taking a house named Overview? It's as if it was tailor-made for me and my profession. Anyway, the point of this visit is to invite you to consider teaching your bridge lessons at Overview instead of out at the RCC. I would sweeten the pot by having plenty of food to nosh on and an open bar in my great parlor with the fourteen-foot ceilings; and then I thought the free cold readings I would offer after our lesson is over would be that much more effective out on the High Bluff overlooking the river. I even believe there'll be a full moon in a few more days for that extra special effect that I don't even have to pay for."

The proposal caught Wendy slightly off guard, but she soon recovered. "Giving your readings a Halloween-esque feel, you mean?"

"If you want to think of it that way, then yes. But I take my craft seriously, you know. I started getting these psychic flashes when I was just a little girl growing up in Brooklyn. I knew then that I was different from my friends, even though my neighborhood was practically like the United Nations. We had lots of Italian, Irish, and Jewish families everywhere. We all fit the definition of diversity before it was even cool to worry about it."

"I'm sure your life is very different from most people even now," Wendy said, trying to sound as measured as possible.

"You could always go back to the RCC if things didn't work out to your satisfaction at Overview," Aurelia continued with a gracious smile plastered on her face. "I certainly don't want to appear to be forcing your hand, but I can definitely vouch for my skills as a hostess."

Wendy had had some time now to mull over Aurelia's presence within a group that was already far from ordinary. She knew quite well that the woman wanted to use playing bridge as a platform for making social contacts with the sort of people who might come to her for a cold reading and then recommend her to their friends. Her reputation would then spread by word of mouth. More than anything else, it was a business calculation. It had seemed straightforward enough on the surface at first, but something had begun nagging at Wendy all the same. She had been meaning to discuss the matter in greater detail with Ross, but somehow she had let the matter slip, and then his schedule had been all over the map lately.

Now, not only would Aurelia be providing free readings

to the group, but they would take place at Overview, if Wendy decided to accept the change of venue. It seemed slightly theatrical, and the element of control and familiarity that the RCC would provide would vanish into *thin air*. Those last two words gave Wendy pause: Weird imagery was starting to pop into her head. What was that about?

Then, there was this: If Aurelia Spangler were not a genuine psychic but something on the order of a con artist or circus sideshow, would it truly be the proper thing to aid and abet her in any way? Should Wendy avoid the enabling and say, "Thanks, but no thanks," to it all and let Aurelia work things out in Rosalie on her own? Wouldn't that be the more prudent thing to do?

In the end, however, something about Aurelia's serene gaze decided the matter. Or was it more like a spell cast? After telling her that they were on for Overview and Aurelia had flitted off in dramatic fashion, Wendy sat back and reflected further. She decided she was being ridiculous to worry about the whole affair. She would be in control of the bridge lessons no matter where they were taught, and what harm could a handful of free cold readings possibly do in the larger scheme of things?

That evening, Wendy and Ross were sitting in their pajamas at their kitchen table indulging in some of their thawed-out, leftover wedding cake. Off and on, the refrigerator was making its usual, turkey-gobble noises, which the appliance repairman had insisted were nothing to be concerned about and could be safely ignored. It was still cooling and freezing everything just fine, thank you. But Wendy had decided she could no longer ignore her decision to teach lessons out at Overview instead of at the RCC. Ross hardly seemed surprised at the revelation when she finally told him.

"If you want my take, I think the invitation was just part

of the woman's act," he said, after wiping some frosting off his upper lip. "You have to admit that Overview will be quite a spectacular setting up there on the High Bluff. She's not charging admission this time, but that's obviously her end game."

Wendy nodded but did not seem satisfied. "It does seem like an act, doesn't it? Are there statistics on what percentage of psychics are the real deal? You haven't run across something like that in your career so far, have you?"

Ross sat up straighter in his chair, looking somewhat amused. "Afraid not. But there is such a thing as the Barnum effect. Any detective worth his salt knows about that."

"I'm not quite sure what it is. Please explain," she said, frowning.

"It's the way some of these people operate to convince their clients that they really do have these special insights, and other senses are at work that are worth paying for. They throw out these vague questions, and the marks, if you want to call them that, end up providing the answers without realizing it. For instance, a so-called psychic could say that they are suddenly getting an impression of someone in the family going through a crisis of some sort. Well, the chances are excellent that someone in most families of any size is going through a crisis at any given time. Just human nature, and the psychic is just playing the odds with that. Then the mark starts volunteering the actual crisis information, and the cold reading, so to speak, falls right into place as legit. At that point, the psychic has won the confidence aspect of the game, and the battle is over. There's your satisfied customer willing to recommend her to friends."

Wendy considered in silence. "So, when you say the Barnum effect, you're invoking P. T. Barnum, as in 'there's one born every minute'?"

Ross snickered. "Bingo. Pass Go. Collect your two hundred dollars."

Wendy carefully scraped up the last morsel of her cake with her fork and let the sugar high linger. Predictably, it brought forth more questions. "Do you think there's such a thing as an honest-to-goodness psychic, though? Are there really people out there with these gifts that no one can explain away?"

"All I can tell you for certain is that there have been a few that have helped police departments here and there across the country locate missing persons and turn up clues to murders and other crimes like that," Ross added. "That's a fact, even though no one can explain it. So, let me admit to that up front. But as to whether this Aurelia Spangler is one of those with a gift, I have no way of knowing right now. At any rate, your job is just to teach her and the rest of 'em the basics of bridge. After that, what happens, happens."

Ross paused and ran his tongue across his lips. "I'm thirsty. I'm gonna get some milk. You want some, too, sweetheart?"

Wendy said she did and then watched her husband fill two small tumblers for them. Her first generous swig of the ice-cold liquid was exactly what she needed to clear her sugar-coated throat. She was also feeling better about the venue switch now. Ross had helped ground her with his comments, and she saw no reason to give the matter any further thought. Perhaps it would all turn out like a Halloween fun house and make her bridge lessons just that much more memorable and enjoyable. Was there really any reason to think anything else?

It was said that the builder of Overview—a successful, but fierce-looking, mutton-chopped, wholesale grocer named J. Lindford Calmes—had accidentally fallen down the second-floor staircase to his death one week before moving in during the summer of 1896. What an unfortunate tragedy. The tumble had snapped his neck cleanly, and the man never knew what hit him. Despite the coroner's report that there was no foul play involved, there were those who insisted that someone—presumably an opportunistic relative—had pushed him in order to inherit all his money and the house besides, but nothing had ever been proved. No one had ever been accused of anything. Nonetheless, Overview had always had clouds of suspicion hanging over it, as well as a succession of owners who had never been happy living there. Something always seemed to go drastically wrong for them, and they all ended up moving away not only from the house but from Rosalie, itself, for various reasons. It wasn't so much that Overview was haunted as that it seemed cursed with bad luck for its various owners—financially or otherwise.

Yet it continued to hold a morbid fascination for Rosalieans, frowning down as it did on the river below from its perch on the three-hundred-foot High Bluff. It was supposedly near that very spot that the French had first planted their flag in the early part of the eighteenth century. In the millennium now, a series of white Corinthian columns positioned across a sprawling veranda gave the house a commanding view that was unequaled up and down the entire length of the Mississippi from its source in Minnesota to the mouth in Louisiana. No wonder Aurelia Spangler had chosen to be the latest to try her hand at soaking up those cinematic sunsets with a bottle of good wine in hand. It was said that there were no more beautiful sunsets in the entire United States of America than on the formidable bluffs of Rosalie. The rich streaks of pink and gold were said to be heaven-sent, giving those below a glimpse of what believers thought lay ahead of them.

Finally, the evening of the first bridge lesson had arrived. It was just a little after seven o'clock that the last of the five newbies—Sarah Ann O'Rourke wearing blue jeans and a short-sleeved blouse—was greeted in the foyer by Wendy and Aurelia together. Wendy was pleased to see that everyone had taken her suggestion and dressed on the casual side—the exception being Aurelia in one of her floor-length, kaleidoscope creations; the last thing Wendy wanted was the pressure and pretension that formal wear sometimes added to any event. She was going to be teaching them the game of bridge, not ballroom dancing.

The high-ceilinged parlor, itself, was decorated throughout with pink and purple crêpe myrtle clippings—Rosalie's prolific summertime, street tree blooms—in an assortment of antique vases; off to one side near an enormous Victorian bay window was a Chinese cloisonne sideboard groaning with ceramic bowls filled with nuts, crudités, dips, crackers, sliced fruits, and dark chocolate chips for snacking. There were also wineglasses and tumblers, an ice bucket with tongs, and a generous selection of liquor and mixers on a neighboring table, though Aurelia had chosen not to employ a bartender for the occasion. Finally, the aroma of incense further lifted the parlor's ambience out of the ordinary into the exotic.

"I thought I'd let everyone serve themselves as they pleased," Aurelia told the gathering once they were all assembled before her generous offerings. "Wendy has also asked that you take care not to spill things on the cards once we get started, though."

"But please don't get obsessed to the point you don't enjoy yourselves," Wendy added, trying to inject a note of levity. At the moment, she thought Aurelia was overdoing it a bit in the meticulous department. Exerting control seemed uppermost among her priorities. "It's not like the decks are made of gold. They're just ordinary Bicycle cards. And please turn off your cell phones so we don't have any distractions that way. I can't believe people have to be reminded of that all the time, but since phones keep going off even in places like theaters and churches, I feel obliged to mention it."

After a bit of congenial snacking and sipping, everyone eventually took a seat at the circular dining table in the center of the room, and the group's introduction to bridge began in earnest. Wendy had dealt each pupil an opening hand of thirteen cards using several decks to illustrate point count.

"Each ace counts four points," she said as she slowly moved around the table. "Each king counts three; each queen, two; and each jack, one point. You need thirteen or fourteen total points to make an opening bid when it's your turn. The dealer bids first, if he or she can. Then the auction, as it is called, proceeds around the table clockwise. There are four people seated at each table, playing in teams of two. You and your partner will try to win the auction by outbidding the opposition and securing the final contract. Thus, the name contract bridge. There are thirteen tricks to every round, and every bid will consist of six tricks called a book, and anywhere from one trick to seven tricks over that. Four tricks over a book in major suits is a game, whereas it takes five over a book in minor suits. Six over is a small slam, no matter the suit, and seven over is a grand slam, the highest contract it's possible to make. It's rare to see it made too often, but it does happen from time to time, particularly among the best players. It is, of course, the gold standard."

Everyone seemed to catch on to the fundamentals quickly, although Sarah Ann made a fuss about the ranking of the suits. "I mean . . . why are the clubs the lowest suit and spades the highest? Umm . . . why aren't they all equal?"

Here, Wendy sensed she needed to tread carefully and relied upon the most soothing, bedtime-story tone she could manage. "We don't know when, where, and by whom, but it seems that long ago in a magical land unknown, it was decided that the ranking of the suits from lowest to highest would be clubs, diamonds, hearts, and spades. Since then, it's been pretty much a reality that there's no equal opportunity in almost all card games. The element of luck figures in prominently."

Sarah Ann nevertheless pressed on. "So you're saying it was just an arbitrary decision?"

"That's as good an answer as any I can give you. But as far as bridge is concerned, it's not worth dwelling on. It is what it is and can't be changed. We need to move on."

"Well, I just question everything. You have to understand that about me. It—well, it drives my mother crazy. We get into arguments all the time."

Wendy felt herself losing control slightly, so she flashed Sarah Ann a smile and then quickly focused on the types of opening bids it was possible to make. "Sorry to hear that, but if you have a choice of bidding one of the major suits—the hearts or spades—over the minor suits, you'll want to do that. Tricks are worth more in the major suits—twenty points per trick in the minors versus thirty points in the majors, and you can get to a game of one hundred just that much faster. Let's pause a moment to take that in, shall we?"

Wendy had decided beforehand that she should not try to cover too much ground this first time out. It would be counterproductive to make bridge seem more daunting than it actually was, especially if anyone overindulged in cocktails and developed a bad case of muddled brain cells. So she had her five newbies practice bidding various hands she dealt out to them. After a short time, they all seemed to be getting the hang of it, although Aurelia and Vance turned out to be more successful at it than the other three, but every one of them made plausible bids at least twice. After a productive hour had passed, Wendy brought the first lesson to a close.

"Next week, we'll discuss the requirements for a no-trump bid versus the suit bid, and the strengths and weaknesses of both types. Playing a no-trump game is an entirely different creature and requires a bit more planning and patience, or you'll end up running your game off the rails. A no-trump bid also outranks all four suits and literally means that there are no-trumps when the game is played. The higher cards in all suits are the ones you want to have."

Then Aurelia rose from the table, thanked Wendy, and pointed to a door just off the parlor. She made quite the to-do about it, moving her fingers as if sprinkling something magic but invisible there at the finish.

"In there is my cold reading room. I would like to invite each of you to take advantage of my gifts free of charge just for the fun of it. Of course, if you'd rather not, I'll understand that completely. Over the years, I've found that psychic readings just aren't everyone's cup of tea. But a reminder—please keep those cell phones turned off. One of those crazy ringtones in the middle of a reading could pull my focus and ruin everything. And I mean crazy literally. I was interrupted once by a client whose phone played Patsy Cline singing 'Crazy.'"

"Oh, I just love her music," Sarah Ann said, clasping her hands together. "The crossover artist of all time."

"We're getting off the subject a bit, though," Aurelia said, slightly annoyed. "I'm ready to do my readings now."

"If you ladies and Milton don't mind," Vance said, popping up, "I'd like to go in first.

As long as I'm down here in Rosalie doing all this research, I think I should be game for just about everything. After all, this is a pretty quirky little town, so why not indulge in a cold reading? I've had a thing about volunteering, and I've always made a great guinea pig besides."

Wendy and the others had no objections and watched Vance follow Aurelia eagerly through the door and into her room. There was about it all the suggestion of a puppy wagging its tail as it obeyed its master. Was Aurelia Spangler truly capable of casting spells in such a manner? The more rational lobes of Wendy's brain brought that train of thought to a screeching halt.

"I've decided I'm going to wait and see what Vance says when he comes out before I make my decision to participate or not," Charlotte said. "Right now, I'm pretty much on the fence."

"Well, I do like to question things, but I'm not undecided at all," Sarah Ann said. "I mean, what could it hurt? She'll either be spot-on or way off base, the way I figure it."

No matter what, Wendy had already made up her mind to take a reading with Aurelia. When she got home, she could share the experience with Ross and see what he had to say. One thing was for certain—her first bridge lesson had gone well enough, and she felt she now had five apt pupils on her hands. Perhaps this was going to be a piece of cake, and she had worried needlessly about the outcome.

CHAPTER 3

Vance Quimby emerged from Aurelia's cold reading room about ten minutes later with a look of astonishment frozen on his face. He barely seemed able to blink. Aurelia followed close behind with an expression of supreme satisfaction, and it was she who spoke up first.

"I'm quite pleased to announce that Mr. Quimby has told me he wants to share his reading with the rest of you, haven't you?" She made a delicate, sweeping gesture as if blessing the entire room.

Vance turned and shot her a brief glance, then approached the others. "I did say I wanted to do that. It's just too incredible not to share. Mainly because I just can't believe she knew what she knew. I simply wasn't prepared to hear what I heard because I'll be the first to admit that I really didn't think I would be taking anything seriously. I intended to play the role of the amused skeptic all the way."

"Then by all means, share it with us," Charlotte said, beckoning him with her hands. "I've already told the others that I would wait for your reaction before I bought into any of this."

Vance took his seat at the table again and began as everyone gave him their undivided attention. Wendy noted with a slight sense of envy that none of them had been quite that focused throughout the bridge lesson. "Aurelia took my hand, and after a little while, she said that she clearly saw this vision of a service dog of some kind—you know, the type that helps the blind or with other disabilities and—"

"It was a German shepherd, as I recall," Aurelia interrupted with a gracious smile.

Vance nodded and continued. "Yes, it was definitely a German shepherd. Anyway, it was on a leash sniffing around a dark, back alleyway, where the body of a dead female tourist guide was eventually found in a Dumpster." He turned quickly toward Aurelia as if looking for guidance. "You also said you were certain that I was somehow involved in the entire affair. Of course, I nearly fell out of my chair when you said that. I was speechless."

"Wait . . . what?" Charlotte said, her voice somewhat breathless, and there were gasps from some of the others. "What did all that mean? Did you have something to do with the death of a tourist guide here in Rosalie? You don't mean to tell me that we are in the presence of a murderer?"

Vance took his time, taking a swig of the bourbon on the rocks he had left behind. "No, certainly not. I'm nothing of the kind. What she said she saw . . . well, it's remarkable because I can vouch for the fact that it never happened. At least, not that I know of."

"I'm totally confused," Charlotte continued, shrugging her shoulders. "Why are you so impressed with the reading if you're sure it never happened? Suddenly, I'm not understanding the English you're speaking. I know you're a writer, but I just don't get it."

"Well, I'm afraid I don't, either," Wendy added, exchanging puzzled looks with the others.

Milton quickly joined in. "I'll third that notion."

"Just give me another moment," Vance said, finishing off his drink and letting the bourbon course through his veins a bit, evidently for courage. "What Aurelia said she saw was in reality the germ of the plot I'm busy concocting for the novel I'll start writing soon. It's going to be a murder mystery that takes place in the Deep South. I've shared nothing of the ideas I'm hatching with anyone so far. So, there it is, folks. How could she possibly know anything about what I haven't even written yet? It's all still locked up in my brain, but somehow she found a way to get at it. I have goose bumps just thinking about the whole thing."

Aurelia bowed her head slightly, trying for a hint of modesty. "To be honest, that was all I could come up with. I don't know what happened to the tour guide—if anything really did—or who did it or anything like that."

"That's because I haven't plotted much further than that. But wasn't what you did see enough?" Vance said. "Vague generalities were more along the lines of what I was expecting to hear from you. Now I feel like you've drilled into my skull and yanked out my brain."

"That's quite a graphic image, but I report only what I see," Aurelia continued. "Nothing more, nothing less. As I told Wendy when we first discussed my offer to the group, this is not a game with me. I know there are much simpler ways to make a decent living, but it seems I'm stuck with this."

"I'd like to go next, if no one minds," Charlotte said, her voice brimming with excitement. "Except I can tell you right now that I'm not making any shocking things up in my head like Mr. Quimby. My life in recent years has been real enough without anything like that."

Aurelia again pointed to the door. "This way, then."

★　★　★

When Charlotte emerged from her session not too long after, she seemed no less stunned than Vance Quimby had been. Unlike Vance, however, she said nothing to the others. Instead, she made straight for the bar and quickly mixed herself a scotch and soda. Previously, she had nursed a glass of white wine but obviously needed something stronger now.

Wendy turned to Aurelia and said, "Is she okay?"

"I'm afraid I was a bit too on the nose for her," Aurelia said. "That sometimes happens. As I told all of you, I hold nothing back in my readings. It comes with the territory."

Charlotte took a big swallow of her drink. "Some bad memories got dredged up, that's all."

"I'm truly sorry if you're upset," Aurelia added. "But I assume you wanted me to tell you the truth."

"And you did," Charlotte said, the liquor calming her down somewhat. "I suppose I should have expected it since you were so accurate with Vance."

"She's two for two apparently," Vance said. "That's pretty remarkable, if you ask me."

Sarah Ann excitedly caught his gaze and then focused on Aurelia. "Well . . . I guess I'd like to be next and you can try to make it three for three."

Aurelia's tone became solicitous. "Are you certain? I'd like to emphasize again that it's not my mission to upset people. I've had people tell me that they're jealous of my gifts, but they can also be a burden to carry around, believe me. There are times when I wish I could look people in the face and not know a thing about them other than what they tell me."

But Sarah Ann just shrugged. "Don't worry about it in the least. My mother and I get into it all the time."

Once Aurelia and Sarah Ann had disappeared to begin their session, Charlotte decided to open up to the others, even though none of them had pressed her. Perhaps it was the liquor at work. "About my reading—it's just that I haven't discussed this subject with anyone since I moved to Rosalie a few months ago, yet somehow Aurelia knew what had happened."

"I hope you understand that you don't have to explain anything to us if you don't want to," Wendy said. "These are private matters." Then she turned toward Vance. "The same applied to you, of course. You didn't have to tell us anything about the plot of your novel or what Aurelia said."

"I realize that," he said, sounding very upbeat. "But these things don't happen every day, you know. It's probably just the writer in me that couldn't help but blurt it out to all of you. It's not business as usual."

Charlotte took another sip of her drink, and that seemed to strengthen her resolve further. "He's right, of course. Perhaps it's better if I just get it off my chest finally." She took a deep breath and then continued. "The reading concerned my late husband. I've told people that I'm a widow, which is true enough. But unfortunately, I did not lose Jimmy Ruth to natural causes. I expected us to be together for many more years. He committed suicide on me a few years back—swallowed too many sleeping pills, and it was no accident. He'd known his correct dosage for years. It's taken me a while to get over it, and I'm still not there. Moving to Rosalie was my attempt to try and truly make a fresh start. The point is that very few people know about my husband's suicide, but somehow Aurelia did, and it really caught me off guard."

Wendy was the first to say it, gently rubbing Charlotte's arm. "I'm sure we're all so sorry for your loss."

The others made sympathetic noises, and Charlotte said, "Thank you all for your concern. Aurelia said the same thing to me after her words came out. I suppose Jimmy's suicide had to see the light of day sooner or later. You'd think it was my fault the way I've been acting about it all this time. I keep thinking that maybe there was something I could have done to prevent it from happening. Who knew he was that depressed? Do we ever really know what's going on deep inside the people we love? I try not to beat myself up, but there it is."

An uneasy silence fell over the group as they exchanged bewildered glances, but Wendy finally broke through. "Grief is one of the most difficult things in life to deal with. I know what I'm talking about. When I lost my mother to pneumonia when I was only fifteen, I thought my world had come to an end. I couldn't see tomorrow coming. All the juvenile concerns of high school seemed ridiculously unimportant to me at that point, and the friends I had faded away. None of them knew what to do or say to me, and I withdrew from them anyway. High school and death just weren't meant to go together. Dying is supposed to be for much later on in life. Fortunately, my father helped me get through it all. So please don't beat yourself up, Charlotte. Cut yourself all the slack you need."

"Believe me, I'm trying. That's the main reason I decided to take up bridge. I'd heard it was a great way to meet new people."

"And you have already," Vance said, pointing to himself with a smirk on his face. For a split second, it appeared that he might even be hitting on her. "No telling how much we'll end up knowing about each other by the time we become bridge experts, right, Wendy?"

There was welcome laughter all around, and Wendy said, "I certainly hope that's the end result. We're all pretty chummy in the Bridge Bunch out at the RCC, where you'll eventually be playing if I'm any kind of bridge instructor."

"How long do you think that'll be?" Charlotte said. Her mood and tone of voice had finally returned to normal.

Wendy gently patted her shoulder. "I'll know when all of you are ready. As I told you, I'll ease you in so you won't be overwhelmed."

Sarah Ann sounded not the least bit disturbed when she returned from her cold reading. "I'm happy to report that Aurelia is three for three," she began, making the peace sign above her head. "She absolutely nailed it, and I have no doubts whatsoever about her gifts."

Aurelia tried to sound self-deprecating but missed the mark. "Maybe I'm on a roll, but I don't know. I can have my off days."

"Are you going to share with us, Sarah Ann?" Charlotte said. "As Wendy said, you don't have to. Maybe I shouldn't have."

Sarah Ann emphatically pointed her index finger at the ceiling. There was a quality of strength in her voice that hadn't been there before. Had that been a perk of her cold reading?

"Gladly. It's not that complicated. Aurelia told me she saw this image of a Bible being thrown to the floor by someone in a fit of anger. She said she could hear the loud thud clearly and saw a cloud of thick dust rising up, and I made sense of all that immediately. My mother and I have been arguing a blue streak these past few months about my wanting to stop going to church with her—even leaving the church entirely. She practically has a stroke every time I bring it up. What it comes down to is I've told her that I want to start thinking for myself and not take all these passages in the Bible literally the way she does. She applies them to everything that happens in today's changing world, and I've told her that I think it's irrelevant. We are not living thousands of years ago. She insists that some things about faith are timeless, though, and she gets very angry with people who disagree with her."

"Religion can be a touchy subject," Charlotte said. "I've

found it best to avoid discussing it with most people over the years. It's a trigger for certain types. My older sister is still not speaking to me because I stopped going to church altogether. Meanwhile, she goes several times a week. She says, 'Just to make sure,' whatever that's supposed to mean. She's a good person, but she acts like she's some sort of monster unless she shows up in church."

"There's much more to it than attendance, as far as I'm concerned," Sarah Ann continued in a lecturing mode. "My belief is that too many people use their religious beliefs to hurt rather than help others, and I don't think that's right. Mother's from a different generation, and she says that we have to abide by everything in the Bible or else face these dire consequences at the end. So when Aurelia said she saw an image of someone slamming down a Bible, I interpreted that to be me in opposition to my mother's views. I didn't even have to think twice."

"Do many people know about this debate going on between you and your mother?" Charlotte said.

"We've kept it mostly private. We don't air the family's dirty laundry as a rule. That's why I was so impressed when Aurelia brought it all up. How, indeed, did she know about it?"

"If I were you," Charlotte continued, "I might think twice before telling your mother about discussing all of that with Aurelia at length. She could lose it."

Sarah Ann dismissed the comment with a cavalier wave of her hand. "It's way too late for that, I'm afraid. Mother already disapproves of my taking up card-playing, if you can believe it, and when I told her about Aurelia being a psychic, she hit the roof. 'That kind of thing is the work of the Devil,' she said. 'It will only lead you further astray, and I cannot be responsible for what happens to you.'"

Aurelia addressed the entire group, sounding not the least bit defensive. "It's not my place to come between mother and daughter, you understand, but I think Sarah Ann must assert herself if she is going to live her own life the way she wants. We're all on our different journeys."

Sarah Ann nodded emphatically. "Exactly. As far as Mother is concerned, I've already hurled myself off a huge cliff and can hardly be saved. Things couldn't be any worse between us. Frankly, I don't think learning how to play bridge and going to a psychic make me a bad person, but she does."

Then Milton Bagdad, who had been taking everything in mostly in silence, stepped up. He could not have sounded more eager and childlike. "I wonder what you have in store for me, Miz Aurelia? I'd like to be next, if you don't mind."

"Of course. But please—call me, Aurelia, like everybody else does."

"You got it," he said, as the two of them headed toward the reading room.

The oddest thing about the behavior of both Milton and Aurelia when they emerged from his session ten minutes or so later was that they both appeared to be under the influence of something. Was it alcohol, or was it a drug of some kind? Had they indulged inside the room? Or was there something else in play entirely? Milton staggered slightly as he led the way, and Aurelia's signature poise and knack for gliding effortlessly across the floor seemed to have abandoned her completely. Her movements were suddenly awkward and choppy. It also seemed that gravity had done its best to pull their facial muscles downward in an exaggerated manner that defied description.

"What on earth is wrong?" Wendy said, although everyone else was surely thinking the same thing.

Milton seemed unable to speak, and Aurelia shook her head slowly. "I'm sorry to have to say so, but I think what was discussed in the room needs to be left private between the two of us. That's ordinarily the case in my practice, but some of you have chosen to open up with the others."

Milton agreed quickly with a nod of his head, and then as a couple of the others had done, he, too, resorted to the bar to steady himself.

"Sometimes, these readings can be overwhelming, often when you least expect them to be," Aurelia added. "At other times, some sense can be made of them, but this is not one of those cases."

The words had a foreboding, almost numbing effect on Wendy at first. She wondered if she should just tell Aurelia to skip doing a cold reading for her and call it quits for the evening. Then, something Ross had said to her earlier in the week bubbled up again. He had explained the Barnum effect to her and that some things that psychics did or said just might be part of the act, done entirely for effect. Wendy did not, however, bring any of that up to Aurelia. Instead, she thought better of her misgivings and said, "I'll take you at your word, then. But do you think you have enough left for one last reading? I think I'd definitely like to take my turn."

Aurelia seemed to recover her composure somewhat. "Of course. I've rarely conducted this much business in one evening over the years, but I'm quite sure I can wind things up with you, Wendy."

The word *conducted* stuck in Wendy's head for some reason, but she did not think she had consciously brought it forth.

Moments later, Wendy found herself sitting directly across from Aurelia at a small table covered with white lace. There was no crystal ball, nor any tarot cards and traditional props of that kind. The room, itself, was very small, with the walls painted a bright red, suggesting a warmth that did not exist within it. Instead, it felt uncomfortably cold. Two large potted palms flanked the table, and a few of the more mature fronds stretched toward the high ceiling as if trying to touch it.

The first thing Aurelia did was to take Wendy's right hand in hers. She held it there loosely for a while. "Please look into my eyes quietly," Aurelia said. "But don't forget to blink. This isn't a staring contest."

The comment made Wendy chuckle as she began to do as she was told. A minute or two passed. Wendy tried her best to keep her mind blank, even though from time to time she could hear snippets of the muffled conversation of the others out in the parlor. If this was all about reading minds, then perhaps she should try and make it as difficult on Aurelia as she could. But she soon discovered that it was somewhat of a chore to keep her mind completely unoccupied. She realized that she had never even tried it before. There had never been a time that she could recall when there hadn't been at least something she was thinking about in there, however trivial it might be.

Words, phrases, and images now kept popping up randomly. It was almost dizzying.

Was someone conducting this symphony of distractions? There was that word again—a variation of *conducted*.

A service dog on a leash . . .

That bewildered expression on Milton Bagdad's face . . .

The Barnum effect . . .

J. Lindford Calmes falling down the stairs and breaking his neck . . .

Waking to thudding noises in the millennium . . .

Overview . . .

An overdose of sleeping pills . . .

A dead tour guide in a Dumpster . . .

The Bible thrown to the floor . . .

Honeymoon in Hawaii . . .

That last image completely undid her as her pulse quickened. She was suddenly with Ross lying on a beach somewhere on one of the islands, and he was kissing her fervently. She sensed that there were trade winds blowing against her face, and overhead all she could see were palm trees decorating the blue sky.

"My mother could have painted this," she heard herself saying inside her head. Was Aurelia causing all this?

Then her reverie was halted abruptly when Aurelia said, "Pieces of a puzzle floating in a river."

Wendy came to. "What?"

"I see a wide river in pieces, if such a thing is possible. Does that make any sense to you?"

Immediately, Wendy's beloved mother—Valerie Lyons Winchester—again flashed into her head, filling it to capacity. There was suddenly no room for anything else. Her mother, the promising acrylic artist who had been taken from Bax and Wendy Winchester at such an early age by pneumonia, who had done studies of the Mississippi River with moonlight reflected in the current, then with the bright sun shining down in the same manner. That, at least, was Wendy's interpretation of what she had just heard from Aurelia. Still, Ross's cautionary comments about the methods of psychics dampened her reaction somewhat. Something kept telling her not to go overboard with her reactions as most of the others had.

"I have to admit that I loved putting jigsaw puzzles together growing up. I would often help my parents find the pieces that kept eluding them. Sometimes, all it takes is a fresh eye."

"I often say that about myself," Aurelia added. "I can see things others can't. It's been both a blessing and a curse."

"Offhand, I'd say that some things are merely a matter of detecting patterns in shapes and sizes."

Aurelia seemed restrained by the comment, looking far from mysterious. "That would be one way of explaining it. Perhaps more scientific than anything else."

Wendy decided to press on. "Do you see anything else that might be of interest to me?"

Aurelia remained silent for a while. Then came the one word, "Walls."

"What about them?"

"I now see patterns on the walls. They're your walls."

Wendy continued to pull back mentally. It would not be unreasonable to assume that as Valerie Lyons Winchester's daughter, she would have some of her mother's paintings on display on the walls of the home she now shared with Ross. "I have lots of things on my walls. Most people do."

Wendy's skepticism seemed to deflate Aurelia somewhat, and she withdrew her hand.

"I think that's all I can see at this time."

Thus, the last of the five cold readings came to an end on a somewhat insipid note, and soon everyone was saying their goodbyes out in the parlor. Wendy reminded them all of the time change in next week's lesson.

"It's being moved from seven to seven thirty due to some other business I have to take care of out at the RCC."

"Before you all leave, though," Aurelia said, "I have an important announcement to make." She focused particularly on Wendy as she spoke to the group. "If you don't mind, I think we'd better meet at the RCC instead of here from now on," she said. "I've given out all the free samples I'm going to give here at Overview, and I think the RCC will be the better environment in the long run. Let's just go back to the original plan, shall we?"

Wendy was tempted to debate the issue for a split second but then thought better of it. "If that's what you want, it's fine with me."

To some extent, Wendy was relieved. She had been skeptical from the beginning about teaching at Overview, and now she was more than willing to let Aurelia put the issue to bed once and for all. Yet, there remained something about the way Aurelia had been willing to dump Overview so quickly that didn't seem quite right, just as her expression and demeanor after Milton Bagdad's reading had seemed strangely off balance. At the moment, the investigative reporter in Wendy would have given almost anything to know what was going on inside Aurelia's head.

Wendy was finishing up her impressions of all the cold readings with Ross as they sat on the long beige living room sofa, facing the wall dotted with her mother's Mississippi River paintings. They had split a dozen hot tamales from Fat Mama's on South Canal Street for dinner, washing them down with a couple of ice-cold beers from the Rosalie Brewery, and she had already recounted her successful bridge lesson as well. Then, as Wendy had guessed he might, Ross found Vance's astonishment at the revelation of his plot elements the most compelling of the group to address.

"That's the one that seems the most far-fetched to me," he said. "How do you steal a plot out of someone's brain? How do you raid brain cells? It reminds me of Dr. Frankenstein creating his famous monster. And, yes, as I recall, there was a brain that was borrowed in that instance."

"That's a ghoulish image. I can't unsee it. But I can tell you that Vance was blown away by whatever went on in that room. Looking back on it, though, I'm starting to wonder if there might have been an element of resentment in his reaction. I mean, there she was, stealing his plot from him as easily as if she'd taken candy from a baby. Of course, I could just be reading things into it all."

Ross looked thoughtful. "Offhand, I'd say it was an evening staged for the overactive imagination."

"You're obviously referring to me."

"Among others who were present."

"So you think it was all just a kind of theater or dog and pony show? Just one big hoax?"

"It's a possibility. Don't discount it."

Then Wendy told him about the strange behavior of Milton and Aurelia after they had emerged from his session. "That was the only reading that was not revealed to any of us. Aurelia said it was best kept between the two of them—a private matter, she insisted. Now, what do you make of that?"

"Right now, I'm erring on the side of Aurelia playing to the crowd here," he told her. "It could have been part of her act, and maybe this Milton guy went along with it for his own reasons. You can't rely on surface appearances."

Wendy's frown was a prolonged one. "Well, Merrie and Rex Boudreaux vouched for the fact that Milton's a wonderful singer. They said he graduated in theater arts from LSU. Maybe he's also a good actor because he seemed genuinely upset by whatever Aurelia had told him."

"If she told him anything at all," Ross said with a hint of mocking in his voice. "They could have just sat there smirking at each other inside that room. Perhaps a little money even exchanged hands before that. Maybe at least one of those readings cost Aurelia a few coins. You know, guaranteeing that all of you would be kept guessing and on the edge of your seats."

"I didn't think you'd be quite this skeptical," Wendy added. "Even though I found myself reacting the same way to my own reading. I was questioning everything Aurelia said inside my own head as we went along." She paused and lifted her left eyebrow.

"We're a pair, aren't we?"

Ross flashed a smile as a few locks of his dark blond hair fell into his eyes. He took the time to brush them back with his fingers and said, "Well, I'm a determined police detective, and you're a first-rate investigative reporter. What do you expect from the two of us, sweetie?"

"Good point." But Wendy pursued her earlier train of thought anyway. It was all part of the investigative reporting behavior she had been developing over the past two years at the *Citizen*.

"What if Aurelia actually told Milton something that truly shocked him to his core, though? Isn't that possible? She even seemed a bit shaken by whatever it was, herself. Wouldn't even let it be discussed, whereas she didn't care one bit about letting the others reveal theirs."

"Anything is possible. Neither of us is in a position to say yet whether Aurelia Spangler is the real deal or not, though. At this point, there's nothing we can do unless this Milton comes to the police for help of some kind. You've made it sound like you think he might need a bodyguard or be in danger of some sort. On the other hand, if all this just boils down to him playing a role of some kind for Aurelia, then the hoopla will die down and be forgotten. You've already admitted that Aurelia told you she wanted to seed her brand by learning how to play bridge. I don't think what she's doing is all that mysterious. I'm no psychic, but I do feel like I can see through it all. That's the best insight I can give you at this point."

"You make it sound so uncomplicated and straightforward," Wendy said. "But if that's the case, why do have I this uneasy feeling that something bad might very well happen to somebody soon? What if something really does happen to Milton in the end? Where is this sense of foreboding coming from all of a sudden? You know I have good instincts about people and events."

Ross could not suppress his amusement. "Miz Aurelia Spangler really has got you going, hasn't she? Keep in mind that that was almost certainly her goal from the very beginning. What she did this evening will surely end up enhancing her fledgling reputation here in Rosalie when all of you start spreading the word the way you're doing with me right now. Multiply our conversation many times over. When you come right down to it, I think everybody likes to be spooked now and then. They like the hair to stand up on the back of their necks and those shivers to run up and down their spines. It can all be quite lucrative, too. You only have to look at Hollywood's horror film industry to prove it to yourself."

"The classic or slasher variety?"

"Both have scared people out of their wits equally well over the years. And don't forget the Halloween industry and all that it entails. People spend a small fortune on their monster costumes."

"And candy," Wendy added.

"And parties."

Wendy finally decided to give in. Ross was quite formidable when he chose to be, and it was fine with her if he wanted to continue to play the skeptic. He was, after all, the seasoned law enforcement professional and had put himself regularly in harm's way, coming out unscathed often enough to be given the benefit of the doubt. Not only that, he knew how to keep her calm and centered, which she sometimes needed. She had even been guilty of recklessness when it came to her investigations. Sometimes, fearlessness was not all it was cracked up to be, especially when there was no safety net below to catch anyone who slipped and fell.

"Well, I guess we should just drop the matter completely until further notice," she told him.

"Let's do that for the time being. But thanks for the report, sweetie. It might come in handy, or it might not. By the way, do we have any more wedding cake left? My sweet tooth is acting up again."

Wendy snuggled closer to him and gave him a peck on the cheek. "Nope, I'm afraid we had the last of it yesterday. We have now officially exhausted the remains of our wonderful wedding. But we still have our honeymoon on the horizon when summer's over."

He put his arm around her shoulder, and all was well with his world. "Yowza!" he said with a devilish intensity. "The best is yet to come when we hit the Hawaiian Islands."

CHAPTER 4

Two afternoons later, down at headquarters, Ross was in the midst of some annoying paperwork when he was notified that Rex and Merrie Boudreaux had shown up and were waiting to talk to him immediately about what they described as an urgent matter. He and Wendy had thoroughly enjoyed working with them in planning their reception—the couple had made everything happen that had been requested of them and more—so he was somewhat curious to hear that they had something serious on their minds. It certainly couldn't be about the hefty bill for their services, because that had been promptly paid in full by Captain Bax. The man had been waiting most of his adult life to give his one and only, devoted daughter away to the man of her dreams, and money had been no object for him.

Ross was taken aback, however, when Rex showed up in ordinary street clothes, while Merrie was decked out in a yellow clown suit with black polka dots, complete with garish makeup, but minus a wig of any kind. Ross showed them into the interrogation room and tried his best to repress a smile. What, he wondered, was considered an "urgent" matter for a clown? A lost big red nose, perhaps?

"I know I must look perfectly ridiculous to you," Merrie began, as if reading his mind while taking a seat beside her husband. "But the fact that I had to rush down here in between parties we have planned for today is the reason we need to speak to you right away."

Ross nodded, shot them his best smile, and prepared to make notes. "Please continue. I'm fascinated."

But it was Rex who took up the story at that point. "We think we may need to file a missing person's report. Our Milton Bagdad has missed two events we had planned and one singing telegram delivery over the past two days. That's totally unlike him. He's been prompt, even early to all the jobs we've lined up for him since he was hired, but he hasn't answered his cell or landline or any texts each time we've tried to get in touch. We even drove by the little house he rents, and his car wasn't parked out in front. We also called up his parents down in Baton Rouge, and they haven't heard anything from him, either. He's not down there visiting them on a lark or anything like that. So we're concerned and thought we ought to report this to the police. We did want to give him a little more time to show up in case there were circumstances beyond his control. Strange things do happen now and then, but something is very wrong here. Meanwhile, Merrie had to take his place today as a clown at the children's party we just came from. Thus the outfit. And she did a bang-up job, by the way. She always does. These affairs bring out her inner child."

She pointed to the top of her head and snickered. "I did take off my bright orange wig and left it on the back seat of the car before we came in so I wouldn't look like I'd totally lost my mind, and I just didn't have time to remove much of the makeup. We happen to have another children's birthday party in about an hour or so—summer is our busiest time for those—and we just didn't want to put off reporting Milton's absence any longer. As Rex said, things just felt wrong to us.

I'm sure you would agree. I've tried not to think about worst-case scenarios."

"You did the right thing," Ross told them, finishing up what he had been writing. "Meanwhile, is there anything you can tell me about Milton's behavior leading up to his disappearance? Was there anything out of the ordinary he might have said to you or done that could give us a clue to tracking him down?"

"There definitely was," Rex said. "That was the next thing we were going to tell you. Merrie and I had a late event the other evening when Milton attended his first bridge lesson out at Overview with your wife and that psychic person. He had told us about going to it earlier in the day and seemed very excited about learning how to play bridge and even the free reading."

Given his conversation with Wendy that same evening, Ross immediately understood the significance of what Rex was about to say.

"Milton told us that he was very upset by his cold reading, and once he explained all of it to us, we both couldn't blame him for feeling the way he did. He told us that that psychic woman—"

"Aurelia Spangler," Ross interrupted.

Rex smiled briefly and continued. "Yes . . . well, he said that when she took his hand and looked into his eyes, she gasped loudly and pulled away from him like he was a poisonous snake ready to strike or something."

"That must have been unsettling for him."

"Yes, he said it was. But that wasn't the worst of it. Milton said she then told him she had seen a very disturbing image surrounding him and didn't even know if she should share it with him. It was that terrifying, she told him. But he said that made him want her to share whatever she'd seen all the more.

He said he pressed her on it, telling her that he wanted to get his free reading's worth."

"I can imagine. Adding the element of mystery is a plausible ploy. So, what did she tell him she saw?"

Rex took a deep breath first and began gesturing with his hands. "Milton said she described this very vivid image coming to her of something sharp—maybe a knife—being plunged into a tuxedo shirt. He said she had the sense of this happening to a man wearing a full tuxedo, in fact. Milton said he could see the psychic woman turning pale as she described the vision for him. Then he said that she advised him not to reveal the image to anyone—that it should not be shared publicly."

Ross quickly made more notes and then looked up. "Did Aurelia Spangler tell him why it should not be shared, or did she just leave it hanging? That seems like the perfect dramatic touch to prime the pump."

"Milton said she only emphasized how important it was that the image be kept private and not be thrown out there for public speculation. She must have felt there was some danger in that."

"Very curious," Ross said. "But it's completely consistent with what my wife told me both Milton and Aurelia said when they emerged from his reading. Wendy also said—but I don't think she phrased it quite this tritely—that they both looked like they had seen a ghost and had been completely thrown off balance. I believe there was even a description of staggering about."

Merrie spoke up next. "Since Milton wears a tux so much of the time when he delivers our telegrams, we can see how that vision might be pretty scary for him. He obviously thought it referred to him. He even turned to us and asked, 'Do you think my life might be in danger now?' I think that

was a perfectly reasonable question to ask under the circumstances."

"I would agree. So, what did you say to that?"

"We tried to calm him down, of course," Merrie said.
"He really is such a sweet boy, and I hate to see him in any
kind of distress. We suggested to him that she might not be a
real psychic at all and that she might be playing him. But Milton seemed convinced that there really was a dark cloud of
some kind hanging over him. He said the woman accurately
predicted the plot of this writer guy in the group, and he hadn't
told anyone about it. That does seem to make the case that she
might be a genuine psychic, don't you think?"

"That's possible, but I've also suggested to Wendy that all
of this might just be an act, though," Ross told them. "At this
point, it's impossible to tell if Aurelia Spangler is the real
thing, or if she's just running a clever game. Taking people at
face value can sometimes be a huge mistake. As a detective,
I can assure you that that can sometimes get you in serious
trouble."

"I get that much. But why scare the hell out of somebody
like that?" Merrie said. "Seems like that might end up chasing
them away as a customer."

Ross finished up another of his notes and nodded. "I tend
to agree with you. Offhand, I'd say there's a fine line between
a bit of harmless fortune-telling and instigating terror. I don't
see the benefit in that unless . . ." He paused and shifted his
eyes sideways. "Well, perhaps I'd better not pursue that angle
right now."

"Do you think we're right to be worried, though?" Rex
said. "From what Milton told us about the rest of the readings,
this woman seemed to be pretty accurate. Everyone else
seemed to be vouching for her accuracy. What if something
has happened to Milton that's related to this vision? It makes

you wonder what else the woman might have in her head. Is she the one who's the danger to him? Should he and the others be wary?"

"Not everyone is on Aurelia's bandwagon. I can tell you that my Wendy wasn't as impressed as the others were, although she had certain concerns. But you've done what you should do," Ross said. "We'll give you some forms for you to fill out, and then we can start working with law enforcement officers around the state and also down in Baton Rouge. We can get all the info we need from the DMV about Milton's car and license plate and then issue a BOLO. Once that many eyes start looking for him, he's much more likely to turn up."

"Alive, we would hope," Merrie said. "And certainly not with a knife plunged in his chest. As I said, he's a darling kid—maybe a little too naïve for his own good, maybe too impressionable—but it's so not in his nature to just not show up for work without some sort of explanation. We need to get to the bottom of this. I don't know if I could handle it if something terrible has happened to him."

Ross lowered his voice, trying to sound as soothing as possible. "Try not to go there if you can."

"It's hard to unsee that image of a knife or something plunging into that tuxedo shirt. That's pretty graphic," Merrie said. "If I had been in Milton's shoes during that reading, I'd have been freaked out, too. And your wife might consider whether this Aurelia woman is a good choice for the others to play bridge with when all is said and done, Detective Rierson. I keep getting this image of a fox in the henhouse."

"I'm afraid that decision will be up to Wendy," Ross told her. "But I'll call her down at the paper and bring her up to date on Milton Bagdad, and she can take it from there. Meanwhile, I want to thank both of you again for coming in and reporting this. Sometimes, people wait too late in matters like this."

"You sound as if you expect the worst," Merrie said, drawing back with a slight note of panic in her voice.

"No, I'm not jumping to any conclusions, you understand. I've found it best not to do that in this business. We officers have to stay calm and objective to get the job done right. Who knows? The guy could turn up any minute now with a reasonable explanation for everything that's good for a laugh."

Ross said nothing further, but the young man's sudden disappearance struck him as alarming. The first thing he did after Rex and Merrie had left was to call Wendy on her cell and get her started on what might become her next investigative assignment for the *Citizen*.

Wendy had just settled in across from Lyndell in her editorial office and revealed what Ross had just told her about Milton Bagdad going missing, as well as the details of his disturbing cold reading that Ross had learned from Rex and Merrie Boudreaux. Her tone was animated, her posture restless. It was quite clear that she was more than ready to go into her investigative reporting mode.

Meanwhile, Lyndell began unwrapping a tuna fish sandwich at her desk. It was more of a task than it should have been because the cellophane was not behaving properly, despite its translucence. "You don't mind my eating while I listen, do you? I have a million things to do today and don't have time for a real sit-down lunch in the cafeteria or anywhere else in town. This is it—just me cutting corners and brown-bagging it from home."

Wendy brightened immediately. "Editorial privilege."

"Well said. But this sounds like a developing story we'll want to follow," Lyndell added, after taking her first bite. "You'll want to get Aurelia Spangler's side of this immediately, of course. She'll probably shed an entirely different light on things, which could either clear everything up or muddy the waters further. You have to start somewhere, but I think your path is well lighted in this case."

"I tried to set up an interview as soon as I hung up with Ross ten or fifteen minutes ago," Wendy began. "But Aurelia didn't answer my texts, and her cell went to voice mail. That always especially annoys me. But I left a message for her to call me back as soon as she could. She's probably just temporarily out of pocket, and I'll hear from her any second now."

Lyndell continued to enjoy her sandwich, occasionally taking a sip from her white ceramic coffee mug, which had her name scrawled on it in black magic marker. "It seems your efforts of any kind regarding the game of bridge always lead to some sort of intrigue. I'm sure you've noticed that pattern."

"I have, and I really don't know what to make of it. More than one person has suggested that the gods of bridge are against me and that I should just stop playing altogether."

"Do you think you would ever do that after all you've put into the game? The odds have to break your way eventually, I would imagine."

Wendy thought about it seriously for a while. "The problem now is that after two years of playing regularly, I've gotten pretty good at the game, if I do say so myself. That was my objective all along. I won't say I'm addicted or anything close, but I enjoy bridge immensely. No two hands are ever alike, of course. You can learn something new on practically every deal. I think it's a good thing for me to try to get more people in Rosalie interested in it, and that's the main reason I decided to go ahead and teach."

Lyndell had finished half of her sandwich, wiped the corners of her mouth with a napkin, and caught Wendy's gaze firmly. "There's more than likely a fascinating story behind this young man's whereabouts. Let's go on the assumption that the reason is benign. We always cross our fingers and hope for that when someone disappears. No one wants to end up on a milk carton or in the morgue. So, if you don't hear from Aurelia Spangler soon, I suggest you go out and track her down so she can help you and the police do the best job all of you can."

Then an idea filled Wendy's brain, giving her a tingling sensation at the back of her neck. She found the moment decidedly unpleasant. "What if by some chance she's gone missing, too?"

"Don't get too far ahead of yourself. I think cell phones have made the entire population much too impatient. Life seems to be all about instant gratification these days. That, and not paying attention to where you're going when you're crossing the street, in the supermarket, or on the sidewalk. Not to mention the rudeness I've seen everywhere. As if everyone is interested in your end of a private conversation in confined spaces."

But Wendy wasn't willing to let go of the conversation, despite the fact that she agreed cell phone usage and tweets had conquered the known universe, taking no prisoners.

"I can only tell you that while Aurelia and I were planning the logistics of that first bridge lesson out at Overview, we were constantly texting and talking on our cells. She was always prompt about getting back in touch with me when I needed to clarify something, or vice versa. Rex and Merrie Boudreaux said that it was so unlike Milton not to communicate with them, much less not show up for work. I just this second got that same uneasy feeling about Aurelia. She should have answered my texts and messages by now because she's one of the most organized people I've ever met. I have this terrible feeling that several worrisome things are happening all at once."

"If you don't hear from her soon, don't hesitate to run by

Overview and see what's going on with her," Lyndell said. "I know this sounds corny, but the plot may thicken, you know."

Wendy drew back and frowned. "Funny that you should use the word *plot*. Vance Quimby couldn't get over the fact that Aurelia seemed to know the details of the mystery he's working on—even before he'd started writing on it. How do you grab thoughts out of thin air like that—unless you're the real thing? Or so you think I'm being naïve?"

Lyndell looked puzzled briefly, but that was soon replaced by a rush of recognition.

"Vance Quimby is the writer in your group, right? He was very gregarious at your wedding reception. He even told me that he hoped I wouldn't mind answering a few questions since he was doing research for his novel. Of course, as a journalist, that clicked with me. We are all about research, as you know."

"So you didn't mind, then?"

"Not at all. He was very charming about it, but I made sure he understood that I'm not a native, nor to the manor born, and have only been here in Rosalie myself for a little more than a year. I'm not privy to all the skeletons in the closets and 'what-all's-hiding-under-the-bed,' if that's what he needed, and at times he seemed to be going for *National Enquirer*–type stuff. Even if I were aware of info like that, I doubt I would have shared it with him. That's just not my style."

"Yes, well, what he revealed of his actual plot was what really got everyone on Aurelia's bandwagon as authentic."

"I can't finish this now," Lyndell said, rising from her chair with what was left of her sandwich, again doing battle with the wrapping. "Back into the break room fridge it goes." She checked the time on her cell. "I need to head out to a meeting with the mayor. Meanwhile, you track down Aurelia Spangler and see what else she can tell you about Milton Bagdad's cold reading. I'll check in with you later at the end of the day."

Wendy waited in her cubicle for another fifteen minutes or so to hear from Aurelia Spangler, but there was no contact of any kind forthcoming. Impressions of Overview being an unlucky place for most of its owners to date swirled inside her head. She had been an instinctual person all her life, particularly in the matter of solving puzzles. So when she left the building and slid into the front seat of her Impala to head out to Overview, she was far from calm. Her pulse began quickening on its own, and she had the sense that something out of the ordinary was about to happen. Before she started the engine, she proceeded to text Ross to let him know where she was going. Their unwritten agreement was to always keep the other informed of their whereabouts, unless it was a security breach on his part.

On my way to interview Aurelia about Milton. Will keep you posted.

Then she decided to text Aurelia again.

Headed your way for a chat. Let me know where you are if not at Overview. Need to talk asap.

But although Ross acknowledged her text by telling her to stay in touch, there was once again no reply from Aurelia during Wendy's drive through town toward the High Bluff. She had never been good at handling feelings of foreboding, but these were particularly weighty and uncomfortable. They grew even stronger as she reached her destination and saw that Aurelia's black SUV was parked in front of Overview just ahead of her. She got out of her car and headed toward the impressive veranda. For a moment, she thought about returning and honking the horn but quickly abandoned the idea. She was not in high school picking up a girlfriend to go shopping.

Wendy rang the doorbell and waited. The humidity and ninetysomething-degree heat of late June were unbearable, and there was no breeze of any kind, despite the great length of the veranda to coax it out of hiding. In the short trek from the curb to the front door, she had started to sweat. A minute or so passed. She rang the doorbell a second time and cried out, "Aurelia? Are you there? It's me, Wendy. Did you get my texts?" Then she tried knocking a few times—politely at first, then with more force. Who knew? Aurelia might be the type to take a nap. Or might she be the type to be "entertaining company" and be indisposed?

When no answer still came, Wendy grabbed the gleaming silver doorknob and was surprised to find that the door was unlocked. First, she experienced a rush of adrenaline. Then a rush of cool air embraced her as she opened a crack ever so slowly. She yelled, "Aurelia? It's me, Wendy Rierson. Are you in here?"

The silence both emboldened and worried Wendy. She entered the foyer cautiously and called Aurelia's name out twice more. Still no response. Then she turned to the right, walking warily into the enormous, shadowy parlor where she had taught her first bridge lesson a couple of evenings before. Aurelia was nowhere to be seen, and Wendy's pulse continued to race.

She took a deep breath, knowing what had to be done next. As had been the case several times in the past, her fearlessness overcame her recklessness as she approached the door to the reading room. The latest spurt of adrenaline beneath her chest felt almost like touching a faulty electric socket, and she could not bring herself to turn the doorknob just yet. First, she had to center herself with another deep breath. She even found herself counting to ten in her head. But ten was not enough. The count turned to twenty, then thirty. This was becoming absurd. She was a grown woman acting like a little girl playing a game.

But it was another few seconds before she was actually able to open the door to what now seemed like an inevitable sight to her. Where that perception had come from, she did not know. It was as if she, herself, had become psychic for the task at hand. She wondered if Overview somehow brought that out in people.

All speculation aside, Wendy gasped at the gruesome sight of Aurelia Spangler in her chair, accompanied by the faint smell of beginning decomposition. Her opaque, empty eyes were staring up at the ceiling, and her mouth was agape. There was no doubt that she was dead, but Wendy called out her name twice as a reflex action. No answer, of course. There was also no rise and fall from her chest, and she was as stiff and motionless as a figure in a wax museum. The lace tablecloth that had decorated the table the evening of the cold readings was in a heap on the floor; on the bare table surface, there was a note written in cursive, and nearby were a ball-point pen, a short plastic straw, and the faintest remnants of a powdery substance. While being careful not to touch any-thing, Wendy managed to position herself so that she could lean down and quickly read the note:

> *I'm tired of making my living this way. This has gone on too long. I'm doing more harm than good to people, and it's time for me to leave. I'm sorry for everything.*
> *Aurelia Spangler*

Wendy could almost feel the raw emotion and desperation rising up from the words, but she was still shocked by them.

Suicide and Aurelia Spangler did not seem to belong in the same sentence. Though Wendy had only known the woman for a short time, leaving this way seemed completely out of character. The Aurelia she had worked with was confident and efficient, determined to get things accomplished and achieve her goals. It was difficult to believe that she had abandoned that sort of energy and drive within the space of a couple of days.

Except that there was that uncoordinated, strange behavior from her when she and Milton had practically lurched out of the reading room following his session. If that was part of her act, it was wildly inconsistent with everything about her except this suicide note that had followed days later. That version of Aurelia who had appeared so depressed and down in the mouth at that juncture might have written such a note. So, what was it about the vision of a knife to the tuxedo shirt that seemed to have shaken her as much as it had Milton? Both had made their exits because of it—Aurelia permanently. It remained to be seen about Milton.

Wendy took out her cell from her purse, steadied herself, and punched up 911, calling for first responders and then texting Ross.

Aurelia Spangler is dead. Apparent suicide. Need you here at Overview asap.

Wendy was relieved that his response was almost immediate:

Are you okay, sweetheart?
No, not really. Discovering bodies not my thing.
Hang on. I'll be there in no time.
I'll be okay once you get here but hurry.
Headed over now.

Wendy took her cell with her and walked out onto the veranda, despite the overbearing heat that awaited her. She did not want to be alone inside Overview with Aurelia's body. When Ross and the paramedics arrived, only then would she be up to returning to the air-conditioned death scene to do and say whatever was asked of her.

Overview, with its haughty position well above the river, had claimed yet another victim, it seemed.

CHAPTER 5

Tommy Cantwell, Rosalie's longtime, gangly coroner, turned to Ross and Wendy and delivered the verdict—his narrow, sad face drooping even further. "Looks like a cocaine overdose to me, folks. She's got traces on the tips of her fingers, some in her nose, there's a residue on the table, and I believe she clearly snorted quite a few lines with that straw. I could do a tox panel to verify it, but I think this is a no-brainer. Her liver temp also shows that she's been dead about sixteen hours, so this happened yesterday evening sometime."

Answering Wendy's 911 call, first responders had arrived promptly at Overview, and Ross, Wendy, and Tommy were now huddled out on the veranda. On the sidewalk beyond, a small crowd had gathered with their phones, attracted by Ross's police car, the coroner's car, and the ambulance parked in front. Very few people could resist the pull of such vehicles when they sprang into action with their speed, garish lights, and wailing sirens.

"Will you be performing an autopsy?" Ross said. "Do you think I need to get the CID out here?"

"Doesn't appear to be a crime, so an autopsy may not be necessary, unless it's requested by the next of kin," Tommy told him. "Don't think we need to send this'n down to Jackson to the ME."

"I don't know about the next of kin. She'd just moved to Rosalie about a month or so ago," Wendy volunteered. "She was about to open up her practice as a psychic this coming week. I did get to work with her a bit in planning a bridge lesson we held here a couple of days ago, but she never mentioned any relatives to me. I know for a fact that she was single. She told me once she didn't think any man could put up with the strange life she led."

Ross sounded quite emphatic. "I've taken all the pictures I need to, and I bagged the note. We need to determine if it was actually written in her handwriting. I'll get in touch with the landlord and get a sample of her signature from the rental agreement. Doesn't Bailey Sessions still own this?"

"He does," Wendy said. "He'll be horrified to hear what's happened at his investment, of course. Aurelia was the first person to rent Overview in almost a decade because of its creepy reputation."

"Confirm the signature and that'd about do it," Tommy said. "Suicides are sad things, but they happen all the time. Some say it's the pressure of modern life. Unless that's a phony note, I think we can safely rule out homicide."

Ross wondered if it would end up being that simple but gave Tommy a reassuring wink anyway. "I'll let you know one way or another soon."

Wendy and Ross moved aside and watched the covered body being whisked away on a gurney by the paramedics to the ambulance, and then Ross locked the front door behind him.

"I need to talk to you," Wendy told him as they headed toward their cars while the crowd dispersed after taking their last shots with their phones. "I'll come to the station unless you've got something pressing on your schedule."

He gave her a quick peck on the cheek. "I'm wide open right now. See you in just a few."

Wendy was sitting across from Ross at his desk and would simply not relent. "I don't care what Tommy Cantwell says, suicide is completely out of character for a woman like Aurelia Spangler. I'm an excellent judge of character, and I have to repeat that working with her on the bridge lessons and cold reading sessions was a pleasure. She was certain that it was the right way to introduce herself to Rosalieans, and I agreed with her. She had every reason to be optimistic about her decision to move here. To have her give up like that just a couple of days later makes no sense at all. There's something missing here."

Ross did not answer right away. He had to admit that he had not had the sort of contact with Aurelia Spangler that his wife had. He was careful to tread lightly. "I respect your views, sweetheart. But let me ask you this: Did she ever mention using drugs to you?"

Wendy was frowning now. "No, but not that many people come right out and admit to something like that. I mean, it could end up incriminating them down the line somewhere, don't you think?"

"True enough. But we know that there was a bit of drama after those cold readings took place. We've since learned that Aurelia told Milton about a vision of a knife being plunged into a tuxedo shirt. It obviously affected both of them in a profound way. Milton has disappeared, and now Aurelia has committed suicide, or so it seems. Clearly, that reading had unintended consequences. So, what I'm saying is that the Aurelia you worked with was evidently altered by that vision. The question is: Why did it alter her enough to cause her to take her own life?"

Wendy's face suddenly lit up, and she pointed her index finger at her husband.

"Absolutely. I go back to my original point that it was out of character for her. Why was she unable to handle this particular reading when she no doubt handled thousands of others quite effectively? She told me she'd been doing this professionally for nearly twenty years. She had to have encountered everything under the sun. Why was this not business as usual?"

"Well, our BOLO hasn't turned up Milton Bagdad yet," Ross added. "Why is he on the lam anyway? It looks suspicious enough, but imagine if Aurelia's death wasn't a suicide. Suppose Tommy Cantwell is wrong, and it was a homicide. Did Milton have anything to do with it? Is that why he's disappeared?"

"Just relying upon my instincts, I can't imagine that young man doing such a thing. That seems out of character for him, too."

He gave Wendy a long, thoughtful stare. "You have every right to think there's more to this than an overdose of cocaine. But we need some hard evidence to support that theory."

Wendy rose from her chair, sounding like a woman on a mission. "I can do my part. I'm going back to the newspaper and will let Lyndell in on this. She'd already been interested in my doing a special human-interest piece on teaching the bridge newbies. Now we have an unexpected death thrown into the mix. This changes the assignment entirely. Suddenly, it's not about bridge, it's about death."

"Wait . . . sit back down a minute," Ross told her, gently motioning with his hand. She complied but gave him a quizzical look.

"You and Lyndell need to keep something in mind. If this is a suicide, and there's no next of kin to enlighten us about Aurelia any further, there won't be much of a story to tell. You're an investigative reporter, but what will you be investigating if it's made clear that the poor woman really committed suicide? Aurelia deserves a certain amount of respect. She's entitled to her privacy postmortem. You're still acting and sounding like you're certain this was a homicide. You could be wrong. Don't dismiss the possibility. Work it out with Lyndell."

Wendy felt a sensation at the back of her neck, as if someone or something was pressing on it, and her eyes widened. "You're right. I was. But I can't help it. Something keeps gnawing at me that this wasn't a suicide, and I think you and the CID should go on that assumption, too."

"You know that's not how we operate, unless there's evidence to back us up. Right now, there's not much more we can do. We have to go by what Tommy says. But since you'll be doing this human-interest article, that gives you the perfect opportunity to interview the other newbies and see if anything significant or overlooked comes out of that."

Wendy smiled. "Which puts me right back where I left off. I'm headed to Lyndell's office right now."

The first thing that Wendy did when she returned to her cubicle at the *Citizen* was to text the other newbies the startling news about Aurelia. She'd accumulated all their numbers during the period she and Aurelia had been coordinating the bridge lesson, and she decided not to omit the missing Milton Bagdad. Perhaps the message would bring him out of hiding, wherever he was.

Then, three words followed inside her head that made her shiver: *if he's alive.* She took her time with the text and provided as much detail as she could—she had become quite accomplished at manipulating her thumbs without very many typos to exasperate her.

Next, she covered all bases by sitting down with Lyndell in her editorial office and bringing her up to date on the suicide as well. After giving Lyndell a minute or so to digest the tragic news, she said, "How do you think this changes my assignment on the bridge newbies?"

Lyndell answered quickly and with some authority. "Unfortunately, I think it would be in poor taste to do the bridge lesson article now that this suicide has occurred among your group. You can't treat bridge lessons and a suicide as subjects of equal importance. A matter of life and death versus a card game? It's simply no contest. They don't belong in the same article. The two just don't go together. They'll have to be two separate articles."

Wendy could not disguise her disappointment, and there was a hint of an edge to her words. "Did Ross by any chance call you?"

Lyndell gave her a curious stare. "No, as a matter of fact, he didn't. But I gather from your question that he feels the same way that I do about the assignment. Do I read you right?"

"Yes, you do." Wendy was frustrated but pressed on. "It's just that I have this gut feeling that won't go away. The physical evidence regarding Aurelia Spangler's death screams suicide, but I can't get her positive attitude out of my head. She was just not the suicidal type."

Lyndell sat back in her chair and took her time before speaking. "I've been in this business long enough to know that people sometimes don't behave according to type. You have the time-honored example of the serial killer that everybody says was a model citizen or was so friendly and helpful to the neighbors and that sort of thing. So-and-so would help little old ladies across the street or help weed flower beds and so forth. If you ask me, it has to do with their protective coloration and throwing people off their scent."

"You may be right," Wendy said, putting the palm of her

hand to her temple in contemplation. "They probably go out of their way to look like model citizens beyond reproach."

"Anyway," Lyndell continued, "I think the same thing applies to some people who take their own lives. Friends and neighbors will say that whoever it was seemed perfectly normal and happy going about their daily routine. But deep inside, at that core where everybody truly lives all by themselves, something very wrong or wicked or intolerable was going on all the time. That you can never really know about sometimes until it's just too late and you're stuck with the gruesome headlines."

"I grant you that," Wendy said, her tone less certain now. "Human nature is sometimes a great puzzle, and I understand what you're saying about the article. I just wish there were some way that I could do my job without—"

Wendy's subdued, bell-like ringtone interrupted her train of thought. She leaned forward and picked up her cell on the edge of Lyndell's desk, where she had put it when she first came in; then she glanced at it quickly and saw that it was a call from Vance Quimby.

"Excuse me while I take this. It's from one of my newbies. I'm sure it's about Aurelia's suicide."

Lyndell nodded and said, "Go right ahead and answer it, then. We're almost through here."

Wendy was hardly prepared for the avalanche of anguished words that followed, however, once she had uttered a simple "hello" in normal, even tones, and Vance Quimby had hurriedly identified himself.

"I have to talk to you right now, Wendy. I need to come over there and tell you what's really been going on behind the scenes. Something has gone horribly wrong, and I don't know how anyone found out. All I can tell you is that Aurelia could not have committed suicide. I know without a doubt that someone murdered her. I can't go into why I know this right now, but I do. Once I give you the full story, you'll understand the big picture. So, can you see me now at the paper? Can you make time for me? You just have to."

Wendy finally got in a word. "Yes, of course I can, but is this something you need to tell the police first? It sounds like it to me."

"Yes, I will go to them, but I want to run it all past you first. I'd feel better letting them in on it after you've heard it first—because I have a confession to make. Well, sort of."

Wendy tried to sound as calm and reassuring as possible, even though her insides were churning with excitement. "Of course, I'll make time for you right now. Come right on over."

Lyndell broached the awkwardness that followed the end of the call. "Well, your side of the conversation certainly sounded intriguing. You should have seen some of the expressions on your face. It was like you were going through all the emotions as an acting exercise."

"I'll bet I was convincing, too," Wendy said, and then repeated the gist of the call to her. Both women sat in silence for a while, trying to piece things together. The word *confession* had them particularly intrigued. Was Vance Quimby going to confess to murdering Aurelia Spangler? Had he done something as horrendous as acting out his very own, original murder plot?

Another call on Wendy's phone startled them out of their conjectures, and Wendy shrugged at Lyndell with a hint of a smile. "I don't think I've ever been this popular, but I'm equally sure it's not for the right reasons."

This time the call was from Sarah Ann O'Rourke. As she prepared to answer, Wendy began to wonder what power she had unleashed with her texts. Did Sarah Ann have something she needed to get off her chest, too? Another confession, perhaps?

"I'm shocked by Aurelia's suicide," Sarah Ann was saying, her voice a bit breathless.

"But there's something you need to know. It may or may not be of significance, but I have to get it out there. It's about my mother. And please don't ever tell her that I made this call to you. I'm not at home right now, or I'd never even risk this. I'm at the Student Union at the college, and I was wondering if we could meet in the food court and talk."

Wendy glanced at the time on her phone and wondered how long the meeting with Vance Quimby would last. Well, she could certainly control that, no matter what Vance had to reveal to her. Keeping a tight schedule came with being a reporter of any kind.

"I have some business to conduct for about an hour here at the paper," Wendy said. "But how about we meet at the food court around an hour and a half from now? Can you hang around that long, or would you rather come here?"

Sarah Ann sounded agitated and stumbled over her words. "Well, I . . . guess I could come . . . no, it would be better if you came here. Mother . . . Mother doesn't approve of you because you're teaching me bridge . . . or at least you were before this happened. She says I should stay away from the paper as well. I hate to say it, but she has her spies around town who tell her where I go to eat and shop. It's those church people of hers who quote Scripture in their letters to the editor on just about every subject under the sun. They're like those old vinyl records where the needle would get stuck in one of the grooves. Just recently, there was this blues band playing at Smoot's Grocery on Broad Street, and I wanted to see them, so I did just that. I'm twenty-one, you know, but I didn't order any liquor because, well, I'm just not that interested. Of course, Mother's always lecturing me about that, too—"

Wendy decided to break in. "Listen, dear, I appreciate all the confidence you've put in me, but save something for our meeting. I'll text you if it looks like I'm gonna be late, okay?"

After the call had ended, Wendy brought Lyndell up to speed and then said, "I guess I should prepare myself to hear from Charlotte Ruth and Milton Bagdad, too. Well, I'll tell you what I told Ross. I think this suicide is not what it appears to be, and these calls are only confirming my suspicions."

"Go with your gut," Lyndell said with an encouraging smile. "It's the nature of journalism."

CHAPTER 6

Milton Bagdad threw his cell onto the unmade bed in the cheap motel room smelling of bug spray that he had rented near Rolling Fork in the Mississippi Delta. It also smelled of residual smoke, even though he had specifically asked for a nonsmoking room. He didn't call the front desk and complain about it, though. His mind was on other things. The text he had received from Wendy Winchester a few minutes earlier made him more paranoid than ever. Was there truly a safe place to hide? Would his ultimate fate pursue him no matter where he went? Aurelia Spangler was gone now. Would he be next? He frowned and then shut his eyes tightly, as if that might protect him from whatever danger might be lurking out there. According to Aurelia's vision, he should have been the one to go—and in brutal fashion at that. He was the one who wore the tuxedo shirts. He was the one who should have taken the knife. Still, he was perplexed. Wendy had said Aurelia's death was due to an overdose of cocaine. What did that have to do with knives and tuxedo shirts? What alternate universe was he inhabiting now?

He could not forget the look of pure terror in Aurelia's eyes as she had revealed the crux of her vision involving him—against her better judgment, she had told him. Then she had said, "I've had these moments before, and frankly, they terrify me." She had put the palm of her hand to her forehead as if her temperature were soaring to near-fatal heights.

Taking a great gasp of air, she had said to him next, "I can't see through to any more of this. The beginning and the end elude me, but I know this vision has both. And I can also tell you that there is so much deceit at the heart of this. I see the knife to the shirt materializing soon. It's inevitable. Something has been set in motion that can't be stopped. The upshot is that someone out there is beyond wicked, and no one has an inkling that they are. They don't abide by the rules, and they don't care. But I don't have the ability to see this through. That's been my dilemma for the longest time. I'm being totally honest with you now."

And though he was disturbed by the dramatic intensity of her words, Milton had said, "How do you think this vision of yours makes me feel? You must think it's the truth, then."

Without hesitation, she had dismissed his comment and said, "When we join the others, don't talk about this to anyone. You must promise me that. I must have time to sort this out and decide what's the right thing to do. Perhaps if I concentrate hard enough, the rest of this vision will come to me and I can even prevent it from happening."

He had promised her, but saying nothing to any of the others as he staggered out of the reading room had only made things worse, more fearful, more anxious for him. He couldn't carry around the dead weight of this vision all by himself, he decided, so he had unburdened himself to Rex and Merrie Boudreaux back at Party Palooza headquarters that evening. They had tried their best to calm him down, but their efforts had worked for only a short time. There was just no way they could extract the terror from his body.

By the time he had returned to the little house he rented,

he had come up with what could only be termed a desperate, runaway strategy. None of it made much sense, and he knew he wasn't thinking it all the way through. First, continuing to work for Party Palooza put him in peril, he figured. Wearing a tuxedo with all the trimmings put him at risk. If that knife was going to plunge into a tux shirt, then he would stop wearing one by putting an end to delivering singing telegrams. To do that, he had to quit working for Rex and Merrie, but he didn't have the gumption to tell them so to their faces. Eventually, he must stir up the courage and face his fears. Aurelia had said that the vision would happen soon. He could think of no other recourse than to get the hell out of Rosalie, to give himself some breathing room and decide what to do next.

Could he go to the police about a vision a psychic had seen? They might smirk at him to his face and then belly-laugh behind his back once he'd left the station. He spent a sleepless night turning and tossing, and by the time the sun had come up the next morning, he had reaffirmed his course of action.

He piled some of his clothes and toiletries into a suitcase, leaving his tuxedo and the two ruffled shirts he used for his telegrams behind. To his mind, they were toxic and taboo—articles of impending death. He remembered seeing reruns of that old TV show *The Beverly Hillbillies* on one of those oldies cable stations and found a light moment and a brief smile as he pictured them piling everything they owned into a Model T and heading for Beverly Hills. But the sense of doom, of something dark hanging over him, soon returned. None of this felt remotely like a sitcom. He grabbed his laptop and cell phone, leaving behind the TV set he had intended to replace with a state-of-the-art flat-screen when he'd saved up a bit more money.

Sadly, he knew he would miss those singing telegram tips. All the people who received them didn't appear to be hurting for money. That professor out at the College of Rosalie, for instance, had tipped him handsomely for those anonymous telegrams that he'd delivered to the man's home. The last thing he did after loading up his car was to cash a hefty check at Bluff City Bank & Trust and put Rosalie in his rearview mirror for the time being. For some reason, he stopped short of closing out the account.

But now that he'd done all this running around frantically as if he were in the midst of some kind of improvisational fire drill—where was he actually going to go? How far away from Rosalie should he get? He wasn't thinking at all; he was merely driven by his own fear. On an impulse, the small town of Rolling Fork north of Vicksburg became his first destination. He had no idea why. Maybe it was the unusual name and his fascination with it. How, indeed, was a fork able to roll? How long would he stay there?

He was going to eventually run out of money, despite the size of the check he had cashed. He felt he was losing his mind, totally out of control. Would he live to tell his grandchildren about this helter-skelter episode of his life? He found a moment to smile at that last thought. Grandchildren. Children. That might not ever happen, but he had chosen not to share his doubts about himself in that regard with anyone, not even his parents. That was another issue entirely, and at the moment, he did not have time to wrestle with it as he had for many years. Not with the prospect of death hanging over him.

Perhaps he should allow this text from Wendy to bring him to his senses at last; even though it magnified the notion of coming to a tragic end that he had been feeling ever since Aurelia had revealed her vision to him. Why had he pressed her on it? He would have been better off not knowing what she had seen. It also appeared that she would have been better off not seeing it, too.

Now, according to Wendy, she had chosen to leave the

world because of it. What should he do next? Did he dare return to Rosalie? Without the tux and the shirts, was he now safe, and was it that simple a proposition? No telegrams, no shirt, no knife, no death.

He looked at the stack of money sitting on the nightstand. Mostly twenties and a couple of hundreds. Once again he had to acknowledge the fact that they would not last him all that long. He realized he had to make up his mind once and for all and stop acting like a frightened little child who had just stayed up late and watched a horror movie, wanting to hide under the covers all night.

Then came the startling knock at his motel room door, which sent jolts of adrenaline through his heart. Was the vision catching up with him now, despite everything he had done? Aurelia had said that something wicked had been set in motion that could not be stopped. Was it now on the other side of the door, waiting to plunge a knife into his chest?

But the single word, "Housekeeping," brought the instantaneous relief that he so desperately needed.

He peered through the peephole and then opened the door a crack to a short Hispanic woman. "Checking out today, sir?" she said, flashing a perfunctory smile.

Without thinking, he was surprised to find himself saying forthrightly, "Yes, yes, I am."

Then he closed the door and sat back down on the bed. What he had done so far suddenly seemed absurd. This was no way to live his life. He had to go back to Rosalie and face whatever needed to be faced.

It was as if a different person had put on Vance Quimby's clothes and walked into the interview room at the *Citizen* that Wendy had chosen for their meeting. Yes, his physical features were the same, but the body language and facial expressions had taken on a nervous aura that could not be denied.

The man was also sweating profusely across his forehead and upper lip, although that was not so unusual for people coming in from outside during Rosalie's hellish summers.

"Would you like me to get you a bottled water from the break room?" Wendy said just before sitting across from him.

He hesitated and started to move his lips, but then shook his head emphatically. "I'm okay. Just . . . let's get this over with."

Wendy opened her notepad to a blank page and prepared to write. "I'm ready to hear what you have to say."

"First, you need to know something very important," he began, nervously drumming the fingers of his right hand on the table. "On the way here I stopped by the morgue, where I requested an autopsy be performed on Relly's body and then for it to be transported to a funeral home in Omaha. She'll be buried out there where we grew up. Over the years, she told me those were her wishes. But the most important thing is that . . . I am not a novelist. I did not come here to Rosalie to research and then write a book. Relly was my sister. She was my only sibling, and I'm her only living next of kin. From the start, we were together in this."

Wendy looked up from her notepad, already stunned by his words, but managed a somewhat weak, "I didn't see that coming, but I'm so sorry for your loss, of course." She quickly wrote down in all caps:

AURELIA & VANCE ARE BROTHER & SISTER

Vance's eyes began to water, and his voice, unsteady to begin with, quavered even more. "Thank you. This is very hard on me, but to cut to the chase you're looking for—both Relly and I came to Rosalie to set up her psychic business. It's true that I've been doing research all over town and at the courthouse, but not for a novel. It's been to get background information on a lot of different people and to practice for Relly's actual marks."

"Marks?"

But even before Vance answered, Wendy remembered that Ross had used the term in describing the techniques used by phony psychics and con artists of all sorts.

"Yes, people she would target for a session and then hand them over to me for background checks and so forth. That's just what she did for all of the other bridge newbies, including you. How do you think she knew so much about each one of you that evening? Yes, you can go online and find out a few things about most people. But you'd be surprised how much else you can find out about them just by asking questions indirectly and then continuing to prod. They don't even realize what they're giving away. You tell people you're writing a novel, and they go into an absolute tailspin. They want to know everything about your process, and sometimes you think they might be stalking you. They're delighted to contribute in any way they can. They think for a minute or two that they might even be in it. You know how it works these days—everyone wants their fifteen minutes of fame."

He paused for a breath, and Wendy got in a word. "I have to confess that I, too, was intrigued to be around a writer who was in the midst of a novel. It was exciting."

"We were counting on that reaction from everyone," Vance continued. "Anyway, that was my role in all of this, and it's why I went first at the bridge session the other evening. The plan was to convince you and the others that Relly had actually envisioned the plot of the novel I was writing. There was no novel, and there was no plot. Relly and I just agreed on the business about the service dog leading someone to a dead body in a Dumpster. Sounds intriguing enough, don't you think? We figured that would create instant interest and credibility, and I think you'll agree that it did just that. All of you were duly impressed, which is exactly what we wanted."

"The Barnum effect, after all," Wendy said as a reflex action. "So, you're telling me that your sister was a phony?"

Vance took a deep breath to try and steady himself further, but the emotion still remained in his voice. "No, not exactly. This is the hard part to explain. When she was a little girl of about eleven or so—and she didn't grow up in Brooklyn like she said, she grew up in Nebraska with me—she really did get these flashes of insight about people and places. At first, she was frightened by them. Who wouldn't be? I've often wondered how I would handle something like that."

"I'm wondering if I wouldn't be bothered at all, though," Wendy said, answering his rhetorical question. "I get these flashes of insight that help me solve crimes—not exactly the same way, I would imagine. But it still seems like some sort of gift to me that I can't explain away completely. Is that how it worked for your sister?"

Vance took on a faraway look as he continued. "I can only tell you that I remember clearly the day she came to me and said, 'I think something is wrong with my brain.' I asked her what she meant by that, of course, and if she was just talking about some kind of bad headache or something. She described these flashes, these images that came into her head like scenes from a movie about certain people and places around Omaha, our hometown. She was genuinely frightened by it all until she found out she could definitely use these flashes to her advantage."

"How so?"

"They were just little things, mostly. Nothing out of the ordinary. Believe it or not, she would sometimes see the questions and answers to tests in school in advance. Imagine that.

She knew that it was a form of cheating, but it kept her an A student without much effort. Imagine that. And anyway, how would anyone know she was cheating? She was always in the clear in that respect. None of her teachers ever suspected a thing, and she was not about to try and explain it to them. Think they would've believed her anyway?"

"Anything more?"

This time, Vance shut his eyes, and a tear fell down his right cheek. "Yes, she foresaw our dear mother's death. She said the image came to her of Mom in a hospital bed, and then she both heard and saw that horrendous flat line on the monitor. Now I know for a fact that something like that would've creeped me out, and then one year later, Mom died of a burst appendix. They couldn't rush her to the hospital in time to save her. After that, Relly was deathly afraid of more visions. She didn't want them to come to her. She even went to church, got down on her knees, and prayed that she would be delivered of them; and for a while, they disappeared and let her alone. She thought her prayers had been answered. She thought they were gone permanently, and she could live a normal life. She told me back then that that was what she wanted more than anything else in the world. We all want to fit in if we can."

Wendy was writing as fast as she could and finally looked up during another of Vance's pauses. "I gather from the tone you're using that things didn't return to normal, though?"

"No, they didn't. The flashes began to return not long after she graduated from college. She was working in a bank as a teller and foresaw in one of her flashes the bank being held up and someone being shot in the process. She went back and forth about going to the police, but she didn't think they would believe her. I mean, what police officer would believe a woman showing up insisting that a robbery would happen sometime in the future? Odds are that just about any bank would run that risk during its lifetime of operation. You know they would think she was crazy, wouldn't you?"

Wendy broke in long enough to answer his question. "I know Ross probably wouldn't believe that kind of story. He would listen politely enough, but I don't think he'd take it seriously. How would any police department have the time and manpower to devote to something like that? Post a patrol car across the street from the bank twenty-four/seven? It would never happen. I think only insurance companies take into account what might happen in order to go about their business."

"Exactly the point," Vance said. "Anyway, it was the next day that something told Relly to call in sick when there was nothing wrong with her. That was the day the robbery actually occurred, and the woman who took her place at her teller station ended up being shot. Fortunately, she survived, so at least Relly didn't have that on her conscience."

Wendy stopped writing and caught Vance's gaze intently. "I'm still confused. You seem to be telling me that your sister was both a phony and the real thing. Do I understand you correctly?"

"Yes, she continued to get flashes from time to time, but they were usually incomplete. As the years went by, she realized that she couldn't count on them. But by then she had already decided to try to make a living as a psychic anyway. She was comfortable with it as a concept. That's where I came in. We decided to team up and see how well we could do together, and it worked for us most of the time. Between her flashes and my research, we did okay. But we found it useful not to stay in the same town too long. Fresh faces with their different back stories served us well, and Rosalie was our latest move. We thought it was the best setup ever, what with Overview and all. Yeah, I know, it wasn't really legit and all that, but Relly never did any harm to anyone that I know of."

"That's the problem, though, isn't it? The 'that you know of' part. You can't be sure what people will do or have done as a result of readings that aren't legit. Suppose they *do* end up harming themselves? You would never know about it, but it might happen just the same."

"That's a slippery slope."

Wendy had an uncomfortable expression on her face. "I hope you don't think this is somewhat insensitive of me at this point, but I have to ask you if your sister snorted cocaine. You need to tell me the truth—at least as you know it."

"That's another reason this couldn't have been a suicide," Vance said, raising his voice a decibel or two. "She toyed with it way back in her college days, but not since then. At least, not that I know of. There's that phrase again. I'm not sure where she'd even get it here in Rosalie. Believe me—that's a huge red flag. All of a sudden, cocaine shows up in her life. Followed by death, it seems. She would have told me if she'd started up again. I just know she would. This whole thing is just way out of left field and should raise a hundred red flags."

Then Vance cleared his throat even as he was pointing to it. "I believe I'll take you up on that bottled water. My mouth has gotten so dry, I've been talking so much. This is taking a lot out of me."

"Of course, I totally understand," Wendy said, rising from her chair. "I'll just be right back."

On the way to the break room, a whirlwind of thoughts crowded into her head. A brother and sister con game had been in their midst, ready to strike and take no prisoners. Ross had already suggested such a thing—minus the brother revelation—with his skeptical comments, so it wasn't as much of a surprise as it might have been otherwise. Then there was the notion of murder to consider. Vance had trotted it out right away and had been insistent, while she, herself, had her own strong suspicions.

So, the next thing that Vance must do would be to go to Ross with all these revelations so that the CID could go to work. Overview had to be processed, even though Wendy knew that her DNA and those of her newbies would be all over the place after their evening there. That would only prove that they had all been there, but probably not much more. Unless something startling and conclusive showed up to incriminate someone, and that was always a possibility.

Then, as Wendy pulled a cold bottled water out of the break room fridge, she realized that Ross would have to run background checks on everyone. Were Vance Quimby and Aurelia Spangler really brother and sister? Could Vance really be trusted at this juncture, since he had already admitted to being one half of a con game? Those answers would be determined soon enough, however.

Back in the interview room, Vance twisted the cap off his bottled water with unnecessary force, causing a trickle or two to run down the sides. He ignored the wetness on his hand and took a long swig, but Wendy could not help but notice the brute force with which he attacked the plastic. It was almost as if he were strangling it and was out of control.

"I know I've been throwing a lot at you," he continued. "But the telling thing about all of this is that I visited with Relly out at Overview the evening she died. Yes, I was there—I admit it because I have nothing to hide—and I can tell you that she was far from suicidal. We both agreed that the bridge club readings had gone well enough, although she picked you out of the lot as the most skeptical. Was she right?"

There was a hint of amusement on Wendy's face. "Yep, she was certainly right about that. I did not intend to get carried away under any circumstances, but I also think I was prepared to have an open mind if anything remarkable happened."

"Anyway, we had great plans for our endeavor here in

Rosalie. We were gonna rig up the stairs to make creaking noises every now and then and have other sound effects to exploit J. Lindford Calmes's infamous death. You have no idea how much research I did about that, and we'd even worked out the engineering. There would be a well-hidden remote button that I could push without anyone realizing it, and we were gonna rev up the ghostly reputation of Overview like nobody's business. We were sure that that was only gonna enhance Relly's reputation once she put out her shingle and people started coming to her. We envisioned a virtual gold mine that would never end."

"That definitely sounds like a plan. A bit like a venue at Disney World, but still a plan."

Vance nodded and took another swallow of his water. "What I'm telling you is that Relly was looking forward to opening for business this coming week. She was not depressed. She was sure of herself about that. However, I will say that she was worried about the intensity of the flash she received concerning Milton Bagdad. She told me it was so intense that she believed it was going to happen. She said she hadn't had that realistic a vision in a long time. There were no flashes with the rest of you, though. Just the information I'd turned up about all of you already. But that was her curse, you know. She couldn't control these flashes and never knew when one would pop up. But the one about the knife plunging into a tuxedo shirt threw her off balance plenty. Unfortunately, it threw Milton Bagdad off, too. She regretted revealing any of it to him at all. Now, he's gone missing, so it appears her concerns were justified. Just another reason she sometimes viewed her off-and-on gift as a curse."

He hesitated for a moment, and his expression grew even more troubled. "There's . . . there's a part of me that even believes Milton may have had something to do with this."

"That remains to be seen," Wendy told him. "I'm a bit reluctant to go there at the moment, but I realize we have to cover all the bases. But the next thing you need to do is to go down to the station and tell Ross all of this. I'll text him and let him know you're on your way when we finish here. I'm thinking it will open up a genuine investigation, and I believe that needs to be done. I, too, was very skeptical about the suicide from the beginning, despite the coroner's report."

Vance finished off his water in one huge gulp, causing the plastic to make a crinkling sound there at the end. Again, Wendy couldn't avoid an image of the life being sucked out of the bottle. "It just wasn't Relly's style," Vance continued. "She would never have done something like that. She would have told me she was contemplating it, at the very least, and given me a chance to talk her out of it. After all, she was my livelihood, and I was hers. We were very close, and I don't think I should be doubted on that."

Another tear fell down his cheek.

"Again, I'm so sorry for your loss," Wendy told him. "I know that sounds clichéd and contrived, but I can see what distress you're in. Your sister clearly meant a great deal to you."

"She did. I never have found the right woman, although God knows I've tried, but Relly was married once. To this jerk named Brad Spangler. She thought he was the answer to everything. But the marriage broke up after a couple of years. He couldn't hold down a decent job to save his life. I don't know why Relly kept his name and didn't go back to Quimby. But that was her choice, and I never pressed her on the subject. Anyway, that was when she and I started getting even closer, and the psychic act just sort of fell into place after that. Life sometimes throws people together like that, but she wanted some financial security after living with an irresponsible man like Brad, and who could blame her?"

"When you go down to headquarters, tell Ross everything you've told me. Don't leave out anything," Wendy said, rising from her chair and extending her hand. "I'm sure we'll get to the bottom of this."

Vance shook her hand and sucked in air. "The thing that bothers me most is that apparently Relly couldn't see her own death coming, since I refuse to believe she took her own life, and I don't see her being the one to wear a tuxedo shirt. Her flashes were so inconsistent and piecemeal. This knife to the tuxedo shirt thing—whatever it is, whatever it means—has to be nipped in the bud. I don't know what can be done to stop it, but, believe me, if Relly said it was gonna happen, then it's gonna happen. You law enforcement people just can't stand around waiting. You need to do an in-depth investigation and find out what really happened to my sister and what all's behind it. I'll do whatever I can to help. She made no bones about it to me that something or someone would stop at nothing to achieve their goals. That's the part that makes my blood run cold, and I'm not the type that scares so easily."

He was about to exit the interview room when he turned at the last second. "Something else both you and your husband need to know, even if it might throw suspicion on me. Relly had taken out a life insurance policy on herself, even though it was just for fifty thousand dollars. She said she wanted me to have a little nest egg in case something untimely ever happened to her. I mean, the act wasn't much good without her, was it? So I'll say it to you right now and to your face—I did not murder my sister for that fifty thousand dollars. God forbid. I figure you need to know that up front to save you the investigation time. I realize it gives me a motive, but I'm telling you ahead of time—and I'll tell your husband, too—I'd be one sorry human being if I killed my own sister for any kinda money."

"Thank you for telling me," Wendy said, taken somewhat by surprise. "Just don't forget to tell Ross, too."

"Believe me, I won't."

CHAPTER 7

Because the College of Rosalie was in summer session, there were far fewer people in the Student Union than would have been the case in the fall or spring. In particular, there were no long lines at any of the burger, foot-long sandwich, and pizza outlets that made their living off the current enrollment on their student budgets. Just a smattering of couples and singles here and there, chatting, scrolling on their cells, or obliviously plugged into headphones. As a result, Wendy had no trouble spotting Sarah Ann sitting at one of the small tables in a far corner, typing things into her computer.

"Class assignment," she said, after Wendy had seated herself and the two of them had exchanged greetings. "I'm taking European Lit this summer. I just can't get enough of my major. But it was also the only opportunity I've had so far to get Professor Isaacson for a course. He's so intense, and he makes literature come to life with his lectures. He's also the handsomest teacher on campus. All the female students are positively gaga about him. Okay, I realize that's a juvenile reason for taking a class, but go ahead and sue me."

Wendy gave her a sideways glance and smiled. "So you're in that number of his admirers, I see."

"I'd be lying if I said I don't secretly have a crush on him, but he really is a mesmerizing teacher. I think my crush is within reason, but I happen to know a couple of classmates who sent him singing telegrams, even though they didn't have the nerve to identify themselves. They told me they both sent 'em anonymously from Your Secret Admirer, but then they swore me to secrecy. They said they would melt into puddles if Professor Isaacson ever found out. They prob'ly would, too. But what about him? Is it embarrassing or what for a grown man to be put in that position by his lovesick female students?"

That was a relatively easy question for Wendy to answer, since she was not all that far-removed from her own college years of study. "I suppose it comes with the territory of being a teacher. Students get crushes all the time, no matter their age. I had one at Mizzou on my calculus professor. His name was Erroll Moritz, and there was something about the faces he made when he got into the meat of his lectures. He would stare out above our heads and beyond us like he was admiring spiral galaxies from afar when he talked about equations. I could see them spinning around out in space. That may not make sense to you, but something about higher math stimulates my brain, and that's probably why I love solving problems so much."

Sarah Ann seemed amused, then assumed an impish pose. "That's just a more modern way of saying he looked *dreamy*. I wonder if I'd ever send a telegram, signed or anonymous. Usually, I believe in being much more direct with people. You have to go for what you want in life aggressively and take nothing for granted."

"Speaking of your English major, I know I loved the courses I took at Mizzou," Wendy continued, trying to regain control of the interview. "It's a fact that the literature of the past prepares you for what's going on in today's world. Of course, it goes without saying that down here in the South, some people are still fighting the Civil War tooth and nail. What a hopeless cause. I even saw where certain school districts are removing *To Kill a Mockingbird* from the curriculum because they think it's not politically correct. But let me get off my soapbox, and let's return to the reason we got together today, shall we?"

"Absolutely." Sarah Ann pressed a button and waited for her computer screen to go dark before giving Wendy her full attention. "Down to business. As I told you, I'm finding it hard to believe that Aurelia Spangler would commit suicide. She just seemed too vital a person to me to do something like that. It seems all wrong."

Wendy brought Sarah Ann up to speed on Vance Quimby's revelations and waited for her response.

"That's an incredible story. And here I was, all excited to have met a writer in person. I guess I even thought I might end up in his novel in some form or other—or at least on the Acknowledgments page. We students are so impressionable, you know. But that's another reason that I like to question things. Lies can be part of a curriculum—maybe not intentionally—but it happens enough here and there to serve various agendas."

"Vance's story was a shocker to me, too," Wendy said. "But I have every reason to believe that it's true. I just got a text walking in here from Ross saying that Vance is down at police headquarters telling him everything as we speak. It ought to open up a real investigation that's long overdue, the way I see it."

Sarah Ann scanned the Food Court to see who was nearby, then leaned in and lowered her voice. "I agree that it's coming at the right time, too. What I'm going to tell you may or may not have any significance, but I thought you ought to know—and maybe your husband, too."

"I can hardly wait to hear what you have to say."

"It's about my mother."

"For some reason, I thought it might."

Sarah Ann looked surprised. "Did you? Well, I know you're already aware that my mother and I don't get along. I would have moved out a long time ago, if I could afford an apartment. Just one more year and I'll graduate. But right now, it's cheaper to live at home and commute. Anyway, you need to know about something that Mother told me she'd done. Now, I'm not implying that she did anything wrong when she was there, but the fact is that she went to see Aurelia Spangler the very afternoon this supposed suicide took place. Mother was a bit worked up about it when she got home, if you ask me. But she gets that way at times. You should see her screaming at the TV when some politician or actor with a cause comes on that she doesn't like. 'You are gonna go straight to hell, mister,' she'll yell out, and don't think for a minute she doesn't really mean it. She has a certainty about her that's just not reasonable. People shouldn't let their brains get bronzed that way."

Wendy had not known exactly what to expect from this meeting with Sarah Ann, but this news about Dora O'Rourke did not seem out of place. "So, what all did she tell you about going out to Overview?"

"She said she went to give Aurelia a piece of her mind. Mother regarded her as a witch of some kind that was practicing black magic. So I thought it might be helpful if your husband interrogated Mother. As I said, I can't see her doing any actual harm to Aurelia, but something might come to light regarding their conversation. Of course, you and your husband can't let Mother know I've come to you with this information. I'm on thin ice as it is because I won't go to church with her anymore. I'm already worn out by her quotes twenty-four/seven. Why do I need another huge dose of that stuff at church?"

Wendy thought on her feet quickly as the professional reporter she was. "No, that shouldn't be a problem about you as the source. If Vance Quimby's revelations actually open an investigation, it would be proper protocol to interview everyone who participated in those cold readings and later visited with Aurelia Spangler. Ross could always say that Aurelia had kept notes on all her visitors, and your mother's name turned up. Believe me, he can handle it without arousing her suspicions that you said anything to us. Being married to a police officer and the daughter of the police chief has educated me well in law enforcement tactics."

Sarah Ann averted her eyes, and a certain sadness spread across her face. "I wish Mother and I did get along better and things were different between us. But she can't get past applying these passages to the smallest things in her life—and mine. Not only that, but she cherry-picks. I'll ask her why she abides by this passage but not that one, and she never has an answer. She preaches and preaches, and she may mean well with all of it, but it becomes oppressive after a while. I just tune her out, and I'm sure that's the last thing she wants."

Sarah Ann paused, and her mood and facial expression changed suddenly, becoming more placid, sounding more gentle. "Mother doesn't understand lightness of spirit. I believe we should go out into the world and tread lightly. We're all on our different journeys. But to quote Mother exactly, 'Woe be unto him who disagrees with me on everything under the sun, moon, and tides.' She's a walking, talking absolute, and I realize I'm very young and inexperienced, but I just don't think the world works that way."

"I understand your point of view," Wendy said, breaking into a gracious smile. "It's always been my belief to tread lightly in this world, too. I came to that the hard way when I lost my mother to pneumonia when I was just fifteen. I took it hard, and if it hadn't been for my daddy's guidance and patience—plus a bit of professional help—I don't think I would have made it through that terrible period. Sometimes, we need empathy and compassion and someone to hold us more than the printed word. It's more important and helpful to live it than to quote it."

Sarah Ann caught Wendy's gaze again and seemed almost transformed. "That's beautiful, almost poetic. Anyway, you understand that I'm not about trying to get my mother in trouble here. I just think she had no business going to see Aurelia Spangler like that. I'm sure Mother threw the Bible at her—figuratively at least."

Sarah Ann paused and gasped loudly before continuing. "That was part of Aurelia's cold reading for me. The image of a Bible being thrown down. Perhaps what she saw coming at her was my mother, and not me."

"Hard to say," Wendy told her. "Vance Quimby said that his sister's visions were often hit or miss. It's also difficult to tell at this point what was due to Aurelia's ability and what was due to Vance Quimby's research. He said he had ways of finding things out about people without them knowing it, and I'm quite sure he was telling the truth about that."

"But do you think an investigation will be opened? I just don't think any of us will be satisfied with this suicide verdict."

"I'd be surprised if Ross and my father don't get the CID on this right away."

"What does CID mean?"

"It stands for the Criminal Investigations Division of our very own Rosalie Police Department."

"Oh." Then Sarah Ann reached across the table and took Wendy's hand. "Thanks for taking me seriously. My mother doesn't. She tells me all the time that she thinks I'm a fallen

angel and that I need to listen to her to avoid eternal punishment. I just don't know what to do with that kind of harsh-
ness, but every time she says it, I pull farther away from her. I
mean, what young person finishing up their education with
the prospect of the whole world before them and all the rest
of their life ahead of them wants to be told from the get-go
that they've fallen short of the mark and need to be redeemed?
I'm sorry, but that just doesn't do it for me."

Wendy hesitated for a moment. She didn't know whether
she should say the words, but in the end, she did. "Far be it
from me to speak against mothers, since I lost mine at such an
early age. But try to hang in there. Maybe she'll eventually
lighten up, and the two of you can truly be friends sometime
in the future."

Sarah Ann had a smirk on her face. "Mother's always talking about the 'end times.' That they're very near, and we must
prepare for them. Maybe the two of us will call a truce before
then, but I'm not holding my breath."

When Wendy entered the cramped lobby of the *Citizen*
some fifteen minutes later, Charlotte Ruth was sitting in one
of the chairs, waiting for her; then she jumped up and grabbed
Wendy's arm.

"Oh, here you are at last, Wendy. I was told you'd be
back soon. I hope you don't mind, but I just had to see you
and get something off my chest," she said rather breathlessly.

"I'm assuming this is about the text I sent to all of you?
I've heard from just about everyone else, and it feels like I
could have gotten less of a reaction from a tornado siren."

"Yes, I suppose so. I just have to talk to you right away. I
thought about sending a text back to you, but this is far too
involved for cyberspace. I hate texting anyway. People have
gotten so rude about it, walking around practically running
into walls or even getting run over in the street. I'm all

thumbs, anyway, and I mean that in the traditional and not the technological sense. I needed to see you face-to-face."

"The first thing I want you to do is to take a deep breath and get your heart rate down," Wendy told her, gently rubbing her arm. "We'll talk privately in one of the meeting rooms. Come along with me."

Once they had settled in comfortably, Wendy was surprised to see that Charlotte had still not calmed down one iota. Her broad face was still flushed, and she was nervously fingering the collar of her blouse while flashing an uneasy smile. Finally, she blurted out what was on her mind.

"I feel so guilty, Wendy." But then she volunteered nothing further, making a grim slash of her mouth.

"About what? What have you done?"

"I feel guilty about Aurelia Spangler, of course."

Wendy proceeded logically. "Again, what do you feel guilty about? Did you do something to her? Are you here to confess to a crime or something?"

Charlotte hung her head while she spoke. "Not exactly, but I went to see her the afternoon you said she committed suicide."

"An apparent suicide. But it's beginning more and more to look like there could have been foul play."

Charlotte sighed, and it came off distinctly as one of relief. "Then she didn't commit suicide after all? I'm off the hook?"

"We can't be certain yet, but there's a chance that she could have been murdered. Anyway, what's this all about? You still haven't told me what it is you feel guilty about. Give me the complete picture."

"I think I may have put too much pressure on her and driven her over the edge," Charlotte began, making a sudden pushing motion with her hands. "I went to her that day because I was hoping she could . . . well, I guess this is going to sound silly to you coming from a widow who's still grieving . . . but I was hoping she could make contact with my Jimmy for me on the other side, or wherever he is. Now, you tell me—do any of us really know? But I mean, she knew about his suicide, so I thought maybe . . . well, I thought she might be able to speak to him and let me know if he was okay. I know this sounds even sillier, but I just can't help but wonder what type of . . . accommodations he has. Do some people get better rooms in better hotels or what? Maybe she could tell me how it works."

Wendy tried her best but could not suppress an outright snicker. "I like your thinking. It gives me renewed respect for travel agents."

But the one-liner fell flat, as Charlotte continued without a hint of a smile. "I've never really gotten over the way Jimmy left me, and I didn't appreciate Aurelia bringing it up again the way she did. I guess you could say I just went off the rails a bit, but as long as she'd gone ahead and done that, I figured I might ask her for more. Does any of this make sense to you, or do you think I'm babbling nonsense?"

"No, I don't think so. But let's get to the bottom line here. I assume you aren't confessing to anything diabolical. You have everything to lose by not leveling with me."

Charlotte's eyes widened immediately and she shook her head vehemently. "Of course not. But Aurelia did sort of break down right there in front of me and said that she couldn't help me any further. She told me I needed to leave her house, and she wasn't very courteous about it at all. I was surprised, of course. I really seemed to have upset her."

"So, you were thinking that's why she might have committed suicide? Because of you?"

Charlotte said nothing, but nodded her head.

"I highly doubt that, dear," Wendy said as emphatically as she could manage, seeing clearly she needed to nip this performance in the bud. "Listen to me carefully. If she said she couldn't help you further, she was telling you the truth." Then Wendy quickly reviewed what Vance Quimby had revealed, and Charlotte managed a strange, nervous giggle.

"Well, now don't I feel like the fool? An absolute fool. Here I was worried to death that I had set Aurelia on the path to self-destruction with my otherworldly requests, and she wasn't even the real deal. And Vance isn't even a real novelist. What a deceitful pair. Do you know if people can be put in jail for running a phony psychic operation like that?"

"I don't think so. Not if people come to them voluntarily in person, or it's one of those phone services charging by the minute that seem to be so popular. It happens every day all over the country. It's hard to make the case that people don't know what they're getting into. We've straightened this all out for you, though," Wendy said. "So when you left Aurelia, she was alive and well? She didn't by any chance threaten to take her life because of what you wanted her to do?"

"She was a bit agitated—but nothing more than that. I certainly didn't think she was going to do anything drastic. That's why your text was such a shock to me. Had I inadvertently done something to force her hand? She definitely didn't come off as anywhere near that unstable a person at your wedding and then at the bridge lesson that evening. I just thought she was one of those characters that drift in and out of people's lives all the time."

Wendy was trying her best to sort things out. It was her studied opinion that Charlotte Ruth was all over the map and desperately needed a rest stop. "I think you need to go down to the police station and tell my husband about all this. It's beginning to look like most of your bridge newbies paid a visit to Aurelia sometime during the day she died. It will help Ross establish a timeline and compare that against the time of death.

Except we don't know about Milton Bagdad yet. He's gone missing, and he hasn't answered the text I sent out to all of you. Needless to say, I'm quite worried."

There was a look of consternation on Charlotte's face. "This is getting more complicated by the second, isn't it? I wish now we hadn't taken Aurelia up on her cold reading offer."

"And I wish now I hadn't allowed it when Aurelia first asked my permission. As I said, what Tommy Cantwell called a suicide is beginning to look much less cut-and-dried."

Charlotte rose and offered her hand, though it had started to tremble. "Thank you for easing my mind a bit. But there's still the matter of poor Aurelia. She's still dead, one way or another. No more bridge lessons for her."

"Yes," Wendy said, shrugging, "I wonder how many of the rest of you will want to continue now. I seem to have the most horrific hurdles thrown in my way when it comes to the game of bridge."

Around five o'clock at the police station, Ross was just finishing up scanning an assortment of documents in Captain Bax's office. "The sample from the landlord proves that the so-called suicide note was definitely Aurelia Spangler's handwriting," he was saying, "and the background checks prove that Miz Aurelia and Vance were really brother and sister, born and raised out in Omaha. That's a mixed bag if there ever was one. She really did write that note, but her brother insists it was totally out of character for her to take her own life. So, by our own established standards, do we have enough for an investigation or not?"

Bax was striking his favorite pose, leaning back in his leather chair with his feet on the desk, and said, "Well, it's entirely possible that Miz Aurelia was coerced into writing that note and overdosing on cocaine. That seems to make the most sense to me. Have a seat and let's think it through some more."

Ross arranged all the documents on the desk into a neat pile first and then sat down. "Let's not forget about all these people who paid Miz Aurelia a visit the day she died. So far, we have her brother, and according to Wendy, Sarah Ann O'Rourke's mother and Charlotte Ruth showed up with various agendas that day. Miz Charlotte called up and said she would come down to the station tomorrow to tell me what happened when she visited with Miz Aurelia. We don't know about Milton Bagdad yet because we can't find him, but he could've been in play, too. We need to establish a timeline of who showed up when. My take is that we have enough for the CID to process Overview and see where that leads us. Besides, Vance Quimby has insisted on an autopsy down in Jackson, so we don't want to be caught napping if something unusual comes of that. That could end up being an x factor."

Bax looked satisfied with his son-in-law's evaluation and said, "Despite the handwriting determination, I see things the same way. There were too many opportunities for coercion and foul play that we need to investigate. Miz Aurelia hadn't even put out her shingle yet, and Overview was like a bus station that day. Something just doesn't feel right to me about the whole thing based on my many years of experience."

"We need to get this Dora O'Rourke in here, too," Ross continued. "As I mentioned, when Wendy talked to another of her bridge newbies today—Sarah Ann O'Rourke—the upshot was that her mother seemed to be all bent out of shape after her visit with Aurelia. Something could have gotten out of hand there quickly—something entirely out of character for a woman like Dora O'Rourke."

Bax took his feet off the desk and straightened up in his chair. That always meant he was ready for action with orders to give. "All right, then. We're decided. Let's get our crew out to Overview and make it an official crime scene. You take the lead and interrogate this O'Rourke woman first, and then we'll see if we can make some more sense out of all this."

As Ross left the room, he was certain Wendy would be pleased to hear that there would now be an official investigation into Aurelia's death. She had been lobbying all along against the suicide verdict. By now, Ross knew only too well that his wife had excellent insights into human behavior, as well as puzzle-solving gifts beyond the ordinary. Maybe she would even come up with the solution to this bizarre case, as she had with a couple of others in recent years.

CHAPTER 8

As he was standing behind the Party Palooza counter, Rex saw that the incoming call on his cell was from Mathilde Boudreaux, and he knew better than to ignore it. Merrie stood nearby, looking puzzled as he began his conversation, but understood the moment he whispered the words "Aunt Mathilde" to her with a pained expression on his face. Merrie could only smile and roll her eyes at the revelation. She knew her husband was in for a lengthy call.

"Yes, Auntie, there's no change in Milton's status," he said in response to what was an extended opening monologue at the other end. "No one knows where he is at this point. As I told you, we went to the police about his disappearance and filed a report, and we're still hoping for the best."

"Make sure they leave no stone unturned, Rex," continued the quiet, little voice all the way down in New Orleans. "Stay on them. They're your best bet for tracking him down, and you've said he's the best singer you've ever had."

"Yes, he definitely is. I assure you, we'll hound the police day and night, Auntie," Rex said.

"That recording you sent me of him during his audition

was outstanding. What a glorious voice. And his picture? What a handsome young thing! If I were only a coupla decades younger. Well, just listen to me. Anyway, enough of that. You've done too well up there to lose business over this now."

"Yes, Auntie. We realize that."

"It's worked out just as we'd hoped. Rosalie was the right move at the right time."

"Yes, Auntie. You were on target as usual."

"Please don't let me down."

"No, Auntie. We have no intention of doing that. Have we ever?"

There was more silence from Rex as he nodded over and over again at whatever it was she was droning on about. "I'll be sure and get back to you as soon as possible when we hear something. And thanks for the tickets and reservations. Meanwhile, Merrie and I have a costume party to go to soon. Gotta rake in that money, you know. So, I'll have to sign off now."

But there was a minute more of listening on Rex's part, and then he ended the call abruptly with a "Good to hear from you as always, Auntie." Then he turned to Merrie and said, "You know how she gets. I'm just thankful she doesn't try to micro-manage from New Orleans more than she does. She's the worrywart of all time, but I'm sure that's why she's so successful."

"I think she means well, though. I think it's sweet the way she looks after us like a mother hen."

"But she always seems to call me at the most inconvenient times. I was afraid she'd keep me on forever and make us late for our party."

"So what was the bit about the tickets and the reservations? Sounds like good news to me. I'm already looking forward to our next trip."

Rex's expression softened. "Ah, well, she said on our next visit down, she'd already bought tickets for us to the national tour of the *Company* revival at the Saenger, as well as reservations at Galatoire's."

"Well, there you go. She has such a thoughtful side. She always makes sure we have such a good time when we visit. That ought to be fun. I've heard raves about the gender change of the main character in *Company*." Then Merrie checked the time. "We have exactly five minutes to spare, and it takes three minutes to get there, so we're fine if we walk out the door right now."

Rex gestured in that general direction and bowed low. "After you, madam."

Milton had made up his mind—he would not budge on his decision to quit Party Palooza, no matter what Rex and Merrie Boudreaux kept throwing at him as incentives to stay. He had summoned the courage to walk through their front door after the long drive down from the Delta, surprising them with the bad news that he was determined to find another means of making a living, and that would be the end of it. Despite that revelation, they were both thrilled to see him alive and well, especially Merrie, who embraced him like he was her lost child.

"What would convince you to come back to us?" Rex was saying, sitting on the edge of his desk. He was still dressed as a gambler in the antebellum South, and Merrie stood nearby as a lavender hoopskirted Southern belle from the party they had just pulled off successfully.

"It's hard to find singers as good as you are," Rex continued. "I've had to deliver the last two telegrams myself, and although my speaking voice is quite acceptable, I can't carry a tune. The customers aren't getting their money's worth. You should see some of the faces they make. We'd really like to have you back."

But Milton was still having none of it. "It'd just be too

dangerous. Aurelia Spangler insisted that the vision of that knife and the tuxedo shirt was gonna happen and soon, and I don't intend to be around for it. The way I see it, there are still a lot safer ways of making a living. By the way, Mr. Boudreaux, have you considered that you might be the one who's in danger now that you're delivering these telegrams? You might wanna reconsider that aspect of the business."

Rex made an unpleasant face that distorted his features. "Look, I refuse to live my life in fear, son. I suggest you do the same. Also, you need to drop by the police station and tell them you're okay. We went down and reported you missing to Detective Rierson, and they've had a BOLO out on you all this time. Frankly, I'm surprised a police car didn't spot you on your way back to Rosalie and pull you over. Doesn't make me think all that highly of our state troopers."

"It's not their fault. It's because I took a lot of back roads from Rolling Fork to Rosalie," Milton said, looking rather proud of himself. "I don't know why I thought that was the best thing to do, but I did. It took a while for this panic mode I've been in to lose its grip on me, but it finally did, and I saw my way to sanity again."

"You didn't need to run off that way. Don't be so frightened of everything," Merrie said, now sounding exactly like a mother scolding a wayward child.

"If you could have seen Aurelia's face when she said she saw the vision, you would have believed she was telling the truth. You'd have run off, too. I was frightened out of my wits."

"Well, thank goodness you've come to your senses and come back to where you belong," Merrie added. "We suggest you ignore what that woman said and go about your business. She's no longer around to scare people out of their wits, and perhaps that's for the best."

"I will do one thing you've asked," Milton told them. "I'll check in at the police station and explain what happened. But as to coming back to deliver telegrams in costume . . ." He paused and shook his head. "For now, I just can't see my way clear to it."

Rex and Merrie exchanged disappointed glances, while she threw up her hands and said, "Let us know if you change your mind, otherwise we'll have to place an ad and audition for another good singer. The ones with your talent and personality don't grow on trees, you know. I'll make no bones about it. You were a wonderful asset to us, and we hate to lose you. We wanted the public to think of you as the face and voice of Party Palooza, and you have no idea what that meant to us."

A slight smile crept into Milton's face. "Thanks for the compliment. I do like to think of myself as a professional."

But Milton was no sooner out the door than Merrie brought up the elephant in the room. "Are you gonna call up your aunt and tell her about his refusal to come back to work?"

"Are you out of your mind? This isn't over yet by any means. This was just our first try. Now that we know he's okay and can relax about that part, there'll be other offers on the table—and hopefully one he can't refuse."

"How much is this gonna end up costing us?"

Rex made a smug face. "You gotta remember that what seems like a lot to a young kid like Milton may not be all that much in reality. Leave it up to your husband to handle it just the right way."

Down at headquarters, Ross was finding Dora O'Rourke difficult to communicate with in the interrogation room. Agenda-driven and consumed with working Scripture into practically every sentence uttered, she was distracting in the extreme. So he decided he had nothing to lose by politely laying down the law.

"Miz O'Rourke, I understand that you have strong religious views to which you are certainly entitled, but do you think you could refrain from trotting them out long enough to tell me what happened between you and Aurelia Spangler the evening you visited her at Overview? I am only interested in that and not what could happen to me at the end of my life."

Dora drew back with a look of surprise on her middle-aged, fleshy face, which featured no trace of makeup. Her lips were severely pursed, as she sucked air into her generous bosom; and with her hair fixed in a towering bun, she could not have looked more judgmental had she been delivering a sentence for a crime.

"I thought I'd been cooperatin' with you so far," she said. "I did you the favor of comin' here for all these questions, though I don't know what good it'll do you. I can't help you where the woman's death is concerned. She is beyond help."

"Yes, but please do me another favor and omit the Scriptures when you answer these questions. We're not in church or Sunday school." Ross was careful to keep his tone courteous and soft.

Dora took her time considering his request and finally said, "As long as you understand that I am a godly woman."

"Yes, I do understand that, Miz O'Rourke. I have no intention of trampling on that. So please continue with what you were saying about your visit, and concentrate only on that."

Apparently satisfied that she was being afforded the proper respect, Dora continued where she had left off. "Well, as I said, I had introduced myself to that Miz Spangler as Sarah Ann's mother who was very upset about her occupation, and then she led me into that cramped, little room with the Devil's red on the walls. Believe me, I did not wanna go in there because I could sense the wickedness just waitin' for me. Then she up and says to me, 'What can I do for you right now?' as if she hadn't listened to anything I'd said to her before that. It only convinced me all the more that I was bein' led into a chamber of Hell. I can sense when people disrespect what I stand for, and she had no respect, I can tell you for sure."

"I'm sure you can. Please go on."

"Anyway, I told her that I wanted her to stop fillin' my daughter's head with the Devil's lies." Dora paused to stick her nose in the air.

"And what did she say to that?"

"If you can believe it, she said that my daughter was a grown woman and had the right to live her life any way she wanted. She had the gall to tell me that there always comes a time in a child's life when she has to break the tie that binds. Can you imagine? A stranger buttin' into what's rightfully between a mother and daughter. That's just not the way it's supposed to be."

Ross noted the intensity and decibel level of Dora's voice. "That obviously angered you. Did you do anything about it?"

"What do you mean?"

Ross saw no point in holding back. "Did you threaten her in any way?"

Dora's look of disdain became even more pronounced. "Are you implyin' that I took her life?"

"No, not at all. I was just asking if there were any threatening words on your part in the heat of the moment."

"As I said, I just told her to stay away from my Sarah Ann. But she was smart-alecky about it all and said that she could not stop my daughter from comin' to her place to seek her services." Dora leaned in and made slits of her eyes. "The services of the Devil, I say. Conjurin' up evil is what she did for a living. And it makes perfect sense to me that she couldn't take it no more and ended it all the way she did. Just the definition of evil, I tell you. But justice was done."

"How can you be so sure of that?"

"Vengeance is mine, saith the Lord."

Ross decided to change tactics. "Miz O'Rourke, are you familiar with the drug cocaine?"

Dora's voice rose yet another decibel. "Not personally, if that's what you're gettin' at. All I know is that it leads people astray and ruins their lives. I've had friends tell me about their children who've gotten hooked on these drugs, and I wouldn't wish that life on anyone."

"I'm quite sure you wouldn't, and neither would I, but I bring it up because Aurelia Spangler died of a cocaine overdose. At least, that's what we think right now. She's being autopsied down in Jackson by the state medical examiner as we speak to verify the cause of death. Sometimes, these autopsies can reveal surprises. We take nothing for granted."

"I'm sure that's none a' my business," Dora said, bowing her bun slightly. "What she did to herself and how she pays for it in the end is up to her Maker and nobody else. That's the truth of the matter."

"You are very consistent, if nothing else, Miz O'Rourke," Ross told her. "You do stick to your guns."

"From your tone of voice, I'm not sure that was a compliment, Detective. But if it was meant to be, I thank you for it. I believe what I believe, and nobody can talk me out of it."

Dora struck a defiant pose there at the very end, and it flashed into Ross's head just how formidable a woman she could be at times. He could also easily envision the tense showdowns that must be taking place constantly between herself and her daughter.

"You'll get no argument from me," he said. "I'm quite sure they couldn't move you with a crane."

There was the slightest hint of a smile from Dora, and she said in a more softened tone, "Let me tell you somethin', Detective. I know that people make fun a' me because of my beliefs. Even my own daughter does, and it hurts me. It really does. I'm not stupid, you know. It's just that when my husband ran out on me and Sarah Ann when she was just a little girl, I had no place to turn to but my church. I was welcome there, and it's what got me through those tough times. Now, make fun a' that if you want, but I think we all need to believe in somethin'."

"You don't have to justify yourself to me, Miz O'Rourke. As my wife says to me all the time, 'We're all on our different journeys.' That's for you and your daughter to iron out between you. Seems like that's part of life for just about everybody. But I do need you to do one last thing for me, please. I'll need a sample of your DNA and your fingerprints for our investigation."

"Is that where you do the Q-tip thing I've seen on those crime shows? I watch 'em 'cause I like to see justice done to bad people. There's a lot a' them in this world, you know, and you can't tell just by lookin' at 'em which side they're on. Matter a' fact, the face a' evil often comes wrapped in pretty packages. You just think about that for a while."

Ross nodded as he pulled a swab from the pouch lying on the table. "I don't have to. I see you keep up with the times."

"Yes, Detective," Dora said. "I'm a lot more savvy about a lot a' things than you and my daughter think. Everyone only thinks they know me." Then she obediently opened her mouth wide.

The next day, it did not take long for the CID to verify the DNA and fingerprints of Wendy and her five bridge newbies at Overview, along with those of Dora O'Rourke and someone else who they could not identify. This biological evidence was found all over the parlor and in the reading room particularly, but that made perfect sense. Every one of those people had been there for bridge lessons, readings, or on another day for their private meetings as well, as in the case of Dora O'Rourke, Charlotte Ruth, and Vance Quimby.

Ross and Bax were mulling over the report from the criminologists in his office, and Ross said, "Well, this really doesn't tell us anything we don't already know, except for the unidentified prints and the wisps of African-American hair in the kitchen. I'm pretty sure we can zero in on who that was. Wendy spent some time out at Overview working with Miz Aurelia on the bridge lessons, and she mentioned to me once that there was a black housekeeper who came in once a week to straighten things up. Overview is an enormous place, you know. I'm sure Wendy knows her name, and we can get the woman to come down and give us her DNA. That'll likely clear that up."

Bax was once again lounging with his feet up on the desk, and Ross had set up shop in the chair across from him. "I'm also assuming your interrogation of Milton Bagdad today turned up nothing new or you would have said so."

"Correct. When he showed up at Party Palooza, Rex and Merrie Boudreaux told him they'd filed a missing person report and to come down and check in with us right away. He explained that it was just a case of panicking that he left town, plain and simple. But he did hand in his notice to them. No more delivering singing telegrams for him, he said."

Bax sat up and rapped his knuckles on the desk a couple of times. "So at first glance, his going missing seems to have nothing to do with what happened to Miz Aurelia. If we are to believe him. What next?"

"We do have to wait on the autopsy," Ross began, "but the deeper we get into this, the more the case can continue to be made to keep suicide open as an option. The interviews with the three who admit to visiting with Miz Aurelia after the bridge lessons seem straightforward enough. Miz Dora just doesn't seem like the type that would have the wherewithal to off anyone, what with her religious beliefs and all. Miz Charlotte was clearly ready to take the blame for the suicide, but she certainly didn't come off as a killer, either. And then there's Miz Aurelia's brother."

Bax broke in. "Do you think there's a possibility that Vance Quimby is playing us? That something happened between him and his sister that caused him to do away with her, and now he's covering his tracks by making sure we know about the life insurance policy? Now that we know he was down here on false pretenses to start with, do we take everything he told us literally, even though we know they were definitely brother and sister?"

Ross shot his father-in-law a skeptical glance, even though he loved these brainstorming sessions at the station. Both men had benefited from talking things out and sharing each other's perspectives on more than one occasion. "Killing the goose that laid the golden egg for fifty thousand dollars seems a bit shortsighted to me. According to him, his sister was his livelihood. I totally believed him when he told me all about their plans to rig up Overview by exploiting that creaky old story about J. Lindford Calmes falling to his death on the staircase. It made sense to Wendy when Aurelia told her, too. You know as well as I do that Rosalie is tailor-made for those who believe in ghosts and strange voices and things that go bump in the night. They even have those tombstone tours of the Rosalie Cemetery, where the locals portray famous people buried there. They're quite entertaining. Think of what all the antebellum attics, basements, and closets in this town have witnessed. Anyway, Vance and Miz Aurelia had a workable scheme in place, even if it wasn't exactly on the up-and-up. But someone put an end to it before it even began. Why did that happen? What did they have to gain?"

"Or lose," Bax said. "Maybe the real motive for this is something completely unexpected."

"Money's involved more often than not, as you well know. But there's always the outlier—the wronged lover and the crime of passion, or the wrath of the self-righteous crusader."

Bax made an unintelligible noise under his breath, which was usually a prelude to choosing an option. "That last thought makes me go back to Dora O'Rourke. She was highly opinionated about the harm she thought Miz Aurelia was doing to her daughter—and surely others as well. And we have her DNA now to confirm that she was really there when she didn't have any business being there at all. Her version of what happened between herself and Miz Aurelia may or may not be the truth. She may not be just quoting Scripture, she may be hiding behind it for her own self-serving reasons."

"On the other hand," Ross countered, "it was Miz Dora's daughter who put us on to her visit to Overview in the first place. Wendy found all that out when she interviewed Sarah Ann O'Rourke out at the college. There's a lot of really bad feeling between mother and daughter. Still, it's doubtful that it reached the level of Sarah Ann trying to frame or implicate her mother."

Bax was frowning now, but there was a measure of incredulity to it. "So you're suggesting that Sarah Ann O'Rourke might have killed Miz Aurelia? That seems the unlikeliest explanation of them all, son."

"You know this business, Bax. We've both seen enough of those out-of-left-field solutions to last us a lifetime. I got the unshakeable feeling that this is gonna be one of 'em."

"Could be. Meanwhile, you get the name of Miz Aurelia's

housekeeper from Wendy, and we'll see if that turns up anything helpful. But there's something else we need to consider, and I'm surprised you haven't brought it up yet."

Ross leaned forward in his chair, giving his full attention to his mentor. "And what's that?"

"There's the matter of the cocaine. Vance Quimby claims that his sister had not relapsed into using it. What if he was wrong, and she had started snorting again behind his back and didn't have the nerve to tell him? Where did she get it, then? A few years back, we shut down the two most notorious dealers in town and bundled them off to their sentences in Parchman. We know she couldn't have gotten it from them. Or if she hadn't started using again, and someone forced it on her, where did they get it? We need to go to our old reliable street informant, Earl Jay Doxey, and see if he knows anything about who's still dealing in Rosalie. Whether Miz Aurelia committed suicide or was murdered, there could be a new player in this crazy old town, and Doxey might help us find out who it is."

"Aurelia's housekeeper's name is Lula West," Wendy was saying as she and Ross sat at the dining table that evening, munching on a dessert of fresh fudge she had bought that day from Darby's on Main Street. It was always Wendy's go-to when she needed to keep Ross's sweet tooth satisfied. "My guess is that she's probably in the phone book."

"We think the unidentified prints and DNA may belong to her, then," Ross continued. "We'll track her down and ask her to come in tomorrow."

Wendy took a sip of milk to balance the sweetness of the fudge. They were the perfect complement to each other. "If it's hers, I doubt it'll lead to anything. Aurelia told me that Lula had only been working there for a few weeks, but I had to blink when Aurelia told me how much she was paying her.

I see no reason Lula would have wanted to do away with an employer who'd given her a job that lucrative."

Ross's face was full of creases as she spoke. "Can it be possible that Miz Aurelia really did commit suicide? Don't tell me you've fallen back on that again. Nothing has come to light to convince me that she did such a thing. I continue to believe that someone forced her hand and actually committed murder. I've had a very strong feeling about this since the very beginning."

Ross's creases disappeared as he gazed at his wife with a smile. "You know I have all the respect in the world for your instincts. I just hope we can make some headway in this case. Your father and I were throwing everything we could against his office wall today to see if anything would stick. For every reason we had to suspect someone, there was an equal and opposite reason to dismiss them. Of course, we haven't gotten the report yet from the ME. Maybe something will turn up there."

"And if it doesn't?" Wendy said, deciding to play devil's advocate. "What if the autopsy reveals that Aurelia died of a cocaine overdose and nothing more? Do we have to accept Tommy Cantwell's original call of suicide, barring any new evidence to the contrary?"

"I guess it could come to that," Ross said, looking down at the last bite of fudge on his plate. Then he caught Wendy's gaze with a sheepish expression. "Do you think I should have another piece?"

She snickered. "Only if your pants are still fitting, my dear, sweet husband. Are they?"

He stood up quickly and pointed to his waist with a look of achievement on his face. "Haven't had to go to another belt loop in years. I mean, not since just right after college. Belt loops don't lie."

Wendy laughed and sauntered over to the large clear jar

on the counter, where she kept all the sweet treats, pulled out one of the smaller pieces of fudge for him, and put it on his dessert plate.

As he gleefully attacked it with his fork, she said, "I think it's pretty obvious that the key to this case has to be Aurelia's vision of the knife to the tuxedo shirt. It truly spooked Milton Bagdad, and from what you say he told you at the station today, it wasn't business as usual for Aurelia, either. You said Milton told you he had quit his job at Party Palooza because he feared for his life, and that Rex Boudreaux was now delivering the telegrams. If there was any truth at all to Aurelia's vision, shouldn't Rex be in danger now? Isn't that where you and Daddy and the force should concentrate before something else terrible happens?"

Ross swallowed a bite of fudge and said, "But concentrate on what? How can we concentrate on something that hasn't happened yet? Rex Boudreaux hasn't asked for police protection, and frankly, we don't have the manpower to follow him around all the time for something that might or might not happen. I really don't think he'd go for that anyway. He's a big physical specimen who can certainly take care of himself if the occasion arises."

Wendy's expression remained skeptical. "I don't think this is about Rex in that way. After all, he really wasn't there to experience Aurelia's vision."

"For that matter, neither was Milton if you think about it. He had to take Aurelia's word about what she claimed to see. She either saw something terrifying, or she was lying."

"In the latter case, we really have nothing to go on."

"I wouldn't go that far," Ross said, as husband and wife seemed to be switching places in their discussion. "We have a dead body, no matter what."

"I wasn't denying that part, of course. Somehow, we've gotten off track."

Her remark caused Ross to crack a smile. "Okay, then. Milton may have taken that vision seriously—or too seriously, I might add—but apparently, Rex Boudreaux is not. My impression from Milton is that Rex is going about his business and not paying attention to Miz Aurelia's vision at all. Maybe that's the most reasonable approach for all of us to take anyway, because the evidence we do have is not really helping us in this case."

But Wendy was shaking her head emphatically. "If you have any regard for my sleuthing skills—and I know you do—you can't just shrug this off and accept Tommy Cantwell's verdict as gospel at this point. Yes, I'm well aware you have to follow the evidence, but I don't care what anyone says. I know without a doubt that Aurelia Spangler did not commit suicide."

CHAPTER 9

It had been over a year since either Bax or Ross had availed themselves of Earl Jay Doxey's services. A former dealer of a smorgasbord of drugs in his wild, younger days, he had finally gone straight by buying and running a successful tow yard; but he was still privy to what was going down on the streets of Rosalie and was happy to share such valuable information with the police department. He had even cleaned up his act enough to take a wife and buy a house out in Whiteapple Village, which was a most respectable address. Himself the product of a mixed marriage with his rich café au lait complexion, welcoming smile, and trademark gold rings in his ears, he was considered a friend to both black and white Rosalieans; and his relationship with Bax, particularly, went all the way back to the police chief's rookie days when Earl Jay had frequent run-ins with law enforcement.

"So, what can I help you with today, Chief?" Earl Jay was saying, as he nursed his beer at the Simply Soul Café on the north side of town. As was usually the case, a B.B. King tune played in the background as early lunch customers began to drift into one of Rosalie's most popular neighborhood haunts.

But Bax wanted to shoot the breeze just a bit with his old

friend before getting down to business. "First, how's that married life treatin' you? I never thought I'd see you so settled, Doxey."

"My Mary Liz is the best thing that ever happened to this ol' rascal, I tell ya. She won't let me get away with a thing, ya know. I used to be able to stay out as late as I want, but Mary Liz has all kinda rules I never thought I'd pay attention to. But I do, and I tell ya somethin' else—I like it. It suits me. I needed tamin'."

Bax stared down at his coffee cup and smiled. "Marriage'll do that to any man if he honors it. My Valerie had me wrapped around her little finger, and I loved every second of it. I miss her like all get-out."

"I heard that, Chief."

Both men went silent for a while, and then Bax switched to the reason for their meeting. "You remember we sent Poley Johnson and Larry Ventner and their pals up to Parchman for at least thirty years a while back, right?"

"Sure do. They got a lotta young kids hooked on coke in their day, and those hustlers got what'z comin' to 'em. They even had a few ODs on their hands."

Bax took a healthy swig of his coffee and caught Earl Jay's gaze intently. "Do you happen to know of any new player in town, Doxey? We have reason to believe there might be— and a very clever, ruthless one at that."

Earl Jay frowned, looking past Bax in contemplation. "Lemme see, now. I cain't say I have, though. Nothin' new goin' down on the north side a' town that I know about. Somebody woudda said somethin' by now. Why do you think it might be a new player out there?"

"Well, we had a cocaine overdose suicide the other day— or at least we think it was—and it kinda caught us by surprise. I mean, we're not naïve enough to think that Rosalie is clean and sober as a whistle even now and that nothin' at all goes on, but it was plenty messy, what happened, and I told my son-in-law that it couldn't hurt to get in touch with you. Our suicide wasn't somebody off the street who might be using, black or white. She was a well-off white woman, and there are some aspects that seem suspicious to us. We've got a full investigation ongoing."

Earl Jay hitched his mouth to one side. "And you want me to keep an ear and an eye out for ya, right?"

"You got it."

"Done. If it's anything goin' on at all, I should be able to sniff it out sooner or later. I have my ways. By the way, you wanna hang around a little longer for some lunch with me? It'll be my treat."

Bax shot his friend a look of genuine regret and then threw up his hands. "You know, I wish I could, Doxey, but I got lots on the agenda today, including a lunch meeting with the mayor about makin' room in the budget for buying a coupla new police cars. Gotta get that request in early or some other department will, and then the money'll be gone like that. But if I could hang out a little longer, it'd be my treat, not yours."

"Just like the old days, huh?"

"Just like."

Earl Jay finished up his beer before it got too warm and said, "Well, I think I'll stay and order me some greens and pinto beans and another cold beer. Does that make you wanna stick around a little longer?"

Bax glanced at his watch and winced. "Don't get my stomach growlin' now. You know I'm hooked on the food here, but I really gotta run."

The two men rose and firmly patted each other on the back the way men will do. "I'll get back to ya, if I hear anything, Chief. It may take me a while, but you know I'll cover all the bases."

"I know you will, Doxey."

It was Merleece Maxique's day to clean for Wendy and Ross in the morning and Bax out on Lower Kingston Road in the afternoon, but Wendy was looking forward more to sharing with Merleece her latest bridge-related catastrophe— namely, that one of her earnest newbies had met with a shocking and untimely end. Merleece had never failed to give her down-to-earth advice and counsel over the past couple of years, and Wendy was hoping for more of the same on this particular sweltering Tuesday morning in June. Over coffee and blueberry muffins at the kitchen table, Wendy gave her friend and confidante the details of what had taken place at Overview and then what disturbing news had followed a couple of days later.

"That is some sorry bid'ness, Strawberry," Merleece said, shutting her eyes and shaking her head as her ordinarily pleasant smile disappeared. Then she patted the top of her close-cropped hair a couple of times absent-mindedly. "I don't cotton to suicide much. Seem to me they's always some way outta any kinda depression that deep. Now, I don't wanna be judgin' somebody and all like that, but I don't think you can just give up on life thataway."

Wendy picked off part of the top of her muffin—she felt that it looked messy to eat below the paper, and crumbs got beneath your fingernails besides—and popped it in her mouth, washing it down with a sip of coffee. "That's the thing, though. I've told Ross and Daddy from the beginning that I don't think Aurelia Spangler committed suicide. I think she was murdered. I think someone forced her to overdose on cocaine— by whatever means. I'm sure of it, even though I don't know why someone would have done that to her yet."

Merleece made a gentle, sympathetic sound. "But you gotta prove it was murder first, right?"

"Doesn't matter who gets there first—whether it's Daddy, Ross, someone else on the force, or me. It's my strong belief that if the coroner's report of suicide is allowed to stand, that someone will be getting away with murder. Of course, we still haven't gotten the results of the autopsy from the medical examiner down in Jackson. We do have to wait on that."

Merleece made a face and shivered at the same time. "That autopsy stuff—cuttin' up someone with a knife that way—I don't see how folks can do that to another body for a livin'. Kinda creepy, you know what I'm sayin'?"

"Well, someone has to do it, although I'll grant you, it's not the most pleasant thing to think about," Wendy said. "But look at it this way. There's a lot of justice done because of it. The autopsy is a way for the dead to speak to the living without any doubt."

Merleece swallowed a big bite of her muffin and said, "I guess so. Anyway, you told me you didn't know why somebody'd wanna kill that Miz . . . Spangler, was that her name?"

"Yes, Aurelia Spangler."

"Well, when you start lookin' for answers, don't forget to look up, down, all around you, and straight ahead."

All the lines in Wendy's forehead revealed themselves at once at that one. "I'm not sure what you're getting at."

Merleece produced the sliest of her smiles and took a deep breath. "Just somethin' that did actually happen the other day with Miz Crystal."

The very mention of the woman instantly relaxed Wendy's facial muscles and she said, "I can't wait to hear this."

"It was nothin' much—just somethin' simple," Merleece began, puffing herself up a bit more with every word. "You know how she always get to dressin' up like she's the Queen a' England no matter what party or where it is?"

Wendy laughed out loud. If there was one thing she particularly looked forward to on Merleece's visits, it was the skinny on the latest escapades of Rosalie's perpetual social climber, the very wealthy and widowed Crystal Forrest of Old Concord Manor. Not that there wasn't plenty to observe when the woman played with the Bridge Bunch out at the Rosalie Country Club, but it had been Wendy's experience that Merleece was never guilty of what could pass for mean-spirited gossip. The hardworking, loyal cook and housekeeper was always about the unvarnished truth, warts and all, even if she was inclined to give people the benefit of the doubt first.

"I'm familiar with most of her wardrobe excesses, yes," Wendy said, still conjuring up images of the woman gallivanting about town at times in what amounted to outfits just shy of period costume.

"Well, she was really out to impress somebody the other evenin'," Merleece continued.

"I think it was some prissy lady comin' into town who was with some group about white people's ancestors or somethin'. They's plenty that get all worked up 'bout that here in Rosalie. Anyway, Miz Crystal was wearin' her opera gloves and one a' her sparkly gowns that near 'bout blinded me when the overhead lights hit it; but then she got herself all worked up. 'Merleece,' she say to me, all outta breath and talkin' British through her nose the way she always doin', 'where is my tee-ahhh-ruh? I simply must have it on my head tonight, but I cahn't seem to find it anywhere. Do you possibly know where it could've got to?'"

Merleece paused to roll her eyes and cackle. "Now, who do you know anywhere that talk that way—*where it got to?*"

Wendy stopped laughing long enough to say, "You always do a fabulous imitation of her, you know."

"I ought to. I heard her talk that way long enough. Anyway, then I look her straight in the eye, I mean, I'm starin' her down, chile, and I say, 'Miz Crystal, you already wearin' the tiara. It's right up there in that hairdo."

"No, not really," Wendy said, continuing to laugh.

"Yes, really, Strawberry. You shoudda seen her reachin' up to feel for it, and then her face got all pink, and I have to press my lips together so hard, they hurt just to keep from laughin' in her face, but I manage not to do it."

When their present laughter had died down, Wendy said, "That was funny, but I forget—why were you telling me that story?"

Merleece put her coffee cup down and leaned in. "Now, pay attention. What I mean is that sometime what you lookin' for is right in front a' you, more or less in plain sight."

Over the years, Wendy had found that particular phrase a bit confounding—*hiding in plain sight*. Did people really get away with things by *not* hiding them from others? Did they really just count on people overlooking the obvious—or if not the obvious, then the cleverly disguised? But not so cleverly that an inquisitive mind could probe deep enough to figure it all out. That would be Wendy's mission in such a case, and she felt that this one certainly qualified.

"Thank you for reminding me about that," Wendy said. "What I think I need to do is to apply it to everyone who was at Overview, either on the evening of my first bridge lesson or later in the week on their own. What might I be overlooking about any of them or their stories? Are any of them too clever for their own good?"

Merleece resumed sipping her coffee thoughtfully and then said, "I can see the wheels turnin' already, Strawberry. Seem like they always do start when we get together and catch up with each other."

"That's a fact. You are very good for my sleuthing skills. You coax them out of hiding."

"And I don't even charge you."

"Is that a hint for a raise?"

Merleece enjoyed the kidding between the two of them and pointed her finger playfully. "Now, you know it's not. You pay me plenty. Between you and Miz Crystal, I'm stout at the bank."

"Stout?"

Merleece added a wink for good measure. "I'm mighty comfortable is what I mean. Stout—well, that's just my word for it. At this stage a' my life, I'm truly thankful for that."

Wendy had been putting it off long enough. Did the remaining newbies want to continue bridge lessons at the Rosalie Country Club or not? She and Lyndell had already decided that the article about them being taught had been dealt a fatal blow—literally—by Aurelia Spangler's death. It would just be in bad taste. But that didn't really preclude more lessons from the others if there was continued interest, and she had to be the one to determine that.

When Merleece had finished her cleaning after the two of them had resolved all the troubles of the world over their coffee and muffins, Wendy drove to work and settled into her cubicle with phone calls to the rest of the newbies as her top priority. For some reason that she did not bother to question, she chose the following order: Sarah Ann, Charlotte, and finally, Milton.

Vance had already made it clear to her and the police department on another occasion that he intended to stay in Rosalie to help solve his sister's death in any way he could, but that playing bridge would seem disrespectful to her in the extreme. Wendy had agreed with him at the time by nodding in silence, but in the back of her mind, she had filed away the observation that Vance had been overly emphatic about everything, flashing his temper when it was unnecessary to do so. They were all on his side, thoroughly sympathetic to his loss. So why did he think he needed to convince them of anything? And then there was the fact that he had made sure they all knew about his sister's life insurance policy. Was that overkill?

As it happened, Wendy reached Sarah Ann at home right off, rather than at the college, and put the bridge question to her immediately.

"Yes, I'd like to continue," she said with girlish enthusiasm. "That is, if you're still willing to teach us. I'm an adventurous person, as you well know, just in case you were at all worried that I was afraid that someone was going to pick the rest of us off one-by-one. Do you think I'm paranoid?"

Wendy was taken aback by the comment. It showed an odd, even morbid sense of humor, and she allowed herself a few moments to consider her reply. "That's an idea that hadn't occurred to me, I can assure you. I'm going on the assumption that Aurelia's death was a single, isolated incident that will hopefully not be repeated in any way, shape, or form."

Sarah Ann laughed off the comment, then continued her curious narrative. "You know, I was just thinking that it's too bad Vance Quimby really isn't a novelist, because what happened at Overview absolutely has the makings of a good book. Don't you think so? I know I'd want to read it."

Wendy again had to think on her feet. "Well . . . perhaps in the true crime category, once it gets solved."

"Do the police have any real leads?"

Suddenly, Wendy realized that it was she who was being interviewed and not the other way around. Sarah Ann was being awfully nosey. Or was it just natural curiosity because she and Aurelia had become friends in the short time they had known each other? The phone call was supposed to be about continuing bridge lessons, but it was turning out to be anything but.

"I'm not privy to that sort of information," Wendy said, with an edge to her voice. "But I can assure you that Ross and my father and the entire department are hard at work as usual."

Sarah Ann pressed on. "Do they ever tell you anything?"

"No," Wendy said, nipping that line of questioning in the bud. "Anyway, can I put you down for more bridge lessons at the RCC?"

"Yes, of course."

"I have to check with Charlotte and Milton, but if we have at least three, we'll continue because I can always sit in at the table as the fourth. It might even work out better that way. In any case, I'll let you know."

Wendy thought their conversation had ended at that point, but Sarah Ann kept it going. "Guess what crazy, compulsive thing I've done? I decided to go ahead and send Professor Isaacson an anonymous singing telegram just like my classmates did. It's being delivered tonight. I talked to my friends Mandy and Patricia about it, and we agreed it would be fun to keep the pressure on him."

"What do you mean? Surely the three of you aren't foolish enough to think you can date him. I'm sure that's against the rules."

"No, we weren't going that far. It's more like keeping him wondering which of his students were sending them and seeing what he eventually does about it."

Wendy was rapidly becoming annoyed. "I would think he's not likely to do anything but ignore every one of them. College professors don't have time for that kind of foolishness."

"It prob'ly is silly. But you're only in college once. Didn't you pull some crazy stunts?"

Wendy felt no obligation to continue the conversation but made a mental note of Sarah Ann's peculiar attitude. "I forget.

Anyway, I've got another call incoming, so I need to take it. Bye for now."

"I'm having trouble getting Aurelia's death out of my head," Charlotte was saying over the phone after Wendy had put the question of more bridge lessons to her. "You helped me realize that I probably shouldn't feel guilty about that visit I had with her, and I thank you for that. But I still feel sad. I don't think I'm well. Dealing with two suicides in one lifetime is not something I'd counted on. You'd have to have gone through it to truly understand."

"I'm sure you're right," Wendy said. "I'm sure we all feel bad for Aurelia, and if you don't want to continue with the bridge lessons, that will be that. Sarah Ann wants to continue, but I've already told her that we need at least three—plus me, of course—to make a table."

There was a long pause—so long that Wendy thought the call had been dropped, or Charlotte had put her phone down and wandered off for a drink of water or to go to the bathroom. "Charlotte?"

"I'm sorry," Charlotte finally said, sounding as if she were about to burst into tears. "I've been so out of it lately, thinking about my Jimmy because of what happened. It just dredged it all up again. I've been considering going to a psychiatrist. Does Rosalie have one that you could recommend? I'm still so new here. I'd appreciate any help you could give me."

Wendy was as surprised by Charlotte's emotional response as she had been by Sarah Ann's strange, cavalier comments. "The only one around is Dr. Henshaw. He's been practicing here for years. I could put in a good word for you, if you like. Along with my father, he helped me get over my mother's death when I was a teenager. I'm sure he's got a busy schedule considering all the crazy Rosa—" Wendy cut herself off as she realized she was veering into gossip.

"Anyway, I could see what I can do to get an appointment for you. I might not be a doctor, but my referral might be just as good as one."

"That would be wonderful."

"But I do have something further to say to you. Bridge is not only a social game, it's highly therapeutic. In the time since I've more or less mastered it, I've seen that it can take your mind off your problems, if only for a few short hours. But during that time, you are with friends who are happy to see you, have a bite to eat and drink with you while competing with you in a friendly competition. Believe me, I think you'll feel better about yourself if you learn the game, and you'll also save money, since psychiatrists don't come cheap."

Charlotte sniffled and then exhaled. "Well, you know what? I believe you've talked me into it. I still want you to give that psychiatrist a call for me. But the next lesson is on Saturday at the RCC, then?"

"If I can get Milton to come aboard, yes. I'll get back with you and let you know one way or another."

"Good." There was an awkward pause. "Wendy, tell me something. Do you think I'm an old fool acting the way I am?"

"Certainly not. Your grief is real, and you shouldn't ignore it. Don't apologize for your feelings."

"Thank you, dear. I really am beginning to think that learning bridge will pull me out of my funk or whatever else is the matter with me."

When the call was ended, Wendy picked up a pen and started making notes. It was that inner sleuth of hers, nudging her, gnawing at her. She wrote in all caps:

SARAH ANN—ON BOARD, CAVALIER ATTITUDE
CHARLOTTE—ON BOARD, EMOTIONAL MESS

She frowned when she read her own comments. What was she doing? And then she remembered what she had said to Merleece at the breakfast table. It was this *hiding in plain sight* business that Merleece had brought up. Were these two women genuine suspects, or was she overthinking it? She had been successful at solving crimes before by digging deeper and examining things from a different angle, and even though Lyndell had canceled the article on teaching the bridge newbies, she could not cancel Wendy's interest in every aspect of this bizarre case.

"Guess where I am?" Milton said, after Wendy had said hello to him over the phone. "I'm at Party Palooza. Rex and Merrie wouldn't give up on me, and they've finally made me an offer I can't refuse to return to my singing telegram job. Apparently, they just can't do without me, and they kept raising the ante until my eyes were filled with dollar signs. It took some doing, though, 'cause that vision really freaked me out but good, but Rex is even gonna go with me on the delivery tonight to show me there's nothing to fear. I mean, he's been delivering them in my absence for a few days, and nothing awful has happened to him. Maybe Aurelia Spangler's vision died with her."

Wendy was amazed. All three of her newbies had totally surprised her with their unexpected attitudes and responses. "If you're comfortable now, I'm happy for you." Then she asked Milton if he would consider being the third newbie to continue the bridge lessons, and he didn't hesitate to answer.

"Well, I was having fun before all the cold readings, so my answer is an emphatic yes." Then Wendy's curiosity got the better of her. "If you wouldn't mind, could you tell me if by any chance that telegram you're delivering tonight is to a College of Rosalie professor?"

There was a gasp at the other end of the call. "Matter a' fact, yes. How did you know that?"

"Never mind my sources."

"Are you gonna be the psychic now?"

They both laughed, and Wendy said, "Hardly. I'll just stick to my investigative reporting, thank you. Anyway, with you on board, our next bridge lesson will be at seven thirty Saturday out at the RCC. Charlotte Ruth, Sarah Ann O'Rourke, and myself will make up the table, since Vance Quimby has withdrawn."

There was a long pause. "So, the original five newbies are down to three, then."

"Afraid so."

Then Milton began an unsolicited monologue. "I just sort of lost it for a while when Aurelia shared her vision with me, but I'm back now, thinking straight, thanks to Rex and Merrie. The way I see it, Aurelia was an actress of the highest caliber, but Rex said that I just couldn't allow myself to be taken in by her. She relied on hysterical reactions to build her reputation and get the word out on the street. I guess I'm a prime example of going overboard."

"Apparently so."

After Wendy hung up, she made a third newbie notation beneath the other two she had written earlier:

MILTON BAGDAD—ON BOARD—DELIVERING
ONCE AGAIN

Then to wrap things up neatly, she added three more, even though one was not a member of the original five newbies:

VANCE QUIMBY—NOT ON BOARD—PART OF
THE ACT

AURELIA SPANGLER—SUICIDE OR MURDER?
DORA O'ROUKE—SCRIPTURE CRUSADER

For the first time, Wendy began to wonder if Tommy Cantwell's COD was going to end up standing after all. This case, she decided, was the most complex she had ever encountered in her brief career as the amateur female sleuth of Rosalie. Everything and everyone seemed out in the open. But therein lay the dilemma if what she and Merleece had discussed carried any weight at all.

Hiding in plain sight, if done expertly, covered up the truth to perfection. It was the boldest of moves, full of risks, but with the ultimate payoff of getting away with murder. Literally. So what or who was she missing or overlooking? There was still a part of her that was making her terribly uneasy with the status quo. She simply could not let go of Aurelia's sudden departure. Almost as important as the *who* was the *why*.

Perhaps once she got some inkling of that, she would discover the truth.

CHAPTER 10

Milton was beginning to feel like his old self again as he drove through town to Professor Isaacson's house on Wisteria Drive in one of the newer suburban developments outside Rosalie. Undoubtedly, one reason for that was due to Rex Boudreaux sitting in the front passenger seat as his faux bodyguard; at the moment, Rex was in the midst of a pep talk to end all pep talks.

"We got so many calls from delighted customers after practically every one of your deliveries," he was saying. "I'm afraid I ran a distant second to you in that department. I didn't even try to sing on my deliveries because I think our customers would've run out of their own homes screaming. Reciting the words just doesn't get the job done, you know. Let's face it, Milt, I was dragging Party Palooza down without you. We need your talent and your youth to continue to be successful with our telegrams. You'll put the singing part back. Thank goodness you changed your mind, and I hope that's for good."

Milton let all the praise sink into him like a professional massage. Only it was his ego being stroked, not his muscles.

He had been someone who was easily swayed one way or another all his young life, and this particular instance was doing the trick. "I'm not planning on getting any more cold readings anytime soon, if that's what you're implying."

"Good deal. I think you could prob'ly go the rest of your life without another one. I'm sure we're all sorry about what happened to Aurelia Spangler, but we have to get on with our lives."

It was nearing eight forty-five in the evening, the fireflies were out, and the summertime light was fading drastically, but Milton didn't have to bother with his GPS this time out because he already knew the way to Professor Isaacson's house. Twice before, he had delivered anonymous telegrams to him. The first time, the man had been mildly amused and tipped him handsomely, even after getting no satisfactory answer to his question, "So you have no idea who sent this to me?"

"The owners know," Milton had said to him. "But when the customer wants to be anonymous, they don't tell me."

The second time, Milton's tip was not as hefty, and Professor Isaacson did not disguise his annoyance. "I guess you don't know who sent me this one, either, right?" the man had said.

Milton had answered with a somewhat sheepish, "No, I'm sorry, I don't know, sir."

But even though this would be the third time he would be delivering an anonymous telegram to Professor Isaacson, Milton wasn't particularly nervous. Rex Boudreaux would be with him this time—in a tuxedo outfit, no less—to field any questions about anonymity and the identity of the "secret admirer."

Surprisingly, however, Professor Isaacson did not do a double take or shoot an exaggerated frown at Milton and Rex when he answered the doorbell. Dressed smartly in a brown smoking jacket that matched nearly perfectly with his thick brown hair and mustache, he behaved cordially with a smile plastered across his strong features.

"Come in, come in. I've given up resisting these musical outings. I know you guys won't tell me, but I'm sure these are the work of some of my female students out at the college. I'm not naïve. I understand the teenage libido. But it's also what I get for being stubbornly single."

"That's the spirit," Rex said. "I'm here just to lend moral support, but Milton here is gonna do the honors of your delivery."

"He was most melodious the first two times."

Once they had moved from the foyer into the well-appointed living room, which featured a large hearth, Persian rug on the floor, and chandelier overhead, Milton pulled the pitch pipe out of his tuxedo jacket and sounded a middle C. Then, as Rex and the professor watched with great interest, he got down on one knee with the widest smile he could manage affixed to his face and began singing to generic-sounding music:

I have an English teacher with a history,
He turns it into something more than mystery,
He brings it all to life with every spoken word,
And makes it the most lively stuff you've ever heard,
In case you don't know who this song is all about,
I'm happy to inform you as I twist and shout,
Professor Marvin Isaacson's the cat's meow,
And how he really does it, I just don't know how,
It really doesn't matter, just keep teaching me,
I bet my final grade goes down in history.

Then Milton spoke his signoff with a smile in his voice: "Or should I say 'my grade goes up'? Signed, Your Secret Admirer."

Rex and Professor Isaacson applauded generously, and then Milton got to his feet and reached into his pocket, handing over the tuxedoed rag doll. "The usual souvenir," Milton added. "You know the routine by now."

It was clear that the professor was making a mighty effort to maintain a sense of humor, and he said, "Now I've got three of these floppy things. I don't have any idea what to do with them. I don't have any nieces or nephews to give them to. Maybe I should donate them to Goodwill or something so someone can use them around Christmastime. Hey, it's almost Christmas in July anyway."

Rex snapped his fingers. "I have an idea. Why don't you harness all the frustration they've caused you and just rip 'em apart? And I have some good news for you, sir. If we get another one of these anonymous telegrams for you, we'll just refuse to take it. We know what you're up against with these fawning females, but enough is enough is enough."

Professor Isaacson's handsome face lit up. "That's a spectacular idea. I believe I'll take you up on it."

He then excused himself, disappeared into another room, and quickly returned with two more of the rag dolls in his right hand, while in his left was a letter opener. Then he methodically and energetically plunged the letter opener into the front of each of the dolls, tearing open their tuxedoed shirts. Straw stuffing fell out all over the rug as Rex nodded his great approval.

As for Milton, his eyes widened, as it suddenly all crashed down upon him, and he stabbed the air with his finger a couple of times. "That's it," he cried out. "That's it!"

"What's it?" Rex said.

"The vision," Milton added. "Don't you see it? That's what Aurelia Spangler said she saw. A knife being plunged into a tuxedo shirt. She somehow saw into the future, captured this exact moment in time, and scared the hell outta both of us. That's just gotta be it."

Professor Isaacson gave him a quizzical look, but Rex said emphatically, "Well, I'll be darned. I never even thought of that."

"Me too," Milton said, still mesmerized by what had just happened. "She interpreted it as something dangerous and frightening happening, but it was . . . it was only this. And she got all upset, and I got all upset, and it was all for nothing—" He came to an abrupt halt, and his face was overcome with sadness. "Well, I don't suppose you can call committing suicide nothing."

"I'm not going to ask what the two of you are talking about," the professor said. "But I have to tell you, it felt good to rip into those dolls. I was a good sport about it tonight, but these anonymous telegrams weren't much more than a nuisance to me. Students making goo-goo eyes at me are one thing, but these telegrams are a bit much. Maybe if I announced an engagement to all my classes, these female students of mine would hang it up and leave me alone."

"As I said, you don't have to worry about that now," Rex told him. "I'll tell my wife not to accept any more of these anonymous telegrams to you. Your ordeal of extreme admiration is finally over."

"Thank goodness for that." Now it was the professor's turn to snap his fingers. Then he quickly turned to Milton. "Give me a second while I run to get my wallet. I thought this third rendition was maybe your best from a singing point of view, young man. In fact, all three telegrams were quite professionally sung. I have no quarrel with that part. You have a terrific voice."

"Thank you, sir."

Once he had left the room, Rex said, "See what I mean?

They all love you. Merrie and I want you to continue to be the face and voice of Party Palooza. I'm afraid it's just me and my croaking without you."

Milton proudly stuck out his tuxedoed chest. "I have to admit I feel like a million bucks now, especially since we've put that terrible vision to rest."

"I told you all along not to worry about it."

"Seems you were right."

Professor Isaacson entered the room briskly and promptly handed over a twenty- and a ten-dollar bill to Milton. "For your talent and your trouble. Perhaps someday I will see you in a theatrical production of some kind."

"Much appreciated, sir. And it's my intention to try for the top. I'm sorry I won't be delivering any more telegrams to you, though. That is, unless you get one from an admirer who's willing to identify themselves."

"That'd be a nice touch for once, I'm sure." He gestured toward his liquor cabinet against the wall across the way. "Can I interest either of you two gentlemen in a little nightcap before you leave? Just not enough to negate one of you being the designated driver, right?"

Milton and Rex exchanged brief, wide-eyed glances and then nodded. "I think we can take you up on that," Rex said. "We should drink a toast to all that got accomplished and resolved tonight."

"We got Miz Aurelia's autopsy report this afternoon," Ross said to Wendy as he walked slightly hunched over into their kitchen after a lengthy detail that had kept him out late on the other end of town.

Wendy rose from the table, where she had been nursing a glass of Rosalie muscadine wine, hugged him hard, and kissed him lightly on the lips. "And what was the final verdict?"

"COD was definitely a cocaine overdose as Tommy Cantwell diagnosed. Nothing else of interest was in her system. Nada."

Wendy took the sentence in stride, but first things first. "Are you hungry? Did you eat tonight? I could warm up some of the chicken and wild rice I had earlier."

No thanks," he said. "Pike and I grabbed a cheeseburger and some fries and had a ketchup-fest in the car. I think we may have gotten more on the seat than into our mouths."

"I wish you wouldn't eat that stuff as much as you do," she said. But then she immediately felt guilty about what she had just said. Ross was in excellent physical shape, and she knew his schedule often forced him into whatever was most convenient to eat. "Don't mind me, please. Just a faithful wife worried about her law enforcement hubs."

"I would like a cold beer, though," he said, sitting down at the table and loudly letting the air out of his chest.

She moved quickly to the refrigerator, reached way in to the back of the shelf to get the coldest bottle possible, and then joined him at the table, where they began to sip on their drinks together in a thoughtful silence. Finally, she returned to the pressing subject of the autopsy.

"So, where are we now in this investigation?"

He shrugged. "Stuck at this point. Nothing of interest to report. Your daddy got in touch with our longtime informant, Earl Jay Doxey, to ask him to be on the lookout for anything on the street about a new coke dealer in town. Bax says Doxey's got everyone snooping around, but nothing to report yet. What we do know is that Miz Aurelia got that cocaine one way or another. She either did herself in with it, or, as you've been theorizing all along, someone forced it on her with fatal results."

Wendy was swirling her wine absentmindedly now. "Are

you saying that we'll pretty much have to accept the original suicide verdict unless we can come up with something new?"

Ross suppressed a belch after taking a swig of his beer. "Yes, no matter what we might suspect. The case will go cold on us without anything more than we have right now. I mean, the best we have is that Vance Quimby admits he knew about his sister's life insurance policy, but it's hard to turn that into a case against him without strong evidence."

"I still can't help but think we're missing something despite the evidence to the contrary."

"We miss things all the time," Ross continued, offering up a wry smile. "I mean, *we* as in law enforcement in general. Cases go cold because of that one crucial thing we overlook or misinterpret."

Wendy decided that it couldn't hurt to bring it up. "Such as evidence hiding in plain sight? Merleece and I were discussing it when she came over to clean."

"You and Merleece?"

"Don't sound so surprised. Merleece Maxique is a very intuitive woman just the way I am. She often gives me the germ of an idea that fits right into my sleuthing skills. I think we both have natural gifts. We've almost become a team."

Ross chuckled a little longer than he should have. "Is that so? Wendy and Merleece, Crimefighters Incorporated."

"Don't be so smug about it. Besides, you know she calls me Strawberry because of my hair, so it'd be Strawberry and Merleece, Incorporated."

Ross adopted a more serious tone. "Okay, so tell me your interpretation of this hiding in plain sight business."

"Nothing complicated. You've heard it before. Just the idea that somebody is getting away with something by putting it all right there out in the open. Only they're so successful at it that nobody suspects a thing. I've been going over all my

other newbies in my head, plus Dora O'Rourke, and trying to
come up with something that makes sense."

"And have you come up with anything?"

Wendy didn't bother to hide her frustration and even
managed a pout. "Not yet. But I'm not giving up by any
means. This Saturday, I'm giving my second bridge lesson at
the RCC to the three newbies who are still sticking with me,
and something may come of that."

Ross frowned and said, "You really think so? Well, who's
still left in your original group?"

"Sarah Ann O'Rourke, Charlotte Ruth, and Milton Bagdad. As you already know, Vance Quimby opted out because
of his sister's death."

Ross perked up a bit. "Vance Quimby. He told us he was
staying here in Rosalie to help us, and he's kept in touch. Of
course, I'm not sure there's much he can do anyway. Unless . . ."
Ross didn't finish his sentence as his eyes shifted back and forth.

"Unless what?"

"I'm playing devil's advocate here. He acknowledges that
he visited with his sister the day she died. He's the one who
told us about her cocaine habit in her younger days, but we
have no way of knowing if that's true or not. Yet we now
know he wouldn't be lobbying for suicide because he wouldn't
inherit the life insurance money, and he insists that his sister
would have told him if she had actually relapsed into the coke
habit. I just don't see much that's helpful or provable there."

Wendy put down her wineglass and stared at it as she
spoke. "Yep, you're right. I know we've all considered the al-
ternative before."

"To borrow the phrase that you and Merleece seemed to
find so irresistible, maybe that's where your hiding in plain
sight comes in. Maybe Vance is the one who's doing it, as I
said. What better way to throw all of us off the scent than to
put everything out there for public consumption? Maybe he

wants us to come to the conclusion that a loyal brother like himself couldn't possibly have murdered his sister for such a small amount of money and also gotten rid of his one reliable source of income."

Ross suddenly began speaking in an alternate voice, supposedly that of Vance Quimby: *"Yes, I was there that day. Yes, she was once a user. Yes, I'm devastated by her death. Yes, my sister and I were about to implement a slick scheme here in Rosalie. And so forth."*

Then he resumed in his normal tone. "Unfortunately, we have no reason to call the man in again with no new evidence at our disposal. He'd view it as police harassment if we took a hard-line approach now, and that would get us nowhere but in a big hassle with his lawyer, which he'd no doubt go out and hire. And in the end, he may be genuinely on the up-and-up about his sister's death."

Ross sipped more beer in silence, and then continued. "By the way, we did track down that housekeeper out at Overview that you told me about, Lula West, and she came in and cooperated fully with us. That unidentified DNA all around the house was indeed hers, and she still seemed quite upset about Miz Aurelia's death. I read her grief as genuine. Why would she want to off her employer? I told your daddy that I thought she was just another dead end."

"So, where does that leave us?"

Ross's expression was deadpan. "With a woman who officially committed suicide. At least for the time being, that's the party line."

CHAPTER 11

Wendy intended to go all out to impress her newbies with their second bridge lesson—the first to be held at the RCC. Sporting one of her signature caftans, Director Deedah Hornesby was eager to help in the planning to ensure its success, given what had eventually transpired out at Overview, and her ever-flamboyant son, Hollis, dressed in one of his retro, psychedelic outfits, had even offered his services during their Friday meeting in the cavernous great room.

"If you need someone to sit in as a fourth while you give some personal attention to one of your fledglings, I'm your man," he said.

Wendy had enjoyed an invigorating belly laugh. "The words you use sometimes, Hollis . . . *fledglings*." Of course, Wendy still hoped that the time would come when she could integrate those same fledglings into the general membership, despite the traumatic start they had all endured.

"I'm the most literate artist in Rosalie," he added. "Just a walking dictionary of delights."

"And understand that if Hollis is not available for a fourth, I'll be right over there," Deedah said, pointing to the office wing.

In truth, Hollis and his mother were among the most delightful of all the Bridge Bunch regulars that Wendy paired with from time to time. Of the two, Hollis was the better, more attentive player, but Deedah was perhaps the best sport in the entire club. She had the ability to sit through an afternoon of being dealt hands with nothing close to opening points without complaining; she would simply traipse over to the marble-countered bar, where Carlos Galbis held sway in his tux, and order up another of his famously potent mint juleps. After a couple of those, she no longer cared if most of her cards were faceless.

Wendy had almost wound up her wish-list session with Deedah and Hollis when the finishing touch occurred to her. "Why not have Carlos fix them all mint juleps before we get started? They'll be on me. That way, they won't be all uptight and nervous about the lesson."

Hollis couldn't resist. "You don't think they'll fall asleep on you?"

"I'll take that chance," Wendy said with a smirk. Then she turned to Deedah. "So, I think we're all set for tomorrow. What snacks we'll have, what liquor we'll offer, you and Hollis as subs if needed. Have I left anything out?"

"Just the intrigue," Deedah said. "Let's have no more of that. Just a quiet, friendly lesson in the basics of bridge. No disturbing glimpses into the future. The present is difficult enough to deal with."

Wendy nodded and said, "Amen to that."

It was Saturday evening, and Wendy was pleased with how well things were going so far in the great room. The three newbies seated at the table with her seemed to understand the concept of the no-trump bid versus the suit bid, but she repeated it just to make sure. She would shortly be dealing out examples of no-trump hands for each of them to handle.

"Again, now, whereas you can generally open with a point count of thirteen or fourteen in a suit bid, particularly if you have five cards in that suit—major preferred over minor, of course—it takes anywhere from sixteen to eighteen points to open with what is called no-trump. Not only does that tell your partner you have a strong point count, but it implies that you have fairly even distribution among all the suits. There will literally be *no-trumps* in a no-trump contract. High cards in every suit are of equal value. No suit will be higher than any other. Does everyone understand that?"

Wendy quickly glanced around the table to see if her newly named fledglings were truly on board. There were lots of broad smiles flashed at her, and Sarah Ann said, "I think I do." But she followed that up with, "This mint julep sure is delicious. You know, I've never had one before, don't you?"

"There's a first time for everything," Wendy told her.

Charlotte wasn't far behind in praise of Carlos's specialty. "Well, this isn't the first julep I've ever had, but I have to say that it's the *best* I've ever had. And it's gone straight to my head."

Sarah Ann made circles around her right temple with her index finger. "So I'm not the only one feeling this way, right?"

"Right," Charlotte said.

Then Milton chimed in with his boyish enthusiasm. "I have to agree with the ladies on this one. That Carlos can sure whip up a mean cocktail. I'm gonna have to leave a little something for him in that tip jar on the counter."

"I didn't even think of that because he brought them all over here for us," Charlotte added, clasping her hands together.

"I know," Sarah Ann said, rising up slightly in her chair as if someone had lit a match under her. "Let's take up a collection and someone can take it over there."

"That's really not necessary," Wendy told them all, keeping a smile in her voice. "I've already taken care of Carlos's compensation myself."

"But why not let us?" Sarah Ann continued. "What will it hurt?"

It was at that point that Wendy realized she might have made a mistake with the juleps, at least with the decision to serve them first off. The focus of the group was clearly turning out to be the liquor rather than the lesson. It also came to her that she was going to have to put her foot down about allowing seconds, at least until she had finished with her instruction.

For now, however, she just said, "Go ahead, then. You all do that while I take a minute or two to arrange these no-trump hands for you." Then she began doing just that with several decks at the adjoining table.

Wendy was still creating the hands when Milton returned from handing over the combined tips to Carlos. "He told me to tell all of you how grateful he is for the extra gratuity," Milton said. "At first, he didn't want to take it, but I told him he just had to let us express our appreciation."

"I guess he hit the jackpot today, and he didn't even have to go to the casino Under-the-Hill," Wendy said, as Milton took his seat. "I'm almost ready now to give each of you an example of a no-trump hand. It won't be too much longer."

"Don't worry," Sarah Ann said. "I think we can find something to talk about. For instance . . ." She paused and shot Milton a come-hither glance. "How did you like my little poem, Milty?"

He took another sip of his julep and said, "What poem are you talking about? And call me Milton, please."

Sarah Ann exaggerated her reply. "*Verr-ee welll thenn, Milltonnn.*"

"Are you drunk?" he said, frowning.

She shook her head emphatically. "Who knows? I have

absolutely no point of reference. Anyhoo, to answer your question about the poem—it's the one I wrote for Dr. Isaacson's singing telegram. I thought it was awesome, myself. I would love to have heard you sing it."

Milton put down his julep cup and cocked his head. "So you're the secret admirer, then."

"The one and only."

Wendy, who was already privy to that information, chimed in. "So how did the delivery go?"

"Very well," Milton said. "In fact, you'll all be happy to hear that we solved that scary vision that Aurelia gave me in her cold reading. We couldn't believe that it was just a big fuss over nothing."

He now had Wendy's full attention, as well as everyone else's.

"*We* solved? Who is we?" Wendy said.

"Rex Boudreaux and myself. He went along for moral support, but as it turned out, I didn't need it."

Everyone nodded, and Wendy ended up speaking for them all when she said, "So tell us what happened with the vision. That's what we really want to know about."

It was truly Milton's moment to shine, and it appeared his theatrical training was bearing down full bore. His voice took on a dramatic element often used in storytelling, and he gestured frequently. "Well, it went down like this, folks. Rex and I arrived at Professor Isaacson's house, and he didn't seem to be at all upset with what was his third anonymous delivery. I should know, because I delivered all three—"

"And I happen to know who sent the other two, if anyone is interested," Sarah Ann managed.

"Maybe later," Milton said, glaring at her briefly for the hammy interruption. "Anyway, when I finished singing your poem, Sarah Ann—and, yes, I do think you did a good job with it—I handed over to Professor Isaacson his third tuxedoed rag doll. So, he says to me and Rex, 'I don't have any idea what to do with them.' So Rex says, 'Why don't you harness all the frustration they've caused you and just rip 'em apart?' And that's just what Professor Isaacson did. He went and got all his rag dolls and he tore into 'em with a letter opener. And that's when I connected with Aurelia's vision. She said she'd seen a knife plunging into a man's tuxedo shirt. Boom! There it was, just as she'd seen it. Only she misinterpreted it. It wasn't something scary and dangerous happening to a real person, it was just an act of harmless frustration taken out on a rag doll. How about that?"

"Wow!" Sarah Ann said. "That's somethin' else."

"It does make sense," Charlotte added.

"Yes, it puts it into a believable context now," Wendy said. But her brain was in high gear. She could hardly wait to discuss it with Ross and her father, but that would have to wait for a while. She had a bridge lesson to teach to some slightly inebriated newbies. Yes, back to the original term. She decided she was tired of thinking of them as fledglings and would no longer use Hollis's word, as amusing as it had been, for a while.

It took a bit longer for further discussion of the delivery and the vision to die down, but once it did, Wendy transferred the no-trump hands to the playing table and cleared her mind as much as she could.

"Let's all please look at the hand I've arranged here for Charlotte," she began. "You will note that the point count is sixteen in this case, and that the distribution among the suits is—"

A strident shout interrupted Wendy's instruction. "Sarah Ann O'Rourke!"

All heads turned to the great room entrance, where a middle-aged woman with a great bun of a hairdo and clothed in a white robe pointed in the direction of the bridge table. Then she began advancing slowly and steadily while continuing to point, her voice still impolitely loud as she finally stood near her daughter.

"*Ephesians 5:11* . . . 'Take no part in the unfruitful works of darkness, but instead expose them' . . . ! I am the Avenging Angel!"

Sarah Ann gasped as she rose from her chair. "Mother . . . will you please leave us alone?"

The others rose slowly as well, as Dora O'Rourke resumed her performance. "I will do no such thing. I see you have been drinkin' liquor here. I can smell it on your breath. I can see that all of you have been drinkin'. No tellin' what all this will lead to in the end."

Wendy motioned to Carlos, who had been observing everything from across the room, to come to her aid and said, "Miz O'Rourke, this is a private club, and you are intruding upon a private gathering. You will have to leave."

Carlos moved quickly to Wendy's side and said, "You will have to do as Miz Rierson asks."

Then Wendy texted Deedah, who was in her office, visiting with Hollis.

Come quickly. Trouble with non-member.

When Deedah and Hollis arrived, both breathing heavily, the standoff between Wendy, Carlos, the bridge newbies, and Dora O'Rourke seemed like the freeze frame of a movie. There was a tension that was of such substance that it seemed to reach all the way up to the vaulted ceiling above, but it was quickly broken by Deedah.

"What's going on here, Wendy?" she said.

But Dora prevented a response by loudly quoting Scripture again. "*Ephesians 5:18* . . . 'Do not get drunk on wine, which leads to debauchery. Instead, be filled with the Spirit . . .'"

"I'm sorry, Miz Deedah, my mother has intruded on our bridge lesson," Sarah Ann said, tearing up.

"This is Dora O'Rourke. She's been asked to leave by both myself and Carlos," Wendy added.

Firmly but gently, Deedah said, "I'm sorry—Mrs. O'Rourke, is it?—but you are going to have to leave this club immediately with this kind of behavior. It's simply unacceptable to us."

The anger in Dora's voice was pronounced. "I am Sarah Ann's mother. I know what's best for her. I'm askin' her to come home with me now instead of continuin' to indulge in all this debauchery."

Sarah Ann held her head up and practically spat out the word, "No."

The hand that Dora had been pointing with so emphatically began to tremble. "We will discuss your punishment when you get home, then."

"I'm not coming home after this display. I'm tired of all this. I'm twenty-one years old. I will go to the Rosalie Women's Shelter if I have to. I can't keep living in the same house with you," Sarah Ann said, finally breaking down into tears.

Wendy moved to her side and patted her shoulder several times. "We're here for you, Sarah Ann."

"I'm sorry, Mrs. O'Rourke," Deedah said, "but this is not the time and place for you to discuss family matters like this. Your daughter is here to learn the game of bridge, and that is all. We again have to ask you to leave so that we can continue our planned activities."

"I'd like to know when a country club became more important to a child than her mother."

"Mother, this isn't a custody battle. It's just a simple card game among friends," Sarah Ann said.

Dora glared at her daughter one last time, then turned on

her heels, and marched resolutely to the front door without another word. It appeared that the Avenging Angel had been silenced for the time being.

Wendy and Sarah Ann were seated on Deedah's office couch after the interrupted bridge lesson had been completed and all of the other newbies had left. Deedah, Hollis, and Carlos had also called it quits for the day, but Wendy had sensed that she needed to huddle with Sarah Ann after Dora O'Rourke's overbearing display. The idea that some physical harm might come to the young woman at the hands of her obsessed mother did not seem altogether out of the realm of possibilities, and Deedah had given Wendy carte blanche to use her office and then lock up the RCC after that.

"Do you really not want to go home?" Wendy was saying. "Won't you need your computer and some other things for your schoolwork? Not to mention your clothes and shoes and all that."

Sarah Ann sniffled and managed a mock smile. "That's the key to my getting away from Mother, you know. Graduating and then getting a job of any kind. I'm not sure I want to stay here in Rosalie, to be honest with you."

"No one says you have to. But I'm concerned about where you're going to stay right now. I do have a suggestion. Why don't you come home with me and spend the night in our guest room? Then Ross can accompany you back home tomorrow so you can pick up all your necessities. I'm sure your mother will want to cooperate with a police officer in the house. I'm not sure how long you can stay at the women's shelter, but maybe they can work something out for you."

Sarah Ann's smile went from mock to genuine. "That would be awesome if I could stay with you tonight and think about what I should do next. I don't think I'd be able to thank you enough."

"Think nothing of it."

"In a way, I'm glad this happened today," Sarah Ann continued. "You see what I'm up against at home now, don't you? Mother's gotten worse and worse the older I get. I think she resents my growing up because . . . well, I think I've figured it out. She knows that once I graduate, I'll be on my own at last . . . and she'll be alone. But I can't help that. I have to live my own life."

Wendy managed a sigh. "The empty nest. You always hear it's hard on a lot of parents."

Sarah Ann's smile disappeared and her voice quavered. "All of that may be true, and if that's all there was to it, I'd feel a little bit better about . . . well, what happened to Aurelia."

"What do you mean?"

"I mean, I can't prove it, but I have a very bad feeling about Mother and what may have happened between her and Aurelia when she visited Overview. You see how she gets. She finds passages and throws them at people and expects them to fall in line without questioning anything. She hates questions. She believes in absolutes. And lately, she's starting referring to herself as the Avenging Angel. You heard her today." Sarah Ann shivered for a few seconds. "It makes me wonder what type of avenging she may already have done."

"You know that my husband has already interrogated your mother down at headquarters, don't you?"

Sarah Ann said nothing, but nodded.

"He doesn't seem to feel that your mother is capable of murder, and he wonders where someone like herself would have the wherewithal to get her hands on cocaine and force someone like Aurelia to overdose on it. I also highly doubt your mother is the type to know her way around the streets. Does your mother own a gun?"

"Not that I know of."

"Then how did she pull all of that off, if she actually did it?

I'm wondering if she could have had help, which is a totally different issue."

Sarah Ann took a deep breath and exhaled all in one smooth motion. "I don't know about all that. I'm just telling you what I suspect, and your husband and the rest of the police department can take it from there. I just consider that I'm only doing my civic duty."

"I promise you that I'll be discussing everything that happened here today with Ross when I get home. Including what you've told me. Or you can tell him yourself. It may be helpful since it appears the case is going nowhere fast. Officially, Aurelia's death is still considered a suicide."

The two rose from the couch together and hugged for a good ten seconds. Then Sarah Ann pulled back slightly and said, "Thanks for caring about me, Wendy. You're practically a saint. Of course, I know you're not old enough to be my mother, but I wish you were."

Wendy found herself blushing. The words gave her the sort of warm feeling that she frequently got from being around Ross. "I'm not sure I'm quite ready for motherhood yet, much less sainthood, but I tell you what. You follow me in your car, and we'll stop by the drugstore and get you a few things like a toothbrush on the way to my house. I think I have a pair of pajamas for tonight that'll fit you, too."

"Oh," Sarah Ann said, bringing her hands together prayerfully. "Would you mind if I run to the ladies' room real quick before we leave? With all the crying I've done, I must look like a raccoon with my mascara running and all. Do you mind if I fix my face up a little?"

Wendy chuckled softly and waved the tips of her fingers. "Run quick, like a little bunny rabbit."

"Will do."

As Wendy watched Sarah Ann leaving the room, she found herself tossing around the word that had been brought up in such a complimentary fashion just a few minutes earlier—*mother*. She had told Sarah Ann that she thought she wasn't ready to become one yet, but Bax had not so subtly dropped a few hints here and there about becoming a grandparent. Namely, when was it going to happen? He let it be known that he was leaning toward the sooner rather than the later option.

She and Ross had discussed it more than once, to be sure. They both wanted children eventually, and as had been the case with Ross on the issue of getting married in the first place, he had gotten there first. She had told her father not to be impatient and that it would come in time.

"But I don't wanna be so old that I can't hold your babies," he had told her with a gleam in his eye. "I wanna do things with 'em."

She had smiled back at him and said, "You're young yet, Daddy. And so am I. I'll know when the time is right."

CHAPTER 12

The next morning, Ross had just finished bringing Bax up to date on his chaperoning duties for Sarah Ann O'Rourke, as the two of them were seated across from each other in Bax's office.

"I've never felt such tension in a house before," he concluded. He made fists of his hands and brought his knuckles together like opponents in a prize fight.

"Mother and daughter at war with each other," Bax said, shaking his head. "A sad story. Things were so different between Wendy and her mother every precious day that Valerie was with us. That's the way it should be for everybody in every family."

"I think Dora O'Rourke was in shock as we left with the last few things, though," Ross continued. "You could see in her face that she couldn't believe what was happening. Maybe this will be a wake-up call for her. Her daughter wasn't bluffing. But that's too bad because from what I've observed and what Wendy's told me, Dora was the one who caused all the trouble in the first place. Anyway, Sarah Ann is settled in at the women's shelter for a while. Wendy's gonna look in on her later and see what can be done after that."

"My daughter, the investigative reporter, the amateur sleuth, and now the social worker. I've known for quite some time she's a multitasker."

Ross smirked. "That about covers it."

Then Bax handed his son-in-law a sheet of paper. "This is the timeline I've worked out for all the visitors Aurelia Spangler had at Overview the day she died, based on what they all told us. Obviously, any of them could be lying. The one thing that's fixed is Aurelia's TOD, according to the coroner. According to the housekeeper, Lula West, she had the day off. We've checked, and her alibi holds up there. So the deal appears to be that if all of them were telling the truth, then Vance Quimby was the last person to see his sister alive. But note the huge gap between the alleged times of all the visits and the TOD."

Ross began scanning the neatly typed document with great interest:

2:30—Charlotte Ruth visits (says took 20 minutes)
4:00—Dora O'Rourke visits (says took 15 minutes)
5:30—Vance Quimby visits (says took an hour)
8:00 to 9:00—Aurelia's approximate TOD

"I see what you mean," Ross said, finally looking up from the page. "According to this, if Charlotte and Dora are telling the truth, they inadvertently confirm that Miz Aurelia was definitely alive when they both left her. Which brings us back again to Vance Quimby. His sister would have been alive when he left her, according to the TOD."

Bax leaned over his desk and took the sheet back, then made a disdainful face. "Here's the thing that gums up the whole works, though. There's a huge gap between the time Vance said he visited and the time his sister died according to the coroner. There was plenty of time for any of the others, including himself or someone we don't yet know about, to return or show up for the first time to take care of some nasty, unfinished business. That's the x-plus factor here, and it seems to be doing its best to elude us completely."

"And there's still that one last possibility, unfortunately," Ross added. "That Aurelia Spangler really did commit suicide for the reasons she described in that note she left on the table, despite what her brother told us about her mood in general. I've read that some suicides aren't planned all that far in advance. They just happen like spontaneous combustion."

"We're not making much progress, are we, son?"

Ross stuck out his chin and winced at the same time. He hated when cases reached a standstill like this, and it happened all too frequently. So frequently that a healthy percentage of them went cold.

"Doesn't look like it," he said. "We have everyone's DNA, but that doesn't help us much because we already know they were all there at one time or another. And if there was somebody else we don't know about yet, then they were damned careful not to leave a trace of themselves behind."

Bax exhaled. "You know how intent my daughter is on proving the suicide diagnosis wrong, of course."

"Does the sun come up every morning?" Ross paused briefly. "Nothing more from Doxey?"

"I was gonna tell you," Bax began. "He called me this morning just after I'd first come in and said there might be a glimmer on the horizon. I'm hoping something will come of it."

"Oh?"

"Yeah, he said that one of his homeboys believes there *is* a new player out there, but that they might as well be invisible. He says whoever it is hasn't been dealing on the streets as usual. No one's spotted anything, anywhere. But someone's siphoning off business. Someone's moved in on the sly, and under those circumstances, Doxey and his homeboy wonder how long it'll be before someone pays the price for that. Now, that could get really ugly."

"Well, there'd be an upside. It would likely bring whoever it is out in the open," Ross said, sounding a bit more optimistic.

Then he seemed lost in thought for a while. When he finally came up for air, he began telling Bax what Wendy had shared with him last night about Milton's latest telegram delivery to Professor Isaacson.

"Milton was certain that the letter opener and the rag dolls were the essence of Aurelia's scary vision. But what if that was a gross misinterpretation? What if instead, Aurelia was seeing a representation of violence brought about by this street business being siphoned off? What if the real meaning of that vision hasn't occurred yet? Should we be so willing to dismiss that as a possibility?"

Ross had never seen his father-in-law looking quite so skeptical, and he knew something on the order of a lecture was on the way. "I have to tell you, son, I'm a little uncomfortable factoring these so-called psychic visions into the equation. We already know from Vance Quimby that he and his sister were essentially an upscale carnival act ready to rake it in out at Overview. Now, don't get me wrong. I know for a fact that genuine psychics have been very helpful to law enforcement from time to time—I don't deny that—but do we really wanna spend a lot of time on what Aurelia Spangler had to offer, one way or the other? Don't we have to fall back on more conventional things like the actual evidence? That's our training, and it should be guiding us, of course."

"When you put it that way, I guess not."

But Ross had to admit to himself that living with his Wendy had definitely had an influence on him, and he was not quite ready to dismiss her instincts. They had solved crimes for her before, and he considered himself fortunate to be married to someone with such out-of-left-field talents.

The distinguished Dr. Gordon Henshaw had been more than happy to clear some time for Charlotte Ruth on Wendy's behalf, particularly since he found the story of Aurelia Spangler's suicide more than intriguing. Now graying at the temples, pushing sixty, and a practitioner of his craft for nearly thirty years in Rosalie, he had struck a gold mine in the historic, quirky river port. To his way of thinking, it was simply a fact of life in the Deep South—the older the city, the more people worshiped at the shrine of genealogy, and the more people needed to have their heads examined because of the fallout. The reasons for that were epic and innumerable, if not always logical; but they were all nothing short of lucrative for him.

To add to that, the still-trim Dr. Henshaw had a bedside manner that was soothing and melodious. His soft, smoky voice put his patients—particularly the females—in mind of the celebrated Nat King Cole, even though the doctor never sang romantic ballads to them. Without putting them to sleep, he was somehow able to nearly hypnotize them with his reassuring tone, and that no doubt had everything to do with the fact that practically all of his patients raved about him. In cyberspace, he was always getting those five-star reviews that every professional wants to receive and then publicizes extensively on websites.

Wendy had told him that Charlotte Ruth was a newcomer to Rosalie, however, and he wondered quite frankly if the problems she had brought with her from somewhere outside would yield quite so easily to his particular gifts. He kept his ego in check enough to know that he was not the perfect fit for everyone, however.

"Continue with what you were saying about you and your new friends learning bridge," he was saying to Charlotte a few minutes into their first session, facing her in his comfortable leather armchair.

Charlotte sank back a little deeper into the big green pillows behind her on Dr. Henshaw's couch. On either end of it sat two enormous ficus plants that nearly touched the ceiling, and there were several ferns and potted palms throughout the office to complement the doctor's green wallpaper.

"I just wasn't prepared for the trauma of it all. Here I thought I would just be learning a game for pleasant social reasons, and I ended up deeply involved in this horrible murder."

"But Wendy told me the case is currently considered a suicide, and you said the same thing to me."

"Well, maybe I should clear that up a bit. I went to Wendy and implied that I had caused Aurelia Spangler's suicide. I have to admit I was a mess on that particular occasion."

Dr. Henshaw made a few quick notes and said, "So, you did not cause her suicide, then?"

"No, I lied. It was much worse than that. I actually murdered Aurelia Spangler. I'm the one the police are looking for."

Dr. Henshaw straightened up a bit more in his chair and cleared his throat. He was accustomed to hearing everything conceivable from his patients and was not fazed in the least by Charlotte's remark.

"You murdered her? That's very interesting. Would you mind telling me how you did it?"

"With cocaine, of course. She died of an overdose of cocaine. It was truly quite horrendous for me to observe. It was like she was disappearing before my very eyes the more she snorted it."

Dr. Henshaw did not blink and continued in his trademark beguiling tone. "Was it *her* cocaine?"

"Yes, she wanted me to join her in snorting it. I wouldn't even begin to know where to get the stuff."

"And did you join her?"

"No, I did not. I like to think of myself as a fairly adventurous person, but I wasn't up to that."

Dr. Henshaw made further notes. "So how did she overdose, and why are you responsible?"

"She just kept right on snorting it, and she kept on inviting me to join her the entire time."

"But you didn't."

"No, I didn't. I just watched. She told me it was time for her to leave and that she was very tired of it all."

"What do you think she meant by that?"

"I think she meant she didn't want to make a living by being a phony psychic anymore."

Once again, Dr. Henshaw jotted something down and then looked up. "Is that all there was to it?"

"Isn't that enough?" Charlotte fidgeted a bit. "I murdered her because I didn't call 9-1-1 and just sat there while she kept on snorting right there in front of me with her eyes rolling back in her head. I could have saved her, but I chose not to. So that makes me guilty, the way I see it. I should spend the rest of my life in prison, the way I figure it."

"I understand now." Dr. Henshaw glanced at his notes and changed the subject. "The first thing you mentioned to me was your husband's suicide and how you had never gotten over that."

"Yes."

"Tell me more about that. You sort of skimmed over it before as if it weren't all that important."

"You're wrong about that. It was very painful for me, of course. But I managed to ride it out."

"How did you do that?"

There was a hint of a smile on Charlotte's face. "I stayed close to my friends and what family I had left at my disposal. I forced myself to get out there and entertain to keep my head above water. I was told that the worst thing I could do was to sit around at home doing nothing."

"That was certainly good advice. I would certainly have said the same thing to you had I been your doctor at the time. What kind of entertaining did you do?"

"Believe it or not, I gave lots of parties. Dinners, luncheons, brunches on Sunday with champagne. Had people over for games of bridge and things like that."

Dr. Henshaw paused for a decent length of time. "I thought you said you were just beginning to learn the game of bridge from Wendy with this new group of friends here in Rosalie."

Charlotte's smile grew wider, even mischievous. "All right, then. You caught me red-handed. I already know how to play bridge. I'm actually very good at the game. I've played both party bridge and duplicate bridge for a long time. I've even won a tournament or two, which is not the easiest thing in the world to do. I joined the group here in Rosalie because I needed to make some new friends. Pretending that I didn't know how to play ensured that I would get lots of personal attention from Wendy. Being the expert elephant in the room might intimidate some people and turn them off. I certainly didn't want that to happen. I had an excellent game plan, you see. Is that so wrong?"

"No, not at all." Then, Dr. Henshaw went for it, crossing his legs at the knee. "What else aren't you telling the truth about? Did you really watch Aurelia Spangler snort cocaine?"

Instead of becoming upset, Charlotte looked even more amused. She even puffed herself up a bit. "No, I made that up."

"Why?"

"I-I don't know. I'm not sure why I do these things. Sometimes, I don't even think about them. They just happen."

"Maybe to get attention?"

"Maybe."

"Maybe to feel important?"

"Maybe."

Dr. Henshaw duplicated her smile with one of his own. "You could be playing a dangerous game in this instance. I'm bound by doctor-patient confidentiality to keep this session between us private, of course, and I assure you that I will do just that. But I suggest you not go around telling these types of stories to the police or Wendy or anyone else, for that matter. They might take you seriously. You also might be putting yourself in danger. Is there anything about the story you just told me that *is* true?"

"Yes, I did visit with Aurelia Spangler at Overview that afternoon. I did not let her know in advance. I just popped in, and she was very surprised to see me at the door. Her cold reading had left me tearing up. It wasn't so much that I was upset that she dredged up my Jimmy's suicide as that it . . . well, it gave me something to do, somewhere to go. I like . . . acting out. It seems to be part of my nature. Sometimes, I think I should have been an actress in Hollywood, you know. I'm sure I could have been very, very good at it if I'd applied myself. Perhaps even a Meryl Streep type. She's a chameleon, you know. I am, too."

"That's very high praise for yourself, indeed," Dr. Henshaw said, raising an eyebrow. "Just think. I might have had an Oscar winner sitting before me had you followed through on what you just told me."

Charlotte dismissed his comment with a wag of her penciled-in brows and changed the subject. "I want you to know that I really do miss my husband terribly. That much will always be true. I sort of fell off a cliff onto the rocks below when he left me the way he did. You have no idea how abandoned I felt. The worst part is that I felt responsible for my own loneliness."

"I believe you. So let me get my bearings here. Aurelia Spangler was alive and well when you left her?"

"Yes."

Dr. Henshaw wrote quite a bit in silence, then finally looked up. "Do you want to continue to see me?"

"Do you think I should? Do you even want me as a patient? I can understand why you wouldn't. I'm so mixed up."

Dr. Henshaw laughed gently. "Please cut yourself some slack. You wouldn't be here if you weren't confused about things."

"I suppose that's true."

Dr. Henshaw nodded very slowly, which imparted an extra element of wisdom to his words. "As long as you tell me the truth about things, I believe you may be able to benefit from some extended therapy. But let's keep these stories of yours away from the police, shall we?"

Charlotte's smile finally disappeared. "Dr. Henshaw . . . I am not a bad person. I'm really not."

"No one said you were."

"Then why do I feel the compulsion sometimes to think of myself as one? Is that part of my problem?"

There was an almost paternal aspect to Dr. Henshaw's smile. "It's complicated. But we can get into it as you continue to come to me. I don't want to overwhelm you too soon with too much that's clinical. My approach is to let my patients gradually discover what they've been doing so they can get a handle on getting it under control. That provides them with the best opportunity to succeed, and I do have an excellent track record."

Charlotte's smile returned. "Actually, that sounds exciting to me. I haven't had much control over anything since Jimmy died. I don't know why, but control is extremely important to me."

"That makes perfect sense. But we can work on that, I

promise you. With any luck, we should make some measurable progress together. I have to tell you that it won't be an overnight process, but it will happen."

"I'll look forward to that very much, then. I'm very thankful that Wendy spoke to you."

"I am, too. I'm proud to say that Wendy is one of my greatest successes, and I think you and I are off to a good start."

After Charlotte's hour was finally up in the good doctor's indoor green jungle, and she had made her exit feeling uplifted and actually humming a little tune under her breath, Dr. Henshaw proceeded to his desk to scan his notes again carefully. When he had finished, he turned on his recorder and began speaking into it in that irresistibly unique way of his.

Patient is Charlotte Ruth, fifty-seven-year-old widow in reasonably good health . . . after first session of approximately one hour, patient presented to me a classic case of histrionic personality disorder . . . she needs to be the center of attention and even lies about circumstances to achieve that end . . . the prognosis, I believe, is good with continued therapy, which patient has agreed to . . . I have advised patient not to repeat stories of being responsible for Aurelia Spangler's suicide or murder to anyone, particularly police . . . it is possible that patient will not abide by my suggestion due to her HPD . . . her behavior is a persistent one . . . but I can deal with that should the circumstance arise . . . made an appointment with the patient one week from today at one p.m. and believe she will keep it . . . however, it has been my experience that a percentage of patients like this do not wish to undergo therapy and accept the reality of their condition . . . it is too strong an addiction for them . . . that would likely be the case if Charlotte Ruth does not keep her next appointment.

CHAPTER 13

Milton had his youthful exuberance and confidence back—that feeling that he would live forever like the cast of *Fame* insisted musically while dancing in the streets, and someday make many millions and live the life of a person on the cover of *People*. When he had graduated from LSU with his degree in theater arts, he genuinely believed that he could hurdle any obstacle in the way of his planet-wide success. He would eventually accumulate the power of Zach in *A Chorus Line*. Conquering Broadway? London's West End? Of course he would play them and then later direct. It was a given that people would remember his name. He did not intend to change his moniker, by the way.

Milton Bagdad.

It already sounded like some Hollywood production company or agent had made it up, even though the days of renaming actors Rock Hudson and Tab Hunter were long gone. Ethnic was now in. His name blended the unassuming-sounding—*Milton*—with the intriguing and exotic. Yes, there might be a certain pejorative connotation to *Bagdad*. As in Iraq. The Middle East. Operation Desert Shield. But there was that slight difference in spelling—the insertion of the *h*—

that set his name apart from the legendary city, and he further believed that his blond hair and fair skin pigeonholed him neatly into the favored white American category. He would ask for no favors in that realm, but neither would he turn them down if they came his way. So he was going to continue to be Milton Bagdad no matter what anyone else said.

He could almost hear the announcement being televised around the world in the near future: "And the Oscar goes to . . . *Milton Bagdad!*"

On this particular sultry evening, Milton was going to deliver his first telegram without Rex Boudreaux along as his security blanket and bodyguard. True, he had become used to his hulking employer by his side to reassure him that nothing could possibly go wrong and that he needed to push Aurelia's vision out of his head once and for all. Boom! It had to go. So it was way past time to toss the crutch.

"I'm ready to solo again," Milton had said when Rex handed over a telegram inside the A-frame warehouse of a building that was Party Palooza headquarters. It was to be delivered to a Miss Barbara Kay Beasley from her "ever-lovin'" boyfriend, Robbie Pelton.

"Looks like a straightforward delivery to me," Rex had added. "Nice enough section of town. The high school sweetheart thing is a cinch. You've done these before tons of times. I'm glad you're ready to return to top form."

Merrie had been equally reassuring as she patted him on the arm a couple of times.

"We've got our old Milton back, and we couldn't be happier. Now our customers are getting everything they paid for. So you wear that tuxedo proudly, young man, and sing your heart out." She wanted to add, "Forget about that knife," but she knew she didn't dare.

Then she had lowered her voice and started talking out of the side of her mouth. "I haven't even shared with Rex some of the more graphic complaints we got after his so-called deliveries with you. He wandered all over the scale."

"I heard that," Rex said, smiling good-naturedly from behind his desk. "I'd like to think I was like Rex Harrison reciting songs in *My Fair Lady*. But I'm sure I was more like Frankenstein's monster out there. You know—me grunting a couple of times and then wanting to say, 'Frankenstein *not* sing bad.'"

The laughter that followed filled the room with an energy that Milton eagerly embraced. "I know you're exaggerating, but it really is good to be back on track. Solo is the way to go."

So now Milton was on the way to 105 Powell Street in Rosemont, one of the post-WWII, tin-type developments on the outskirts of Rosalie that had made it possible for returning soldiers to start their families in affordable housing. In truth, these were smaller cottages with limited square footage, even by the standards of the era in which they were built; but they had held up well over the decades since and still functioned as starter houses for younger couples, or even retirement homes for the elderly. It was indeed a safe, stable neighborhood with a general American look and feel to it—far removed from the much-lauded, strictly regulated historical district that had long been Rosalie's calling card.

Milton had turned on the SiriusXM Broadway channel and was happily listening to the rapid-fire Seth Rudetsky talking up a show tune he was about to share with his audience:

"*. . . and we have all these wonderful revivals of* South Pacific *to choose from in addition to the Mary Martin original in 1949. So here she is from the 2008 version performed at the Vivian Beaumont Theater . . . Kelli O'Hara as Nellie Forbush with her toes in the sand singing 'I'm in Love with a Wonderful Guy.'*"

As he was prone to do so often when he was driving around town, Milton began singing along in his rich, tenor voice, ignoring the fact that it was a woman's song, but he never worried about such gender-related facts. He had always been crazy about R&H scores, and the unbridled breeziness of "I'm in Love with a Wonderful Guy" always swept him away in three-quarter time to a Pacific Island beach during wartime.

Now, wasn't that a hoot? A millennial's view of the Big War. If only the actual worldwide conflict had been that worthy of song and full of optimism with an audience applauding at every turn. Curtain and scrim down on danger, nuclear bombs, and all the rest.

So caught up in the lyrics was Milton that he failed to notice that someone had been tailing him ever since he had traveled just a few blocks from Party Palooza—but not so obviously as to give themselves away. There were times when Milton got so carried away with his singing that he forgot to check his rearview mirror for large segments of time. It had even cost him a ticket here and there, and he had failed to have any success arguing his way out of any of them with lines like: "But, Officer, I just got carried away listening to 'The Carousel Waltz.'"

Ten minutes of "singing along with show tunes" later, Milton pulled up in front of his destination, shut off the engine, pulled out his pitch pipe to sound a middle C, and decided to rehearse his telegram out loud before going in:

I'm here to say I love you, my sweet Barbara Kay,
You know I want to say it to you every day,
But this one time I'm singing on this bended knee,
I hope you really like it and you smile with glee,
There's nothing on this earth that I would rather do,
Than spending all the time I have and just with you,
So one more time I'll say it, my sweet Barbara Kay,
I really, really love you,
I say, I really love you,

You know I really love you, Barbara Kaaaaayyyyyy!!!
Your ever-lovin' boyfriend, Robbbbieeeeee!!!

Milton was very pleased with his rehearsal. He wasn't sharp or flat on a single note. He was going to blow Barbara Kay Beasley away. So he got out of his car and walked briskly to the front door with not a care in the world. He was going to make someone's evening, and that was all that mattered. Nothing could possibly go wrong now, and he anticipated another big tip for his spectacular performance.

The driver of the car who had been tailing Milton parked three or four houses down on the opposite side of Powell Street, far enough away to be able to observe things without being noticed. Now there was nothing to do but wait around for Milton to emerge from the house. Patient observation was the game plan here, and it was more than certain to pay off.

But the wait was beyond boring, even angst-producing. There was a time element here to consider. There was also only the radio for entertainment to make the time pass. But it crawled by, no matter what songs were played or what news was being discussed on various stations up and down the dial on both FM and AM. It was all just a boring jumble of cacophony.

Really, now. How long did it take to sing ten or eleven lines of saccharine verse? Apparently, a little longer than expected. Or maybe the telegram recipient was going gaga and had asked Milton for more.

Finally, Milton bounded out onto the small covered portico, and a group of three or four people stood in the front door, waving and praising his singing. He turned and waved back one last time and said, "I enjoyed meeting all of you. Have a good night," before sliding into the front seat of his car.

In the parked car three or four houses down, the thought on the front burner of the very focused brain behind the steering wheel was one note: *Mission accomplished, nothing bad has happened.*

The reality was that Merrie Boudreaux was fast becoming the mother hen of them all.

"I've had this headache coming on all day," she had told Rex just after Milton had left Party Palooza to deliver his telegram. "And it's gotten the best of me now, I'm afraid. I'm gonna go on home and lie down and let you close up as usual."

Fortunately, Rex had complied without an argument and did not suspect what she was up to. "You shoudda mentioned it to me earlier and gone home then. But I've got a few more things to take care of, so I'll see you there. Oh, and I'll pick up a few things we need from the convenience store. I think we're out of coffee creamer and that spicy hummus you like."

Merrie finished reviewing that conversation in her head and then waited a decent length of time for Milton to pull away from the curb and head toward his home. Then she turned the key in the ignition and pulled out herself. As she drove slowly through Rosalie traffic, she felt terribly conflicted. If she and Rex let their guard down, was there still a possibility that something devastating could happen to Milton and, therefore, to their business? Rex had done his part in holding Milton's hand for several deliveries up to now but felt that it was past time to give the young man his wings again and push him out of his nest that he, himself, had built of pure fright.

She knew she had done the wrong thing in developing these feelings for Milton. He was close to the age that a son of theirs might be if they'd been successful at staying pregnant in the salad days of their marriage. Instead, she'd endured miscarriage after miscarriage—the great sorrow of her life. As a result, she had let herself become cynical and been willing to immerse herself in the activities of Party Palooza in Rosalie as she had before in New Orleans, where they had started—with Rex always in charge of the major decisions. She wondered how different he might be now if he had a son or daughter of his own to root for and bring up, instead of planning parties for other people's children and all the rest of it that Party Palooza had become.

After the last miscarriage a few years back, she had even brought up the subject of adoption to Rex, hoping he would be amenable. She felt that a child was the one thing missing in their marriage—and might even save it at some point in time.

"If I can't have one that comes from me, I don't want one that comes from someone else," he had told her. His handsome features had hardened as he said it, daring any further conversation to take place. And so, none ever had again. The couple had continued childless, and their work had occupied all their time.

Still behind the wheel and stopped at a red light, Merrie returned to what had been troubling her for some time now in her job. She had stopped short of making a pass at Milton when Rex wasn't around the office, which wasn't all that often. How very Mrs. Robinson of her had she done so. For that matter, she didn't even know if Milton was straight. She had her suspicions otherwise because of his affinity for humming show tunes and the fluid way he moved his body in general; and, yes, she knew she was being outright stereotypical in her thinking. But he was so guileless and so easily swayed by his elders and those in authority that it hardly mattered what his orientation was. She had never pictured herself as the "older woman" anyway; she could, however, picture the wrath of Rex Boudreaux had she ever attempted such a thing and been found out by her husband.

In any case, she didn't think she could bear it if the unthinkable happened to Milton.

Damn that silly woman's vision that had spun things off so suddenly into a dark, alternate universe that seemed to be so haunting and unending. Had Rex and Milton put it to bed with their delivery to Professor Isaacson, or was it still out there, hanging around in some devastating, unimaginable form— ready to take someone down? Merrie shuddered to think that that someone might be Milton.

Across town, Wendy knew something was up the second Ross trudged into the kitchen with his eyes downcast and his posture slumped. She could almost see the great weight resting on his shoulders. He threw his keys on the marble countertop haphazardly and noisily instead of hanging them up neatly on the little metal hook by the door as he usually did. He did not say hello warmly to his wife, either, and that almost never happened.

"Sweetheart . . . Ross . . . what's the matter?" she said, approaching him cautiously.

He continued his silent journey until he collapsed on the living room sofa and Wendy followed along behind. Finally, he said, "I just need to snuggle with you for a little while." He motioned to her gently.

She quickly complied. "I'm here for you—whatever you need."

He put his arm around her shoulder and got as close to her as it was possible to get. "This feels good," he told her, the tiredness showing in his voice. "It feels safe, and I need to feel that way right now."

"For God's sake, tell me what happened. I've never seen you like this." Suddenly, she stiffened as an emotional bomb hit her. "Wait . . . please tell me nothing's happened to Daddy."

"No, no, no," he said, trying to sound reassuring, but it didn't come off that way at all. "I didn't mean to give you that idea. Bax is just fine. Everyone at the station is fine. But . . . Earl Jay Doxey was stabbed to death tonight."

"Daddy's friend from way back?" Wendy said. Her hands instinctively assumed a prayerful pose as her eyes widened, and she felt something hurting in the pit of her stomach.

Ross nodded somberly.

"Then something's happened to Daddy, after all. His contacts mean the whole world to him."

"You're right, of course. He's taking it pretty hard."

"Is Daddy still down at the station? Do you think I should call him up now or go to him?"

"Yes, he's still there, but I really think it'd be best to leave him alone just now. Take my advice."

Wendy knew he was right, but she was still full of questions. "Did they catch who did it? Or do they at least have a suspect?"

"No, but the murder seems like a hit. Doxey had hinted to Daddy just this morning that he might be onto something at long last, but he had to check out a few things. He wouldn't say any more than that, though. That was Doxey for you—he never spoke unless he was sure of himself, and when he finally did, he was never wrong. He knew the streets and what was going down."

"Where did this happen?"

"Somewhere up on North River Street. The worst stretches of it. You know where they are," he told her.

Wendy quickly reviewed the map of Rosalie in her head and frowned. "Merleece lives around that neighborhood— but the better part."

"I doubt she would know anything," Ross said. "This happened where North River turns into a gravel road near the cemetery."

Wendy shuddered, but that soon turned into a smile. She

was recalling some dares she and her girlfriends had taken at the age of twelve from obnoxious neighborhood boys to roam around near there in search of ghosts during the full moon. Of course, they had never seen anything real, but the boys had dressed up in creepy costumes, jumped out from behind elaborate mausoleums, and caused at least two of them to wet their pants. At least Wendy had not been one of them, although her heart had definitely skipped a beat or two.

"I've always disliked that area. In my mind I've had this notion that if they paved the rest of that road, they would smother the demons that roam around out there with layers and layers of asphalt. Just get it over with once and for all and bury them deep so they can never see daylight again."

"If preventing and controlling crime were only that easy," Ross said with a helpless shrug of his shoulders. "But one thing has come of this terrible tragedy. I'm positive that Aurelia Spangler's death and Doxey's death are linked together by drugs and drug dealing—and as far as I'm concerned, Aurelia as a suicide is off the table. I think it's highly probable that whoever killed Aurelia killed Doxey, or had both of them killed. Bax feels the same way, and he's bound and determined to track down whoever's responsible."

Wendy shivered a little, even though she felt warm and protected up against Ross's strong body. It was one of the things she liked best about their relationship—his strength was always there when she needed it. And hers when he needed it, as well. "I'm really getting frightened now, sweetheart. Somebody in Rosalie obviously means business and will stop at nothing."

"Yes, and your daddy is on the warpath as I've never seen him. That's why I suggested you give him some time to get his equilibrium back. I don't think either of us should be around him right now. Let him come to you when he's worked things out in his head, and he's breathing calmly again and even blinking. He's most likely dealing with some degree of guilt since he asked Doxey to get involved in the first place. Bax does take his job more seriously than any other cop I've ever worked with. I'd be hard-pressed to match his level of passion in certain instances."

Wendy understood what he meant only too well. There were cases that truly seemed to trigger her father more than others: wives being abused by their husbands; children being abused by their parents; animal abuse of any kind; mistreatment or neglect of the elderly in nursing homes; and then there were those cases like Doxey's, where a personal friend was involved.

Wendy knew that her father had the utmost respect for the way the man had stared down his criminal past and made himself available to law enforcement to turn his life around completely. Bax Winchester particularly embraced a "phoenix rising from the ashes" scenario, and Earl Jay Doxey's was one of the best. But Doxey had never revealed his sources and was a big user of burner phones so that their privacy could be maintained at all costs.

"Poor Daddy," Wendy said, resting her head on Ross's chest and finding comfort in the way it rose and fell with his breathing. She was also reminded of the way her father had taken her mother's unexpected death. It was as if a part of him had been surgically removed, and he was never to be whole again.

"I guess it's a little too soon for any information about Doxey's services," Wendy added.

Ross managed one softly spoken word: "Prob'ly.'

"When we find out, let's go together."

"Of course, we will."

Wendy hesitated to intrude on what she knew was Ross's

profound shock but did so anyway. There was no way she would ever be able to retreat easily from her sleuthing gifts. "Did you have much interaction with Doxey?"

"Not as much as your daddy," Ross said. "But what I did have was a trip and a half with him. The man was always straightforward with you and always led you to the truth. He was never wrong about his hunches or leads. I'm sure he was really onto something, because it got him killed."

Wendy couldn't help but wonder if Doxey had left anything at all behind, any clue, any inkling of what he was about to uncover. Maybe when things settled down a bit, maybe after Doxey's services, maybe then she could find out from her father if they were any closer to tracking down the culprit who had staged Aurelia Spangler's suicide and then brutally eliminated the Rosalie Police Department's most reliable informant for a long time now.

Meanwhile, teaching bridge lessons to her newbies seemed like it belonged to another lifetime entirely. Yet, it had somehow triggered everything—the alleged suicide and now this murder. She paused in her head. If only she could return to the days of the harmless mischief of rowdy boys dressing up as ghosts to scare the pee out of girls.

As for the present, what force of true evil had been unleashed upon them all? Would there be even more to endure?

Then, just as Ross was about to turn out the light on his nightstand as they were about to go to sleep a bit later, a rogue thought entered Wendy's head. It struck her so forcefully that she felt she had to let Ross in on it right away.

"Milton Bagdad is not the only person we know who wears a tuxedo," she said, sitting upright.

Ross's voice was beyond drained. "What?"

"Carlos Galbis, our bartender extraordinaire at the RCC. It's his work uniform."

"And?"

"Maybe there's some connection to Carlos with Aurelia's vision. Maybe he's in danger of some sort."

Ross fought through his tiredness to express genuine interest. "I never thought of that."

"Maybe you should go out and question him and see if anything turns up. I realize it could be a long shot, but what could it hurt?"

"Not a bad suggestion," Ross told her, turning to give her a peck on the cheek. "I'll run it past your daddy when I go in. Meanwhile, I gotta turn out the light and get some sleep, or I'll be wrecked tomorrow."

Wendy sank back against her pillows with satisfaction. Had she stumbled upon something that might break the case wide open?

CHAPTER 14

Ross was genuinely surprised the next morning when he was informed that Vance Quimby had shown up at the front desk and had something very important to share with him. All sorts of wild ideas began circulating throughout his brain: Did Vance know something about Doxey's death? Was he somehow involved? Or was there something important he had held back about his sister's death? Ross couldn't wait to get into the interrogation room and find out, because Vance Quimby was the one person who continued to make him frown at a mere mention. What was that about, and was it even fair of him?

"I wanted to come to you immediately with this even though I realize that I didn't have to," Vance was saying once the two of them had settled across from each other at the long table.

From his vast experience with interrogating people over the years, Ross thought that that particular statement smacked of manipulation, of a story well rehearsed. He also could not help but notice how haggard Vance looked, as if he hadn't been getting much rest lately. Not to mention that the white shirt and the gray pants he was wearing were both wrinkled. The ensemble and Vance's face reminded Ross of people he'd run across in his work who were too substance addicted to worry even a little bit about their appearance.

Nonetheless, Ross remained stoic and said, "Please go ahead and tell me all about it, then."

"It's about Relly's life insurance policy," he continued, not making direct eye contact. "The insurance company is going with the coroner's ruling and the autopsy results. They see no reason not to accept their opinions in the matter, and so, they are not going to give me the money, which is what Relly intended, I assure you. She would not want to see me in this situation now that she's gone."

"I hope this doesn't sound impolite, but . . . you have no savings at all? Are you flat broke or something?"

"I have a little in the bank, and I won't starve to death, I assure you. But that's not the point, Detective. Someone robbed both Relly and myself of our livelihood for all time, and I want to see that justice is done. I hope I've conveyed that to you from the beginning."

Ross was staring straight at Vance, searching for tells of any kind. But the man's face was a poker player's blank, even if there was that element of tiredness in it. "So with all due respect, I can't interfere with the decisions of insurance companies. I can't help you there, and I'm sure you're aware of that."

Vance drew back suddenly, and his tone became strident. "But you can solve the case and prove that my sister was murdered. And please save yourself the speculation that I would ever do such a godforsaken thing as kill my own sister. I loved her very much. This is *not* about the money."

Ross decided to play it straight and said, "Fair enough. But is there anything at all you can tell me—tell us, in fact— that would help us get to the solution of this case? Maybe something you've overlooked or brushed aside?"

"Just one important thing," Vance said, leaning forward

with urgency in his tone. "If my sister said that the vision of a knife being plunged into a man's tuxedoed chest shook her to her roots, you have to believe her, and you have to find a way to make some sense of that. Who knows? Maybe it was a representation of something else entirely, but I think it bears repeating. You find out what struck terror into my sister's heart and even made Milton Bagdad skip town the way he did like some runaway puppy, and you'll understand why my sister was murdered."

Ross reflected on the telegram that Milton Bagdad had delivered after which Professor Isaacson had taken a knife to all the rag dolls he had received as a result of his female students' crushes. Those hormonal outbursts surely came with the territory. The CID had effectively put Aurelia's vision to bed with that incident; yet Vance Quimby was demanding—and with what could only be described as a great deal of passion—that he and the CID revisit it, put it under a microscope again. It seemed like an exercise in redundancy to Ross, but there were obviously still two people around to question about the incident, and Milton had already given his full account of what had happened that evening. But what about Professor Isaacson himself? Could there possibly be anything more that he could reveal about what went on that night? Some little detail or insight that might have a bearing on the case?

Ross stood up, and the two men shook hands. "Mr. Quimby, I assure you, we are doing everything possible to get to the bottom of your sister's death. As you said, you did not have to come in today and talk to me, and I thank you for that. We'll keep you posted on any and all developments."

Then Vance revealed what had been obvious to Ross from the minute the two of them had sat down and begun their conversation. "I . . . haven't gotten much sleep lately. My mind just keeps reliving the horrible reality of it all. Losing my sister like this has been driving me crazy. I never dreamed things would end like this. Who would? I thought Relly and I would retire together somewhere, and she would never have to look into people's faces again and coax things out of them. Maybe she'd only have to look at sunsets and sunrises and . . ."

The spurt of emotion in his voice shut him down, and Ross gave the moment his silent respect. He had no trouble dealing with Wendy's various moods, even what he considered the most unreasonable of them, but with men—such as his father-in-law, Bax, and what he was going through with Doxey's death—he was less comfortable, less sure of himself.

Finally, Ross said, "You've given me an idea, Mr. Quimby. Maybe it'll lead to something that'll break the case."

There was a glimmer of hope in Vance's face. "I'd like to think so. And I want to thank you for taking me seriously. This is the most traumatic thing that's ever happened to me, and if I've conveyed that to you today, then I can maybe get a little relief from this terrible weight I'm carrying around."

Ross offered up his best smile. "Yes, I hope you can, too."

After Vance had left, Ross returned to his desk and made a note to himself in all caps:

INTERVIEW PROF. ISAACSON

Then he sat back and also made a mental note. His opinion of Vance Quimby had been clarified somewhat by this last visit. His years of experience and the concept that Wendy had trotted out for him a while back—*hiding in plain sight*—were telling him that Vance was certainly trying his best to give the appearance of being on the up-and-up about everything all along. But that still did not remove him from possibly being responsible for all the trauma, trickery, and sorrow that had begun that fateful evening out at Overview.

All that aside, Ross now had two new leads worth investigating. Just before Vance Quimby had announced himself, Bax had agreed that Wendy's observation regarding Carlos Galbis wearing a tux as his uniform of choice was something they had all overlooked so far. So, his first stop on this day of fresh insights would be to the Rosalie Country Club.

Things weren't busy for Carlos when Ross arrived at the RCC about a half hour later. He had called ahead to make sure Carlos didn't have the day off, and had been told by Rosalie's most celebrated mixologist himself that eleven in the morning was still a bit too early for even the town's most notorious drinkers, with the sole exception of the Bloody Mary devotees.

"Eleven is perfectly respectable for them," Carlos had said with a chuckle. "But none of them have shown up so far."

Ross laughed, too. "I know the type well. But just between the two of us, I think there are certain people in Rosalie who are constantly working toward an even earlier hour to begin consuming those adult beverages."

"Amen."

"Let's sit down at one of the nearby tables, why don't we? That way we can be a bit more comfortable, and you can still keep an eye on your bar," Ross said after he had politely refused the offer of water or a soft drink. As the professional he was, Carlos knew that Ross would refuse anything stronger while on duty.

When they had settled in, it was Carlos who spoke first. "You said you had something important you wanted to discuss with me, Detective? I don't know if I can be of any help to you, though. Have I done something wrong?"

Ross told him he had not and then quickly reviewed what he thought was pertinent about the deaths of Aurelia Spangler and Earl Jay Doxey, particularly her strange vision. Then he added, "I don't want to alarm you in any way, but the fact is that you do wear a tuxedo to work every day. There just aren't many people in Rosalie who do. You can understand my concern, I hope."

The color rose slightly in Carlos's olive skin, and he became fidgety in his chair. "You think Miz Spangler's vision may have had something to do with me?" Suddenly, there was a gasp, followed by definite panic in his eyes and voice. "Oh my, it's happening tonight."

"What's happening tonight? Are you going psychic on me?"

"And I've already paid for it," Carlos added, ignoring the question while the wildest of thoughts erupted in Ross's head.

"Paid for what?"

Carlos was shaking his head now, still not answering the questions put before him. "Do you think she might be in danger? Should I cancel it?"

"Who might be in danger? Cancel what?"

"I decided to pay Party Palooza for a singing telegram for my wife, Elena. It's supposed to be delivered to her tonight as a surprise. Just my way of telling her what a great woman and mother she is to our children. But now I'm worried."

Ross sat back and slumped, looking like all the air had been let out of his chest. "It seems I really have alarmed you unnecessarily. That wasn't at all why I came out here. I had no idea you'd just placed a telegram. My wife and I just thought that maybe I should check up on you. I wanted to ask you if anything suspicious or puzzling had happened to you lately."

Carlos was clearly lost in thought for a while. "Suspicious, no. Puzzling, yes."

"What puzzled you?"

Carlos's mood seemed to have lightened somewhat, and he said, "Figuring out why some of the wealthiest members out here leave me the scrawniest tips. Got any ideas on that one?"

"Afraid not," Ross said, lightening up himself. "Once again,

I'm sorry if I upset you in any way, but I would like you to do
me a favor. Get back to me at once if the slightest thing turns
up that seems strange to you. I mean not only out here but
around your home or going back and forth to work. We have
to look into every lead, of course, and you understand that
this is all that was. You, yourself, are hardly under suspicion,
and don't dwell too much on the tuxedo angle I brought up.
I think both you and your wife will be safe, but if it will re-
lieve your mind, I'll have my partner, Detective Roland Pike,
put on a detail when Milton Bagdad delivers your telegram.
Meanwhile, you just stay alert and keep on making those
monster juleps and mojitos for everybody."

"You got it, Detective, and thanks for the extra protection. I do understand why you had to go into this with me,"
he said, taking a deep breath and finishing with a big smile.
Now all he had to do was wait for the Bloody Mary crowd to
show up.

Wendy and Ross felt emotionally spent after they filed out
of Earl Jay Doxey's services at the cozy North Rosalie Baptist
Church, even though they had both remained silent throughout—and even somewhat in awe of the heartfelt spectacle.
The intensity of the two dozen, red-robed, choral voices and
the energy with which their music floated heavenward were
almost tangible at times. Their version of celebratory sorrow
had a substance to it that neither of them had experienced before in their own white churches. Wendy thought back on
her own mother's funeral a dozen years ago. It had been very
reserved and orderly, but she hadn't paid much attention to
that fact until now—all these many years later. She concluded
that there was a wide gulf between the rituals of bluestocking
Presbyterians and blue collar black Baptists; yet at the same
time, she wondered if "getting it all out of their systems," as
Doxey's friends and fellow churchgoers had done so thor-

oughly and without reservation, wasn't the more satisfying way of saying goodbye to a loved one. At the very least, it had felt joyful to all those in attendance.

In the equally cramped Fellowship Hall next door a few minutes later, Bax was already hugging the widowed Mary Liz Doxey amidst the crowd across the room, but Wendy and Ross lost no time in catching up with him and introducing themselves.

"What a powerful service that was, and such a great tribute to your husband, Miz Doxey," Wendy told her, as her father finally pulled away. "I know you must have taken great comfort in it."

"Yes, it really was a great comfort to me. The choir's singing, in particular," Mary Liz said, perfectly composed and smiling. "Music, it does soothe the wounded soul."

In fact, Wendy had never seen someone so close to the deceased that poised and collected at a visitation; this tall, handsome woman who wore salt-and-pepper dreadlocks down to her shoulders with fashionable aplomb seemed imperturbable. "Earl Jay got to where he loved goin' to church with me on Sundays after we got married," Mary Liz continued. "Sometimes, even on Wednesdays. He never used to darken the door of any church before that, though. Of course, there were times I thought he came on Wednesdays for the supper more than anything else, but I didn't care if it was just all about his stomach. All I wanted to do was bring him into the fold and try to keep him there. He always did things his way for his reasons anyway. Like he told me he wanted a closed coffin and visitation after the services and not before like usual, and so here we all are."

"Mary Liz made a big difference in Doxey's life," Bax added, pointing to his friend. "You were the best thing that ever happened to him."

Mary Liz reached out and took Bax's hand, smiling graciously. "He said the same thing about you, too. You helped him turn away from his life a' crime." Then she gestured toward the table across the way with its generous offerings of food and drink. "Please, help yourselves, won't you? Earl Jay left specific instructions for all a' y'all to party in his memory, and I know you don't wanna let him down. He wanted Simply Soul to cater his funeral with practically everything on their menu that he loved—lots of greens, beans, mac and cheese, fried catfish, and rice and gravy. So don't be shy— please treat yourselves to your heart's content. We have more than plenty. Earl Jay was big on not wasting a crumb when it came to food."

"We'll take you up on that," Ross told her, smiling big.

Over at the busy buffet table, Wendy started helping her plate while lowering her voice to Ross. "Mary Liz is so healthy with all of this. You'd never know she was the widow of the occasion. I doubt I could be anywhere near that together if I were the hostess at your funeral—which I certainly hope and pray will be very far off into the future, by the way."

"I appreciate that, but never try to second-guess the way people grieve," he said, also in a confidential tone while digging into the mac and cheese with the big silver spoon that had been provided. "Some zig, while others zag to deal with it. But no matter what they do, you'll never be able to know exactly what they're feeling. What it looks like on the surface may be very different from what's going on deep inside where they live and breathe."

"Of course, I know you're right," Wendy told him. "After all these years, I'm still not over losing my mother the way I did. I remember clearly that I didn't want to talk about it with any of my girlfriends, or maybe I just didn't know how to do that. Anyway, I drifted away from them all, went to the psychiatrist that Daddy set up for me, and also listened to any advice that Daddy gave me along the way. Still, I never re-member being composed the way Mary Liz is right now, no matter how much time had passed. There was always this enormous void that I was never able to fill. If you're just a small child, death doesn't truly register with you, and the elderly seem resigned to waiting for it patiently. But when you're a teenager or young adult, it seems like a cruel lesson you're having to learn way too soon."

"I wonder if anyone ever completely heals," Ross said.

"I don't think so, but maybe at least enough to keep on going, I suspect. Maybe that's good enough and the best we can hope for."

Ross lifted a large piece of fried catfish onto his plate with tongs and said, "Bax told me that Doxey never shared any of his informant work with Mary Liz. He said that if she never knew anything that he'd learned off the streets, then no one could ever force anything out of her, and she'd be safer that way. At that point, his primary mission in life was to protect her." Ross paused and looked her way. "I should take a tip from Doxey and not leak as much as I do to you."

Putting her plate down briefly, Wendy held her hand up as if she were being sworn in to some office or other. "You know how trustworthy I am; and besides, Daddy's just as bad as you are about that. It wouldn't be fair to start depriving me of little bits and pieces of your cases at this late date. What would be the point?"

"You've given us both a couple of scares at times—that's the point," he said, sounding amused and resigned at the same time. "But you're right. You'd get it out of us one way or an-other."

The two of them made their way to a couple of folding chairs against one of the plain white walls, sat down, balanced their plates on their laps, and began sampling their food. After a couple of bites of green beans, Wendy said, "Does that mean you're not going to interview Mary Liz about her husband's death?"

"I doubt she'd have anything to tell us based on what your Daddy said, and I'm sure she'd come forward if she did."

That brought an odd expression to Wendy's face, as if she couldn't decide whether to smile or look quizzical. "I know I haven't been at this solving-crimes business nearly as long as you have, but isn't it the case sometimes that people don't realize they know something that might be very valuable to the police? That is, until it's drawn out of them?"

"Ah, the art of interrogation," Ross said, smartly piercing the air with his upside-down fork. "And it *is* an art, as you've been finding out since you've become an investigative reporter. Still, I'll leave it up to your father to make that decision about Mary Liz. My guess is that he'll be all about respecting her private grief and leaving it alone. I think she'd have to come forward voluntarily."

Wendy immediately saw the wisdom of dropping the issue and concentrating on eating instead. She was also content to observe the ebb and flow of the significant church crowd. There wasn't much obvious sadness around the room, despite the preponderance of funereal black; tears seemed to have been told to take a hike, at least for a while. Everyone was indeed eating and drinking and managing small talk with laughter as a serviceable accompaniment. There was a pleasant, cocktail-party hum to it all that seemed perfectly appropriate. She concluded that the unrestrained, heartfelt service—filled with hymns like "Blest Hour, When Mortal Man Retires"—had somehow elevated their common grief and sent it packing with some authority to a better place. They all seemed to be following to the letter Doxey's instructions to have a high-spirited celebration in his honor.

That, she also decided, was the only way to go.

★ ★ ★

The next day happened to be Tuesday, and Merleece showed up early to clean Wendy's house as usual, but she had a troubled expression on her face from the moment she stepped into the foyer, and she was rarely without a smile, even when Miz Crystal had driven her crazy with some ridiculous task assigned at Old Concord Manor.

"Is something the matter?" Wendy said, leading the way to the kitchen for their usual coffee and pastry ritual before the cleaning actually began.

"Might be, Strawberry," Merleece said. "I don't know just yet. Might need me another opinion."

"Well, then, you'll tell me about it, and we'll both decide what's what. We're the best two heads together that I know of."

Wendy made busy kitchen noises, fixing up their coffee mugs and setting out a plate of mini blueberry muffins that she'd made from scratch just yesterday. "What's on your mind?" she said, once she was seated.

Then Merleece blurted it out. "It's Mary Liz Doxey. She up and told me somethin' I think you need to know 'bout. And maybe that husband and daddy a' yours, too."

"I didn't even know you knew her," Wendy said, perking up. If Merleece hadn't gotten her full attention before, she had it now. "I didn't see you at the service yesterday. Were you there?"

"Yes, I was at the back a' the church, but I coudd'n stay on after, so I slipped on out. I saw you and that handsome husband and daddy a' yours up front. Miz Crystal had one a' her luncheons I had to tend to right after the services. You know how important all that kinda stuff is to her. But I did come in early to visit with Mary Liz in Pastor Carter's study so I could let her know I was prayin' for her, and that was when she told me what she told me. Lemme just say that she let her hair down and got all the cryin' outta her system with me. She say to me it was better to do it in private with my arms around her than make a spectacle of herself in public. She was like that, you know, even when we grew up together on North River Street. She kep' errything inside. But the deal was my mama knew her mama, and that's how we become such good friends. Back then, she was Mary Liz Johnston, and then she marry Earl Jay. I near 'bout fainted when I heard he got stabbed on the street. What's Rosalie comin' to? I just don't think they's anybody who's safe anywhere now."

Wendy was staring down into her mug with a glum expression. "It was a shock to my husband and my father, particularly. Daddy was very close to Doxey, as he called him. Anyway, what was it that Mary Liz told you that you think Ross and Daddy and I need to know about?"

Merleece straightened up in her chair and silently moved her lips as she organized her thoughts. "Well, first, Mary Liz, she confess that Earl Jay never would let her know what he was up to. It was to keep her safe, he would say to her, and he would always keep his word on that. But that day he got himself stabbed, Mary Liz say she did overhear him talkin' to someone over the phone 'bout a donkey. He did repeat that word, and his voice, it sound surprised. And then, that very evenin', he left this world and not by his own choice. So, she wanted to know if I did think she oughta go and tell the law all about it."

"What did you say to her?"

"I put it on myself. I say to her not to burden herself with it right now. She had services for Earl Jay first to get through and then all the people in the Fellowship Hall to hold hands with and smile, even if that was the last thing she felt like doin'. I did promise her that I'd be the one to think it over and that I'd tell you 'bout it once I finally decide the right thing to do."

"I'm sure you did the right thing," Wendy said. "I have no idea what the conversation means, but I know that Daddy and Ross will appreciate you coming forward with the information. Maybe they can find out who Doxey was talking to from phone records. Ross and I had been discussing the issue of whether he or Daddy should interrogate Mary Liz or not during this difficult period of grief she's going through." Wendy paused and took a sip of her coffee. "Was that all Mary Liz told you at the church?"

"That's it. They was nothin' else. Just the word *donkey*. A coupla times she heard Earl Jay say it, and he was mighty upset. And then she wouldd'n want him to know she was halfway eavesdroppin' and passin' by behind him in the hallway."

Wendy's brain shifted into sleuthing mode once again.

Donkey.

What was that about? She would tell her father and Ross and see if they could make some sense of it. Perhaps it would be the key to the murders of Aurelia Spangler and Earl Jay Doxey, and lead to their solution.

CHAPTER 15

Wendy and Sarah Ann were seated on a little couch in the common room of Rosalie Women's Shelter, and Wendy couldn't help but think that the entire facility needed a huge infusion of funds to spruce it up a bit. The couch, itself, featured cheap upholstery with a few cigarette burns in it, and the rest of the furniture in the room looked like a collection from the proverbial yard sales and flea markets she was so fond of attending. There were also mismatched curtains at the windows that made everything seem as forlorn and hapless as most of the shelter's residents.

"The director says I have to leave at the end of the week," Sarah Ann was saying to Wendy. "My situation is so not typical of what the shelter is supposed to be used for. Fortunately for me, they had a room to spare. But I can't bear the thought of going back home to Mother. I wish I had the money to afford a place of my own, but I don't have a job."

"Have you heard from your mother at all?"

Sarah Ann looked even more distressed. "She called me up once, and she started off by saying that she was praying for me to come home. She's like a broken record, of course."

"Have you thought that maybe that was her idea of a peace offering?" Wendy said.

"You already know that she's not very good at communicating very much except Scripture."

Sarah Ann's expression changed from gloomy to outraged, and her voice rose a level. "But there's something else I just have to emphasize to you again. She said that I had no idea what she had done to try and save me from the error of my ways. She even admitted she had broken one of the Commandments for me. Don't you see what I'm getting at? I'm so afraid she was the one who did away with Aurelia, even though I have no idea how she could have done it. Mother and cocaine just don't seem to belong in the same universe at all, but we all readily admit that 'Thou shalt not kill' is one of the biggest Commandments there is."

"I would definitely agree with you on that," Wendy said, nodding eagerly. "But my husband has interrogated her in-depth, of course, and he doesn't feel she is a likely suspect."

"I don't know what good it'll do," Sarah Ann continued, "but maybe you could talk to her and see if you can get some concessions so I could return without being driven crazy."

Wendy struggled to repress a chuckle. "I don't know why you think she would listen to a stranger who is teaching you how to play a card game and also arranged for you to sip on a mint julep during the lesson. Let's not forget that she caught us all red-handed at the RCC, so to speak."

"Why does that seem like light-years ago to me?"

"Because so much that's disturbing has happened since then," Wendy said. "Aurelia's vision for Milton had Hiroshima-like effects immediately, and there's still some fall-out." Wendy briefly told her about Earl Jay Doxey's murder. "And I seriously doubt your mother had anything to do with that, either. I think we would both agree that she's most definitely not a street person."

"No," Sarah Ann said, somewhat taken aback by the revelation. "She is supremely at home in a church pew and just about no place else. But I still have a bad feeling about my mother and what happened to Aurelia Spangler. I just can't shake it, no matter how hard I try."

"What would you do if your mother does turn out to be guilty?" Wendy said, suddenly playing devil's advocate. "Keep in mind that you do have to be careful what you wish for in this life."

That seemed to stop Sarah Ann in her tracks, and she took her time before she spoke again. "You make a good point. I've been so obsessed with getting away from Mother's eternal quotes that I haven't thought beyond that. Mother does take care of my room and board and all that other stuff I take for granted."

"Parents are generally pretty good at that, though there are exceptions." Wendy paused to think it through and came to a decision. "Listen, I'll do my best between now and your departure date to see if I can talk to your mother and get her to compromise with you."

"Would you? I'd be so grateful."

Wendy noted how much more attractive Sarah Ann was when she smiled—even her freckles seemed more alive—and said, "I make you no promises, but I'll see what I can do."

Ross walked into Professor Isaacson's cramped office at the college with next to no expectations. Yet he knew from past experience that sometimes the most successful results in criminal investigations arose from the most unlikely sources. Perhaps there would be one little thing—however trivial— that the good professor of literature would reveal that might have a significant bearing on the case.

"I wanted to ask you about something that may surprise you," Ross said, after taking a seat in front of many books stacked on shelves reaching to the ceiling and also surrounding him in shorter stacks on the floor. The professor's desk was devoid of a surface; there were only piles of papers from side to side, along with an in-basket that was overflowing with a variety of disparate items. It occurred to Ross that this particular office had not been cleaned in a very long time, and he wondered how that could be allowed to happen. Did they not have a custodian to take care of such things on a regular basis? Did being messy and cluttered come with being an academic? At any rate, the room offended Ross's highly organized and always neat sensibilities, but he did not comment, of course.

"I assure you that there's nothing much that surprises me these days," Professor Isaacson told him.

"This might, though," Ross continued. "I wanted you to give me your version of the singing telegram that was delivered to you recently by Milton Bagdad of Party Palooza. We were also told that the owner, Rex Boudreaux, was along for the ride that evening. Is that correct?"

"Yes, he was there, too, but I must say that I stand corrected," he said, cracking a smile. "That truly does surprise me. Why would you want to know anything about that godawful telegram? I have to tell you that a few of these female students that I teach have gotten it into their heads recently to send me these anonymous concoctions via Party Palooza. The first time, I thought it was cute in a vague sort of way. But the second time, I began to worry that there might be no end to these escapades. I called up and finally complained to Mr. Boudreaux about them, and I asked him to warn me if another one of those things was coming my way."

"And did he?"

"He most certainly did, and we worked out a plan for the telegram you've brought up to me just now."

"A plan?"

"It really wasn't all that complicated," Professor Isaacson began. "Mr. Boudreaux explained to me that his man, Milton, had had a bad scare recently—something about a psychic's prediction that was off the charts. He said he needed me to help him restore this young man's confidence but without the boy knowing about it."

Ross perked up considerably. Perhaps he was getting somewhere, after all. "Please go on. I'm very interested in the rest of what you have to say."

"There isn't much more to it, actually. I was annoyed by the telegrams and those souvenir rag dolls that I had no use for, so Mr. Boudreaux suggested I just rip them up with a knife and that that would help calm down this boy, Milton. At least, he seemed to think it would. I didn't bother to question any further about it."

"And apparently it did."

"It really did. We all relaxed and had a drink together afterward—actually, more than one so there was no designated driver that night—and Mr. Boudreaux's since informed me that he will accept no more of these foolish, schoolgirl crush telegrams. He will gladly turn down the business to keep the peace with me. Now, that's an extremely considerate businessman, I have to admit. How many would go out of their way to do that for you? So that's the end of that."

"It would appear you're right."

All the time Ross had been conducting his interview, Professor Isaacson's rather large head had been blocking a small shelf on the wall directly behind and slightly above his cluttered desk. It suddenly came into view when the professor crossed his legs and shifted his weight to one side. Ross was immediately drawn to the gleaming bronze figurine that was prominently displayed there.

"I've been admiring that donkey on the shelf behind you,"

he said. "Would you mind telling me the history behind it? I know there's got to be one."

"Ah!" came the enthusiastic reply. The professor rose in his chair, halfway turned around, and plucked it from the shelf, then turning it this way and that to catch the overhead light. "I'm more than happy to share him with you. That delightful ornament would be Dapple—I found him in a little gift shop on a trip to Taxco in Mexico on one of my vacations. I bargained and bargained with the shopkeeper until I got him at a reasonable price, although I was still probably taken to the cleaners. They say the merchants start way above what the item is worth so they can still make a handsome profit when they finally settle. Anyway, this is Sancho Panza's donkey from *Don Quixote*, which I always teach in my European Lit course. It's practically my favorite novel of all time. I sometimes fancy myself as Dapple—plodding along, working hard, loyal to his mission in life. My master is literature, of course. The thing is, I want to do more than inspire hormones among these females—thus my irritation at these silly singing telegrams they started sending to me on a whim. I want to expand their minds instead and get them thinking about the significance of a concept like 'tilting at windmills.' An impossible dream, you say? Perhaps."

"I'm afraid I wasn't a big reader growing up," Ross said, missing the reference entirely. "I was more the 'playing-cops-and-robbers' type. But I do admire people who can write. My wife, Wendy, reads all the time, since she's an investigative reporter for the paper."

Professor Isaacson continued in lecture mode, gesturing vigorously, and Ross could see why certain students found him to be so such a dynamic personality. "Yes, I've read your wife's column from time to time. She's quite good at what she does. But there's an entire universe of literature out there for students to explore, if they only would. But I'm afraid there's serious competition in this generation coming up from social media and keeping in touch with each other twenty-four/seven. I can't think of a good reason to do that, if you want my opinion. I'm a man who jealously guards his privacy and time alone with his own thoughts."

Ross glanced at his watch, stood up, offered his hand, and said, "Well, that's all very interesting, and I want to thank you for your time. You've actually given me some considerable food for thought."

"Have I? I only wish that I could say the same thing about myself regarding my students."

"I'm sure you're just being modest," Ross told him with a smile. "You're obviously doing something right, or your courses wouldn't be as popular as they are. One of your students volunteered that information, by the way."

"Do you mind telling me who that was?"

"Sarah Ann O'Rourke, I believe."

The name struck a responsive chord, causing the professor to puff himself up somewhat while nodding his head. "Yes, yes, Miss Sarah Ann O'Rourke. She certainly pays attention in class and has done well on her tests so far. You'd never catch her sending me one of those ridiculous telegrams. She's far too sensible for something like that."

"I'm sure," Ross said, leaving it at that and heading for the door. "Anyway, thanks again for giving me a bit of your valuable time."

"Of course. Glad I could work it into my schedule."

On the drive back to the station, Ross's brain had shifted into warp speed. Perhaps this was the break they had been searching for, after all. There was the donkey, big as life, and with its own literary backstory to boot. What an accomplished animal! The donkey that Mary Liz had overheard Doxey repeating in that emotional phone call he was making to someone—and that someone might even be his killer, and maybe Aurelia Spangler's as well.

Yet it was difficult to picture the erudite Professor Isaacson as a down-and-dirty drug dealer, someone ruthless and brutal enough to murder two people without compunction. He truly did appear to be a genuine academic with those particular lofty priorities and nothing else on his agenda. Street trade, and the money that came with it? That seemed completely off the table.

But, to conjure up Wendy's concept of *hiding in plain sight* once again, suppose that was exactly what Professor Isaacson was doing as the ultimate cover? Was he even supplying some of his students with cocaine? God forbid. Could he be the outlier who had done away with Aurelia Spangler for reasons known only to him? Ross's mind was reeling, and he was unquestionably tumbling head over heels down the slippery slope of all time.

At this point, there was only one thing to do: discuss the interview at great length with Bax and explore the possibility of having Ronald Pike or another officer put a tail on Isaacson to see if there was any suspicious activity that added more to the story. Then he returned to that one word again: *donkey*.

Could it really be as simple as a figurine on a shelf? Or was that just one of those misleading coincidences that by assigning any credibility to it eventually turned a case cold?

The very thick and burly Ronald Pike, the detective with whom Ross had partnered most often over the years, was having a yawner of a day so far, following the routine of Professor Isaacson at the College of Rosalie. Note-taking was at a very low ebb. The professor had not returned to his car in the faculty parking lot since sliding out of the front seat for what surely must have been his classroom duties at approximately 10 a.m. After that, time moved at a glacial pace. Finally, lunch hour came and went, during which Pike sipped coffee out of a thermos and nibbled on a ham and rye that he'd picked up at a gas station. Then, to satisfy his ever-present sweet tooth, he followed that with a store-bought brownie—all of it unremarkable, but it did the trick.

Around 2 p.m., however, the dam burst. Professor Isaacson hopped into his car, having walked at a brisk pace toward it from his classroom building. Pike thought it was more than brisk. It seemed on the order of urgent. In fact, the professor's tires made squealing noises as he exited the parking lot—with Pike waiting behind for just the right length of time to follow without being noticed.

The cars headed into Rosalie proper in a far from obvious tandem, and Pike noted that the professor was exceeding the speed limit by a good ten miles over. But this was hardly about giving the man a ticket at this point in time; it was manifestly about seeing what he was up to, and whether it was legit or not.

Pike began frowning when Professor Isaacson's car turned onto North River Street. He knew the details of Earl Jay Doxey's murder as well as all the other members of the department did. In a very literal sense, the professor seemed to be returning to the scene of that particular crime. The three of them—Bax, Ross, and Pike, of course—had discussed down at headquarters yesterday afternoon the implications of the donkey figurine, coupled with her husband's conversation that Mary Liz Doxey had said she'd overheard. They had all agreed that there was enough of a connection there to warrant a detail that Pike was now undertaking to the best of his ability.

But his frown soon turned into a shaking of his head, together with a biting of his lower lip. "It can't be this easy, can it?" Pike found himself saying out loud. "Where the hell is he headed in such an all-fired hurry?"

A few minutes later, Professor Isaacson ended up parking in front of a modest cottage that was five or six houses down from the spot where Earl Jay Doxey had been so brutally stabbed on the sidewalk recently. Was he possibly visiting the culprit or someone who knew who the culprit was? Or was this a matter of dispensing or acquiring drugs? Pike noted the address from his GPS and finally had something of substance to write about from his vantage point down the street a bit.

When Professor Isaacson emerged from the cottage a good hour or so later, his stride from the front porch to his car was a great deal more relaxed than it had been going inside. It was as if the man were moving in slow motion now. Then, Pike's imagination kicked in, as he played an episode of a police show starring himself across his windshield. In the very first scene he could see himself running up to the man and arresting him for cocaine use or possession or whatever combination existed. The professor would meekly comply, caught red-handed, and Pike would read him his rights. Then he would take him down to the station, where the thorough interrogation by Ross or Captain Bax would reveal that he had been the one to commit both crimes because the victims, Aurelia Spangler and Earl Jay Doxey, were threatening his drug dealing—a wildly successful enterprise using his academic profession as the most respectable cover ever. Who would ever have thought to suspect it but for a donkey figurine on the shelf? Bravo, Ross! Bravo, Bax! But most of all—Bravo, Pike!

Then the episode ended, and Pike returned to the reality of mostly clear glass with a bug splat or two marring its surface, while smiling at himself in the rearview mirror for such a superb diversion. If nothing else, there was certainly plenty to warrant bringing the good professor in for further questioning.

CHAPTER 16

Which of the Ten Commandments had Dora O'Rourke broken? That was uppermost in Wendy's mind as she and the woman faced each other in one of the *Citizen*'s small meeting rooms. In fact, Wendy was surprised that Dora had been willing to come in at all, but here she was, looking as stiff and uncomfortable as ever.

"I have said my piece to my daughter," Dora had told her over the phone in a none-too-polite tone. "She's clearly outta control, and I don't know where she's headed."

"But that's the point. She'll have no place to head after Saturday," Wendy had explained then. "I promised her I'd talk to you about making some sort of arrangement before that happens to her at the shelter."

Somehow, Wendy had managed to convince Dora to at least come to the paper and listen to what she had to say. Maybe that meant there was a crack in the woman's dogmatic armor, after all.

"She doesn't respect me," Dora was saying, once their conversation in the meeting room had begun in earnest. "I'm her mother. I'm entitled to that. Need I remind you of 'Honor thy father and mother'?"

Wendy had been rehearsing very carefully how she would approach the task ahead of her, and so far, she was following her measured script to the letter. "I would agree with you, Miz O'Rourke. But if I could encourage you to remember how you behaved at that age and take that into—"

"At Sarah Ann's age, I had to work. Same job I have now—waitin' on people at the department store on commission and on my feet, by the way," Dora interrupted, pointing toward the floor.

"I can imagine how tired you get waiting around for customers," Wendy added. "But what I was referring to was the fact that you've done such a good job in supporting your daughter that she now has some advantages you didn't have at that age. Remember that you're sending her to college. That's quite an accomplishment, and you should be proud of it."

Dora's hardened expression began to soften somewhat. "Well, I'm glad someone appreciates it. Sarah Ann, she doesn't seem to."

"But I can assure you, she does. She's taking advantage of the opportunity you've given her by buckling down and doing quite well in all her classes. Her grades are top-notch."

A smile began to break across Dora's face. "That much is true. I wouldn't want her to be wastin' her time out there at the college partyin' like some a' them do." There was a pause, and Dora's expression darkened again. "But then, she's exposed to so much I don't approve of."

"Having been to college myself," Wendy continued, "I can tell you that there's a lot I didn't agree with that I was exposed to as well. That's the nature of the beast, I'm afraid. You're given all these ideas, but it's up to you to pick and choose which ones work for you."

"You shouldn't have to pick and choose. You should know the truth already. I know the truth. Why can't everybody else?"

Wendy instantly recognized where Dora was headed and played the "respect" card again. "I know you feel she doesn't respect your beliefs, but I believe that's the wrong interpretation. You know as well as I do how much your daughter likes to question everything under the sun. It's in her nature. At our first bridge lesson, she even questioned the ranking of the suits. To my knowledge, she might be the first person who ever did that. 'But why are they ranked that way? Who did that?' she said, and she was perfectly serious about it. I didn't take it personally."

"But I don't approve of you teachin' her that card game in the first place—and then there was the drinkin' that I walked in on out there at the country club," Dora continued, her nose in the air.

"Well, I apologize if I overstepped my bounds by ordering a mint julep for her, but I can assure you that bridge is a harmless game that has stood the test of time. It mostly brings people together for social reasons, no matter their age."

It was clear to Wendy that Dora was having trouble processing all the patient apologies and concessions being made to her, and there was again a softening of her features as she spoke up. "Well, cards is one thing, but I s'pose you know that Sarah Ann is threatenin' to leave our church, don'tcha?"

"She's mentioned that to me, yes."

"How do you think that makes me feel?"

"I can imagine it upsets you very much. But I do think I have a good idea in that regard."

For the first time, Dora leaned in with what appeared to be genuine interest. "And what's that?"

"See what you think about this," Wendy began. "Welcome your daughter back into your home and tell her that you understand she's still going to college and asking questions. Tell her that you'll always be there for her, no matter what. Believe me, I know what I'm talking about. I lost my mother when I was fifteen, and I can't count how many times I've wished she were still around to be here for me. Don't take your life or Sarah Ann's life for granted. Live in and appreciate the precious moment."

Dora's prolonged silence made Wendy feel hopeful that she might have gotten through. "What you say does make some sense, but the thing is, I'm frightened for my daughter," Dora said finally. "That woman, that fortune-teller or whatever she was—she's dead now—and it all happened because of that bridge lesson that Sarah Ann went to up at that haunted house. What if somethin' happens to my only child now? What if she's next? I . . . feel I need to ward off whatever evil's runnin' around by remindin' Sarah Ann of the comfort I get from my Bible."

Wendy knew she had to proceed carefully now. "I understand your concern as a mother. I know I would feel the same way about my child. But if I may, what you just told me brings up a question I need to ask you. In fact, your daughter mentioned it to me. She said that you told her you had broken one of the Commandments to protect her. She was very concerned about what you may have done."

"Was she?" Dora looked surprised at first, then blushed and hung her head. "I'm . . . not very proud of what I did. I wish now I hadn't done it. I hope I'll be forgiven for it."

"Do you mind telling me what you did?"

Dora continued looking down into her lap. "When you and your husband came with Sarah Ann and took her to the women's shelter, I just lost it. Right after y'all left, I shook my fist at the door and took the Lord's name in vain. It just seemed to explode outta me. I won't tell you what I said or how many times I said it. That's my shame to bear."

Wendy felt washed by a wave of relief and reached out for Dora's hand. This was going even better than she'd hoped. "I feel sure you'll be forgiven, Miz O'Rourke. It happens to all of us from time to time. We know we shouldn't do it, but our temper gets the best of us, I'm afraid."

"I appreciate you sayin' that to me," Dora said. "I feel like you do understand me more than my daughter does."

"Perhaps you underestimate Sarah Ann, though," Wendy added. "Will you give her a little breathing room and the benefit of the doubt while she continues to explore college? Soon enough, she'll be on her own, and you'll be glad for her visits."

"That's true."

"Then you'll welcome her back, and the two of you will try to work things out by talking to each other?"

Dora's smile was hesitant at first but seemed genuine enough. "I believe I might be ready to try."

"I don't think you'll be sorry." Wendy rose from her chair and added, "And maybe you should be the one to go to the shelter and give her the good news?"

"Yes, I think so, too," Dora said, standing up as well. "And thank you for your help. I know I didn't think this little talk was gonna be of any help at all, but it has been."

Wendy smiled but held nothing back. "I have to admit I didn't know how it would go, either."

After Dora had left and Wendy had settled once again into her cubicle, she gave herself an imaginary pat on the back. The communicative skills she was developing as an investigative reporter were paying off big-time for her now. She couldn't wait to tell Ross about her interview with Dora O'Rourke and the conclusion she'd drawn because of it—one he'd already reached and revealed to her.

Dora O'Rourke couldn't possibly be the culprit in either of the murders that had taken place. That would have been totally alien to her belief system. Though misguided at times, Dora's sole aim in life was to do what she thought was in her daughter's best interests, and Wendy could not envision cocaine or knives being a part of that for any reason whatsoever.

The bonus was that the odds had gone up that mother and daughter might indeed be able to call a truce and live together in some semblance of peace.

At about the same time Wendy was conducting her walking-on-eggshells interview with Dora O'Rourke, Ross and Bax were hoping to get some answers out of Professor Isaacson down at headquarters. Father and son-in-law were taking turns throwing out the questions in the interrogation room, but they had just hit a rough patch.

"I told you everything I know about all that telegram business at the college, Detective Rierson," Professor Isaacson was saying. "I was happy to come in and cooperate, but I don't see where all this is leading."

Bax took the time to review the deaths of both Aurelia Spangler and Earl Jay Doxey for him but particularly lingered on the "donkey connection" there at the end. "I'm sure you can understand that we have to investigate further under those circumstances. Please give us your input."

The professor looked incredulous and threw up his hands. "You think I had something to do with that man's death because of my beloved Dapple figurine? Please tell me you're kidding. In my opinion, this borders on police harassment."

"No, I assure you, we don't have it in for you or anything like that," Ross told him. "We were just intrigued enough by pieces of the puzzle that seemed to fit that we decided to have you tailed yesterday. According to the report we received from Sgt. Ronald Pike, you headed right out to North River Street on your lunch break, where you spent an hour at a specific house. As we just told you, it was not far from where Earl Jay Doxey was stabbed on the street. I'm sorry if you think we were unjustified in our actions, but we were just doing what we're paid to do by the taxpayers in these situations. But more to the point, can you explain your behavior, sir?"

Professor Isaacson continued shaking his head in disbelief. "You make me think I need a lawyer, the way you're talking. I mean, I came in expecting that the most that would happen would be that you had something more to tell me about that damn-fool singing telegram. So, do I need a lawyer or not?"

"You're certainly entitled to one, if you wish," Bax told him.

A modest length of time passed in silence, and then Bax added with great intensity, "Earl Jay Doxey was a close friend of mine, and he helped this police department track down some of the worst elements in this town and put them behind bars. I have a vested interest in obtaining justice for him and his widow. If you've done nothing wrong, then speak up. If you have, then go and get that lawyer."

The professor's face fell, and his incredulous expression was replaced by a prolonged sigh. "If it helps you make sense of my behavior, then, well . . . I'll go ahead and tell you what happened. But it's not what you're expecting to hear based on what you've told me already about your reasons."

"We're all ears," Ross said. "We are both fair men."

Then came the one word, "men," from the professor's mouth. He allowed it to sit there, saying nothing else.

"Is there more to it than that?" Ross asked. "Because I have no idea what's going on in your head now."

Sounding more resigned than anything else, Professor Isaacson continued. "I'm a man, just as both of you are. I pride myself on my status as a professor of European Litera- ture, and I think I do a decent job of teaching it. But then there's another side of me that I keep hidden and no one knows about it. I'm not sure I can make sense of it myself." He paused, and his face reflected the turmoil inside.

"Let me take a stab at it, then. Are you addicted to drugs? Did you go to North River Street for a fix? Is that what this has been about all along?" Bax said.

Professor Isaacson drew back with a definite look of disgust. "What? Is that what you think I was up to when that officer followed me? You have it all wrong, but I guess I better get it out, once and for all, although I trust you gentlemen will be discreet with what I tell you. This could ruin me."

Bax and Ross exchanged puzzled glances, and Ross said, "Tell us first. We need to know what this is really about. Now's the time for you to clear your name and then let us take it from there."

Finally, the professor blurted it out and did not stop for quite some time. "It's about my needs as a man, and the truth is that I see this perfectly beautiful woman on North River Street who attends to those needs. I'm sure I don't need to draw pictures for you, do I? But . . . she happens to be black, and I also . . . pay her for those services. Do you get it now? I'm not in love with her, and she's not in love with me—at least not in the conventional sense. It's just an arrangement that works well for both of us. It's . . . it's what I want and need, but there might be people who wouldn't understand and hold it against me or even think I shouldn't be teaching impressionable students. But I assure you, I keep those two parts of my life separate because there is a morals clause in my contract. Maybe I should write a novel about that someday after my teaching career is over—which I don't want to be premature, by the way. The state of Mississippi continues to produce lots of writers of every genre with every passing generation. Do you understand everything now?"

"I think we get the picture," Ross said while catching Bax's gaze.

"Is it necessary to bring her into this? As I asked you before, can you be discreet about all this? I assure you, it has nothing to do with drugs. But I suppose there's the issue of my paying Sammita Jones. That's her name, you see, and you probably already know that because you know her address. Can you please consider letting this go and let me go on with my life?"

Bax spoke up. "You understand that we had to look into this, even though it appears it was all a series of coincidences."

"Yes, I do. But I don't think it would exactly enhance my standing at the college if this got out, do you?"

"Prob'ly not," Bax said. "But one last thing we need from you. Would you mind giving us your DNA and prints? It's more for your exclusion as a suspect than anything else."

"Yes, of course. Anything to get this over with. And you won't bring Sammita into this?"

"We'll need to confirm your story with her," Bax told him. "But we'll make it clear that we aren't interested in anything else. I have never been a big fan of the victimless crime wing of my profession."

"Thank you for that," Professor Isaacson said. "And I wish you luck in finding out who did kill your psychic and your informant. This drug dealing is a nasty business, I hear."

"A fatal business more often than not," Bax added. "No honor among those types of thieves."

CHAPTER 17

"I'm afraid this case is rapidly going cold," Ross was telling Wendy as they sat up in bed that evening in the four-poster of her childhood. "Everything and everybody check out—no hits, no hints or clues that have been productive for us. Doxey used burners when he prowled around for answers, so there are no phone records we can access, and he always kept his wife out of the equation. Even the snatches she overheard of that one conversation of his turned out to be a dead end. In fact, it was more like a comedy of errors."

"Nothing of interest from Professor Isaacson, then?" Wendy said, the disappointment clearly evident in her tone.

Ross was as good as his word to the professor in revealing nothing about the man's private life with Sammita Jones, who had already confirmed their relationship down at the station, and he merely said, "Trust me. It was just a coincidence about the word *donkey*. It all had to do with his fondness for his European Lit course. He even allowed us to search his home without a warrant this afternoon—and nothing. I know I don't have to tell you how often misleading things occur in this business. Your daddy has shared a lot with you over the years about red herrings. They are the bane of our existence."

Wendy snuggled up against her husband, thankful that he was the type of man who truly enjoyed touching on a regular basis. "So . . . do you know what you and Daddy are going to try next?"

"The street's a tough place," he continued, putting his arm around her in protective mode as he spoke. "It rarely gives up its secrets, and it took a man like Doxey to squeeze out what it did give up. But he's gone now, and whoever put out the hit on him is definitely gonna lay low for a while. They know how not to leave a trail of any kind. Meanwhile, the only thing new regarding Aurelia Spangler is that her brother keeps showing up and asking us why we haven't figured out what happened with his sister yet. I've seen this go down before. We can't get the break we need, no one steps up to volunteer anything, and other cases start to take priority. We have the hard evidence on those, and we have to spend our manpower on them."

"But I know how Daddy felt about Doxey. I can't picture him ever giving up on this," Wendy said.

"No, he won't. It's just that it doesn't look good right now. We thought we had cleaned up the town when we put Poley Johnson and Larry Ventner behind bars, but there's obviously someone a lot more clever than either of them were who's still around and will stop at nothing to stay in business. In a sense, whoever this is makes Johnson and Ventner look like Eagle Scouts."

"You make the situation sound pretty ominous," Wendy said with a little shudder.

"Sorry, but murder and drugs are both a very nasty business. I'm afraid there's no other way to put it."

Then his thoughts turned to the meeting in Jackson the next day that he and Bax were attending with the undeniably awkward but vaguely amusing acronym of MAOCOP—Mississippi Association of Chiefs of Police. Its critics had remained steadfast over the years in maintaining that it sounded like a Chinese Communist organization. Yet nothing had ever been changed.

"I appoint you the official alarm-setter," Ross said, giving his wife an affectionate squeeze.

"When?"

"Six. Your daddy is coming by to pick me up right around seven so we can get to Jackson by nine."

"You want breakfast?"

"Oatmeal with raisins and strong coffee to wake me up, please."

"You got it."

After a prolonged good-night kiss and turning out the lights, Ross quickly ran a slide show of all the suspects in his brain, and none of them seemed to fit the bill at this point. Yet, there had to be something about at least one of them that was connected to the solution to these crimes, even if that one person wasn't aware of it. The CID just hadn't found the right angle yet, but it had to be out there just waiting to be discovered. Ross agreed with his wife that Aurelia Spangler as a suicide made no sense, and there was no doubt that Doxey had stumbled upon the truth about her death with fatal consequences. It all had to be connected, but that connection was proving to be very elusive.

As Wendy had said, where were they to go from here?

The invitation was a huge surprise to Wendy, to say the least. She had been in Merleece's little bungalow on North River Street once before to question her about The Grand Slam Murders a couple of years back, but this was the first time she had been invited to dinner there. She'd just given Ross a goodbye kiss and sent him on his way to Jackson when the landline rang the next morning.

"Nothin' against that handsome husband a' yours or any

other man, Strawberry, but it's just gonna be us girls tonight," Merleece was saying to her as the conversation proceeded.

Wendy quickly reviewed the superb calendar she kept in her head and smiled. "I'm definitely free this evening, and I think it was sweet of you to include Mary Liz in your plans. She's prob'ly not even thinking about going out and socializing with people at this point. Grief can really take over your life until you can hardly breathe."

"I heard that. But I wanna get her outta that lonely house a' hers for a change. Plus, I don't think she been eatin' like she s'pose to. I took a casserole over there right after the services, but as I find out later, she just put it up in the freezer 'cause she didn't feel like eatin'. So, you and me, we gonna try to get some food into her and keep her company for a while. You up to it, Strawberry?"

"You bet I am. She's fortunate to have a friend like you. Have you thought about what you'll serve?"

"Now, you know me better'n that. I already got the menu in the works," Merleece told her. "How 'bout some baked chicken, green beans, rice and gravy, biscuits, and then a slice a' my applesauce pie for dessert? Now, you tell me, who in they right mind can turn that down?"

"I know for a fact that I couldn't. But I guess the trick'll be to get Mary Liz to eat all that."

Merleece made a clucking noise. "We gotta try. Otherwise, she gone waste away to nothin'."

"Is it really that bad?"

"Well, maybe not. Sometime, I do exaggerate a little with my friends. But we cain't let her just fold her petals and give up. Right now, Mary Liz Doxey, she's my girlfriend from way back and my project, and that's how you show people you really love 'em—when they in trouble."

Wendy suddenly felt as if the two of them could solve all

the problems of the world, and her natural reaction quickly followed. "Is there anything I can bring along from my house?"

"Not a thing. All I need is you to help me with this just by bein' there. That'll do it."

"Thank you for thinking of me."

"They's nobody else could make it work, Strawberry. We gone do some good. I just know we will."

"You and I, we always get the job done," Wendy said, eagerly looking forward to doing her best to help the bereaved widow find peace.

After she hung up, she texted Ross about her last-minute dinner plans. That way, he wouldn't be surprised by coming home to the disappointing silence of an empty house, not to mention that he and her father would know to stop for dinner somewhere if their meeting in Jackson ran late.

It was Wendy's studied opinion that Merleece had been spot-on about Mary Liz Doxey and her general appearance. As she walked in the front door of Merleece's home on Wednesday evening, the woman's cheeks looked somewhat sunken, and she had applied a bare minimum of makeup, which did not enhance things. Yet, she managed a genuine smile as she shook Wendy's hand warmly during their perfunctory greetings in the living room.

"I remember you at the services. You had some mighty kind words for me," Mary Liz said, as the two women sat on Merleece's cozy, blue afghan-covered sofa together. "So nice to see you again."

"I was pleased to hear that our Merleece had included you in her dinner plans," Wendy said. "I suppose I don't have to tell you how good a cook she is. Everything she pulls outta the oven tastes like it was made for the gods."

"If you mean it's divine, I agree."

The laughter that spilled out of the two women was genuine enough, and Wendy said, "I can tell you and Merleece go way back."

"That we do. Our mothers, they wanted us both to know our way around the kitchen, but Merleece, she paid attention. I'm afraid I ended up looking the other way. I wanted to go out and play ball with the neighborhood kids. I was a little bit of a tomboy, you see."

Merleece settled into her nearby rocking chair and said, "You just didd'n like cookin' is all they was to it, Mary Liz. I remember you sayin' to me way back when, you thought errybody should have a cook in the house but to leave you out." Then Merleece leaned in expectantly. "Would y'all like a glass a' good ole Rosalie muscadine wine? I'm 'bout to have me some. Y'all wanna join me?"

Both Wendy and Mary Liz said they did, and Merleece briskly headed toward the kitchen, where everything was warming on the stovetop or in the oven, while every molecule of oxygen in the house was saturated with all the flavors that would soon delight their palates.

"Your good friend and mine, Merleece, is a bit worried about you," Wendy said, hoping her words would continue their promising conversation. "She knows what a difficult period this must be for you."

Fortunately, Mary Liz responded by flashing another warm smile. "She's gone outta her way to hold my hand, and I appreciate all that, but I know I'm just gonna have to give myself a lot more time to get over my Earl Jay. It was like somebody'd dropped a bomb on me when I got the word that night. He was always so careful; he got me to believe that nothing bad would ever happen to him when he went behind the scenes to dig things out—like he was immortal as a comic book superhero."

"I know just what you mean. Having a chief of police for

a father and a detective for a husband makes me worry all the time, though I try not to show it when I'm around them. It just comes with the territory."

Wendy knew at that point that the connection she had made with Mary Liz was a solid one, and that the woman would continue to confide in her. "I didd'n think straight for a while after it happened," Mary Liz added. "Would you believe I coudd'n even remember the simplest things? The passwords on my computer, an appointment I'd made for the salon to get my hair done, some phone calls I needed to return to friends—they just all went out of my head. I'm slowly beginning to get back to normal, though. I'm at least thankful for that."

"Don't rush things. Take your time," Wendy said.

Mary Liz nodded enthusiastically at first, then became more reflective. "I know that only too well. I got my degree in clinical social work at Alcorn and practiced for a while right here in Rosalie before I met Earl Jay. I saw it in all my patients when they'd lost loved ones to whatever it was. That kind of healing is a slow process for everyone, no matter what."

Merleece returned from the kitchen with the glasses of clear wine on a silver serving tray, offered one each to her guests, and then settled again into her rocking chair with hers. "Y'all been havin' a nice talk, I hope?"

"We certainly have," Mary Liz said, sipping her wine afterward.

"We were just comparing notes on what it's like to have family involved with law enforcement," Wendy added. "You're never sure what's going to happen from day to day. Deep down, you're always wishing they had another kind of job. But you know you can't say that to them because they love what they're doing, so that just isn't possible."

There was a sudden, awkward lull, and Wendy wondered whether it was time for a change of subject. Merleece, however, seemed to have come to the same conclusion and said, "Miz Crystal, she never will tell me much 'bout all those bridge games out at the country club, Strawberry. Is that 'cause of her playin'? She still drivin' all a' y'all crazy?"

"More or less," Wendy said. "She understands the basics of the game well enough, but she refuses to admit when she makes a mistake, like not following suit or trumping a good trick or overbidding or just about anything else that most other players let go with good humor. The fact is that she remains as stubborn as a mule about it all. Her excuse-making monologues are quite annoying to the rest of us, although I'm sure she thinks they are fascinating. Just this last time we played, Deedah Hornesby, the RCC director, took me aside and said, 'I'm not sure it was worth it to accept Crystal's contribution to the country club and then have to put up with this during every bridge game.' She has a valid point, of course, but we're just gonna have to weather the storm and hope Miz Crystal eventually gets her fill of always making herself the center of attention."

Merleece glanced at the ceiling fan whirring above and laughed with conviction. "You got that right. I can just hear her right now carryin' on until the cows come home. You know I wouldd'n call her a good sport by a long shot. If she cain't win, she liable to walk away in a huff."

A strange expression came over Mary Liz's face as she began mouthing a couple of words.

"What's the matter, girlfriend?" Merleece said, watching intently.

Mary Liz continued mouthing for a few more seconds and then said, "I don't know exactly. I mentioned that I've had trouble remembering things because of my sweet Earl Jay's death. But for a second there, something important seemed to flash into my head. Then it went away just as fast. When that kinda thing happens, you know you can't rest until you pin it down."

"Maybe it'll come back to you after you've had some a' my good dinner," Merleece added. "I fixed errything you like, and I happen to know that they all Strawberry's favorites, too."

"You go outta your way to spoil me, Merleece," Wendy told her.

"I'm just aimin' to please, Strawberry."

Soon, the three of them were seated around the cozy kitchen table enjoying Merleece's good cooking, and for a while, everything seemed as carefree as a casual get-together among three friends.

"You know, it's my take that there's a reason they call it comfort food," Wendy said, eagerly spearing a few of her green beans. "You can almost feel it relaxing you once it goes down. Maybe you couldn't exactly prove it scientifically or anything like that, but I know it's always been good for what ails me."

"I know that's right. I always go to it when I cain't deal with the world," Merleece said.

Wendy gave her a knowing grin. "And by that, can you possibly be referring to Miz Crystal?"

"Lord, help me, yes."

"I take it from the both a' you that I could do without meeting this Miz Crystal person?" Mary Liz said in between bites of her chicken.

Merleece snickered. "You best believe it."

But by the time they started digging into their slices of warm applesauce pie, Mary Liz's mood had reverted to that peculiar moment when she had started mouthing words a while back.

"Whatever it was that was on the tip a' my tongue just tried to pop back into my head again," she told them, shaking

her head. "I mean, one a' those things I've been trying to remember very hard since . . . well, since after *it* happened. I
wish there was something I could do about it."

Wendy and Merleece exchanged worried glances, and
Wendy said, "That's the way it works, you know. The harder
you try to force it to the surface, the more it resists. Usually, it
comes to you in the middle of the night or when you're busy
doing something else entirely."

Mary Liz put down her fork and frowned at it as if it were
responsible for her confusion. "For some reason, I think it's
very important that I remember whatever it is. I can't shake
the notion that I made a mistake of some kind, and it has to do
with my beloved Earl Jay. I know that wherever he is, he
would want me to get it right, of course."

"Now you know very well where he is, girlfriend. He's an
angel in Heaven," Merleece said.

Mary Liz smiled graciously. "Yes, of course."

"I'm sure you're both right, but if I may, what did you
mean by mistake, Mary Liz?" Wendy added.

Mary Liz squinted as she focused even more. "I mean that
I think I remembered something wrong. That I was so upset
emotionally, I wasn't thinking straight, as I've already mentioned to y'all."

"Don't go crazy on me now," Merleece said. "You know
I'm here for you if you feel like you losin' it."

Mary Liz managed to crack a smile. "I wouldn't put you
through that. If I haven't gone crazy on you by now, it'll
never happen."

"Maybe so, but don't be so stubborn about this, girlfriend.
It'll come back when it's good 'n' ready to."

Suddenly, Mary Liz had her gasp of recognition. "Stubborn . . . stubborn." She repeated the word a third time.

Wendy chimed in, thoroughly intrigued. "Something
about the word, itself, or someone who was stubborn?"

"Well, it was you who just brought it up," Mary Liz said, pointing to Wendy. "I believe you said that someone was acting 'stubborn as a mule.' That made something click in my brain."

"Yes, I did say that, and that would have been our very own Miz Crystal Forrest at the bridge table. You have no idea just how stubborn and defensive she gets about making the same mistakes over and over. She's trying the patience of Deedah and Hollis Hornesby, just to name two of our Bridge Bunch, I can tell you that. I'd give anything to substitute any of the newbies I'm teaching for Crystal Forrest. They at least would go out of their way to follow the rules and not make a fuss all the time—assuming that I've taught them well so far."

The excitement in Mary Liz's voice grew. "Yes, you said this Miz Crystal was being stubborn about the way she played bridge. Or rather, the way she refused to own up to those same mistakes. That was what finally triggered it for me."

Wendy shot her a quizzical glance. "You'll have to forgive me, but I can't imagine what Miz Crystal would have to do with your husband, though. I highly doubt they ever met."

"I know, I know. I'm sure it seems like I'm not making much sense to you right now. But the deal is, this isn't about Miz Crystal Forrest the way you're probably thinking," Mary Liz continued. "I guess I'm still not making myself clear, but the fact is that you said she was being stubborn as a mule. So I'll repeat the word—*mule*. That's the key here that I'm trying to convey to you. I was in such terrible shock after the fact that I said I remembered Earl Jay's phone conversation as being about a donkey. But that was totally wrong. I'm positive now that I was misremembering it. It's very clear to me at this point that the word he kept repeating over the phone to somebody was actually *mule*."

"I thought a donkey and a mule was the same thing," Merleece said. "Is they really a difference?"

"I don't think that's the point here," Mary Liz said. "It's

not all that much about the animal. It's just that I gave the police the wrong word, and I believe they need to know that
now. Maybe it won't make a difference, but it could. I don't
know one way or the other. But it feels like a huge weight has
been lifted off my shoulders just remembering the right word.
I know y'all have had that happen to you. You'll tell your
husband about all this, won't you, Wendy? Otherwise, I'd
have to go down to the station, and I just feel more comfortable letting you handle it."

"You know I'll be more than happy to do just that. He
and Daddy are out of town today, but they'll be back soon."

Mary Liz continued to look and sound very stressed out.
"The thing is, I've had more than my share of the police station lately, and I'm sure you can understand that the memories are very unpleasant for me. I'm not sure how I ever got
through all that."

"I don't blame you for feeling that way. I understand
completely."

Over coffee in the living room after they had finished their
dessert, however, Wendy could not get Mary Liz's revelation
out of her mind. It distracted her so much that she had to fake
paying attention to the effortless conversation that flowed between Merleece and Mary Liz. A simple nod of the head there
and an easy smile here more than did the trick, and the two
old friends never knew the difference as they traveled down
memory lane together.

Was there anything of significance in changing a single
word? As Merleece had asked straightforwardly: Was there
any difference between a donkey and a mule? Could that possibly have a bearing on the progress of the two murder cases?
Was this the break they had all been hoping for? Or was it just
another of the seemingly endless red herrings these cases had
presented to everyone involved?

CHAPTER 18

Things had gotten completely out of hand emotionally for Merrie Boudreaux now. She had gone from being needlessly protective of Milton Bagdad to falling hopelessly in love with him. If he happened to be straight, she desperately wanted to bed him; if he turned out to be gay, she wanted somehow— the conventional wisdom on the subject be damned—to "turn him around" and expertly show him what it was like to plea- sure a woman. That option particularly appealed to her, even though there was a part of her that whispered she was in- dulging an unlikely fantasy.

As a result, she wasn't eating much these days, had taken to an extra martini before dinner in the evening, and imagined that it was Milton who was making love to her in bed instead of her own very vigorous husband, Rex, with whom she had never had the least little complaint in that department.

She believed he suspected nothing of her inner turmoil so far—at least she hoped that was the case. She kept up a placid front at all times, but each succeeding day was becoming more and more difficult for her to navigate. The fear kept growing within her that she was reaching some sort of breaking point, and that things would not end well as a result. Was there any conceivable way out of this torture?

"You should go to the doctor, the way you're losing weight. At our age that could be a danger signal," Rex was saying to her at his desk as he was putting the finishing touches on yet another of their elaborate children's parties. This one was to bring Peter Pan to the elaborate and expensive birthday celebration of a ten-year-old in the backyard gardens of one of Rosalie's most historic houses: Wayfield Place. Merrie was to disguise herself—and quite convincingly at that—as the "boy who never grew up." Rex, meanwhile, was to portray the villainous Captain Hook, complete with a plastic hook at the end of his hand, along with snarling dialogue that he had written to keep the youngsters wide-eyed and attentive.

"You make me sound like I'm as ancient as the hills. I'm only forty-three, you know. These days that's young. There's nothing wrong with me anyway," she told him, trying her best to disguise her annoyance. "You should just be happy I've dropped a few pounds. That Peter Pan costume was too small for me when I tried it on a while back, and now it'll fit just perfectly for the party."

Rex shot her his best skeptical glance and muttered something unintelligible under his breath.

"What?" she said as a reflex action.

"That may be true about the costume, but you still look tired to me. What's up with you?"

"Maybe I'm tired of all this costuming and makeup and playacting, and that's what's making me tired. Is that so hard to understand?"

"Oh, please. You're not lobbying for moving to another town somewhere again, are you?"

Merrie decided it was in her best interests to lie. Moving to another community might indeed be a way to escape her lovesick dilemma that some might find more laughable than anything else. "Now that you mention it, yes, I believe I am. This place makes me nervous."

Rex put down his colored pencil, temporarily abandoning the sketch he was making, and made a sweeping gesture. "Do you mean this building or our lovely house in a prestigious neighborhood that you just had to have, that we then restored to your very high standards, as I clearly recall?"

"No, I meant Rosalie in general. You may not think so, but it can get on your nerves after a while."

"I don't buy that you feel that way for a second. You've always said you loved it here—the history, the architecture, the people—even though they're hard to get to know with all their complicated genealogy and attitudes. There's something you're just not telling me. We've been married too long, and I know you too well. I want you to come clean with me, Merrie."

Adrenaline settled into the pit of her stomach, and she said, "There's nothing I need to come clean about. Let's just move on."

"And by that I'm assuming you don't mean to another subject, you mean to another town?"

"Yes."

"No way are we gonna do that," he said. "We've got things humming along here. If you wanna move on, you'll have to do it by yourself, and I doubt you could make it on your own. You think about that."

An image of the guileless Milton Bagdad in his adorable tuxedo occupied Merrie's every brain cell as she fumed inside. Her obsession was nearly palpable; it was affecting her sleep, not to mention her breathing every second she was awake. How had she let herself get into such a schoolgirl-like predicament? It had been a gradual process, to be sure, but she had done nothing to stop it. She had nurtured it every step of the way. As she kept reminding herself, she was old enough to be the young man's mother, for Pete's sake.

"Are you by any chance talking about a divorce?" she said, not bothering to disguise her significant spurt of anger. "I know you like throwing your weight around with people in general, but don't you think you oughta take your wife's needs and opinions into consideration?"

Rex frowned while studying her objectively, as if she were a piece of their costume inventory that was missing a button or had an ugly tear that was clearly visible and needed his considerable sewing and mending skills immediately. "No, I'm not talking about a divorce. What the hell is wrong with you? I'd like to know what needs of yours aren't being met at this point in our lives. It's certainly not a lack of money or a lack of sex or no home of your dreams to live in for the first time in your life. Like I said before, I think you need to make an appointment as soon as possible with Dr. Owens and see what's going on."

Merrie avoided eye contact and waved him off. If she could have gotten away with such a thing, she would have marched across the room and slapped him. "As a matter of fact, I already have an appointment for a checkup with my gynecologist, thank you very much, so stop fretting. I'll be perfectly fine."

"You better keep it, too. I've never seen you like this before," he said, picking up his pencil again. "I don't know—do you think that it could possibly be menopause you're going through?"

Merrie struggled for control at his suggestion but surprised herself by somehow managing to conjure up a halfway-calm reply. "No, I absolutely don't think that I'm going through menopause. Men always seem to think their wives are going through menopause every time they get into a serious argument about something if they're anywhere beyond forty. The wives, I mean. Give me a break. In fact, give us all a break."

Rex quickly held up his right hand—signaling a truce—managed a perfunctory smile, and said nothing further.

That hardly settled things for Merrie, however. She considered her bottom line: Was she willing to risk her marriage of twenty years and her place in their lucrative Party Palooza by hitting on a young man who was half her age? And if so, when and where would that even be possible to pull off? She knew she was at a very dangerous crossroads in her life—one she had never experienced before—and she did not know what she was going to do next.

Wendy had no sooner returned from her dinner at Merleece's than Ross texted her:

Meeting ran way late; eating here in Jackson on the Reservoir; home by ten; see you soon, babe

Full of energy from Merleece's good food and having the run of the house until Ross arrived, Wendy decided to sit down at her laptop and Google all the definitions of mule. Mary Liz had more than ignited that puzzle-solving spark she was convinced she was born with—inheriting it from her father—and something told her she was in for a relentless session as well.

Moments later, she was printing out the following definitions:

a hybrid between a male donkey and a female horse (mare)
a self-sterile plant whether hybrid or not
a stubborn person

She dismissed the first two as irrelevant and focused on the last, immediately reviewing all the stubborn people who could possibly be involved in the murders of Aurelia Spangler and Earl Jay Doxey. It did not take her long to realize that everyone fit that third definition to some extent.

Both Sarah Ann and Dora O'Rourke were a stubborn and disparate pair, even if they had recently called a truce, and Wendy took the time to congratulate herself mentally for being directly responsible for that. As a result, they were taking a back seat on her list of suspects, but her investigative experiences of late had taught her nothing if not to take no one's innocence for granted.

Vance Quimby had remained in Rosalie and stubbornly nagged the CID about solving his sister's death and had even revealed the existence of a life insurance policy that seemed to give him a plausible motive for being the person who had done away with her. Was that still highly unlikely, or was he merely being too clever by half?

Charlotte Ruth kept turning up with this or that incredulous confession, stubbornly directing a follow spot upon herself, even though her stories fell apart quickly under pressure. But was she secretly the sort of person who needed not only to be in the eye of the hurricane but to steer it to where it could do the most damage in the first place? It would take a certain type of pathology to do something like that. Did she possibly fit the profile?

Then Wendy considered what Ross had told her about Professor Isaacson. What a surprise he had turned out to be to everyone. An erudite academic with a passion for great literature who was both eye candy for his female students and a stubborn patron of the oldest profession in the world. The dichotomy seemed to be entirely irrational, yet there it was for the taking. And no matter what the rationale, murder was always the ultimate moral transgression at its black-hearted core.

Finally, Wendy lighted on Milton Bagdad. Of all of those under scrutiny, he was the one person who intrigued her the most. She needed to think that through some more. Why could she not shake the idea that everything always seemed to lead back to him? After all, he was the one who had panicked at Aurelia Spangler's vision so viscerally that he had skipped town with neither a short-range nor long-range plan, and according to him, Aurelia had apparently shared his horror at what had popped into her head on that life-altering evening. Yes, the lad had majored in theater arts, so there was no denying that he leaned toward the dramatic approach to nearly everything in his life. It was likely buried within his DNA somewhere.

On the other hand, Milton was the most obvious example of someone "running scared" and gave the impression of being out of control at times and easily swayed to do anything. Despite all of that, he was a highly valued employee of Party Palooza, and Merrie and Rex Boudreaux had gone out of their way to win him back. At first, he had stubbornly resisted their pitches, but then had finally given in and returned to his duties delivering singing telegrams, among other things.

What was it about those telegrams that would just not leave her alone? Wendy clearly remembered all the high praise heaped upon them by Sarah Ann O'Rourke and even Merrie Boudreaux, herself. They were unquestionably charming presentations and ultimately worth the price of admission, and Wendy even recalled Milton saying at her wedding reception that a few people here and there had paid for at least a second helping. She could see how that might happen. Milton was one of those breathtakingly handsome blond males who in California might be mistaken for a surfer or a beachcomber or something else along those lines. But in rural Mississippi, he was merely a dazzling, fit specimen of young manhood—and with a beautiful voice to boot.

What happened next in Wendy's brain was the reason she was born to be the sleuth she had become. The word *rural* practically stood up and saluted her. The imagery was pressing. This was not a learned process of hers, it merely existed. And she paid attention to it immediately.

What was the opposite of *rural*?

Urban, of course.

Why had she even played semantic opposites inside her head? Who knew? Some people were athletes, others were musicians. There was room for everything and everyone in the universe she revered. While others dug in stubbornly to the mundane, she preferred going in search of the incredulous. The rest followed quickly as her brain cells lit up: *urban, urban dictionary, definition of* mule *on Urban Dictionary*.

She was already familiar with that particular definition from watching forensic crime shows on television. Her fingers could not move fast enough for her on the keyboard. But suddenly, there it was, greeting her like an old friend who had been hiding out in cyberspace, just waiting to be found:

> mule: a carrier of things for someone else—often used to refer to a carrier of illegal drugs.

Was that what Earl Jay Doxey had been referring to in his conversation with a person unknown? Perhaps even his killer or someone who knew his killer? That type of mule instead of the more conventional stubborn type—human or animal?

Wendy's brain backed up, and she could almost hear it coming to a screeching halt. Conjecture was burning brightly inside of her. Was it really possible that Aurelia Spangler had been a drug mule for someone? Had something gone wrong, and was that why she was dead now?

She was so excited that she had to text Ross:

Hurry home, I have a new theory of everything

Ross's reply was nearly immediate:

Still at dinner with Bax, you sound almost metaphysical— LOL—the theory of everything—yuk, yuk, you think it's funny, but I'm onto something, see you soon, XOXO

Wendy focused again on her computer, surfing around until she had discovered an article titled, "Drug Mules Gone Wrong." She excitedly printed it out and devoured the paragraphs, smiling triumphantly as if she had discovered the raison d'être for the entire known universe. When Ross returned from Jackson, would she have everything tied up neatly with a ribbon for him? Could it truly be this easy?

The essence of the article was that people sometimes body-packed themselves to smuggle drugs in and out of places, taping them securely to every appendage and their trunks as well; at other times, they swallowed the drugs in many small balloons or condoms, waiting for them to pass out of their systems—hopefully without incident—and then selling them on the streets and elsewhere for an exorbitant profit. Despite Vance Quimby's protestations that his sister had not relapsed from her youthful dalliance with cocaine, had she actually done so and gotten in over her head with fatal consequences?

The case was turning into nothing short of a maze of unexpected twists and turns that kept reinventing itself as time passed.

Wendy struggled to remember the details of Aurelia's autopsy that either her father or Ross had shared with her—she couldn't remember which. She did recall that the nasal passages and snorting were the focus of the cocaine overdose diagnosis. That seemed to fit the recreational use of the drug, but not necessarily the activities of a drug mule. Still, Wendy was left with the lingering impression that there was something that had gone drastically wrong. They had all thrown out the possibility of a suicide long ago.

Then she started watching the clock excitedly. Ross could not get home soon enough.

Over their Amaretto nightcaps at the kitchen table, Wendy and Ross were considering the implications of the drug mule theory; even if Ross was in the midst of scotching it at the moment, perhaps because he was dragging a tad bit from the trip up and back from the meeting—all in the same day. In fact, Bax had turned down an invitation to join them when he had dropped Ross off.

"Thanks, daughter a' mine, but I'm bone-tired," he had said, giving Wendy a quick peck at the front door and then heading off for a good night's rest in his bungalow on Lower Kingston Road.

"But there was no mention of Aurelia's gastrointestinal tract in the autopsy," Ross was saying with some conviction. "The ME's office is quite thorough in cases like this. I mean, I could double-check at the station tomorrow, but I know I'm remembering that right."

Wendy stood her ground, emphatically tapping her finger on the table, although she knew Ross had had a long day. He simply had to grasp and truly appreciate the research she had done to arrive at her latest theory.

"But there are other ways she could have been involved in drug trafficking, and her brother just may not have known anything about it. We already know the two of them were masters of illusion and deceit. They were expertly prepared to dupe as many Rosalieans as they could convince to walk through the front door of Overview into that dark, gloomy Victorian atmosphere. If it hadn't been for that big bay window letting a bit of light shine through, the parlor would have felt like somebody's basement. Anyway, I think their plans would have worked quite well in an old, moneyed town like Rosalie. Most people we know already worship their ancestors here. It's practically a requirement. Why wouldn't they pay handsomely for the opportunity to say hello to them and ask them how they're doing every now and then in Aurelia's parlor? They'd get used to dropping in to Overview to get their fix."

Ross's half shrug was clearly one of agreement more than disinterest, but he said nothing.

"Not to mention the other angle of that whole thing I brought up about hiding in plain sight," Wendy continued. "Vance Quimby has helpfully volunteered everything the CID could have ever wanted to know from the very beginning—the whole psychic scam, the life insurance policy. By pushing it all to the front burner the way he did, he could have been playing all of us by withholding nothing. Maybe it defies logic, but I'm sure it's been done before with very successful results."

Ross let a sip of his liqueur work its magic in silence for a short while, but could not disguise the body language from his drooping shoulders and half-lidded eyes that indicated he was past ready to fall into bed. "We could bring him in again, of course. That's easy enough to do. We could tell him there's a new development and throw the drug mule thing at him and see what his reaction is. Suspects have been known to fall apart completely when confronted with the truth. *If* what you're proposing ends up being the truth."

"I think you and Daddy should do that as soon as possible and not try to second-guess this."

"I still don't see Vance offing his sister no matter what was going on, though," Ross added. "If she was up to something as dangerous as drug trafficking, then I think the more likely scenario is that he just didn't know about it because she didn't want him to know. She could have been on her own and ended up paying the ultimate price by going solo."

"Even as close as he says they were?"

Ross tilted his head, first one way, then the other. He looked for all the world like the scales of justice trying to locate the sweet zone of balance. "But we only have his word that they were *that* close. We've confirmed that they were brother and sister, so that much we don't have to doubt. But we mainly have his version of why they came down to Rosalie and what they intended to do in the first place. Sure, Aurelia had leased Overview, and it does make sense that she needed a setting like that to wave her wand, so to speak. But we were never able to hear from Aurelia on anything substantive. She's no longer here to defend or explain herself to us. Perhaps, you could shed some light on that for me."

Wendy stared at her liqueur glass, somewhat deflated. "Well, she did mention a few things to me while we were together lining up those free cold readings. What a bad idea that was in retrospect. But looking back on it now, I realize it was mostly small talk that she fed me just to build herself up in my eyes. It did seem like she was playing a part."

"There you go," Ross said, pointing at her. "She just wanted to gain your confidence. That's why they call it a con game."

"So, let me get this straight. You don't think the drug mule thing has any investigative value whatsoever?"

"No, I didn't say that. It may end up having everything to do with both cases, and I'm impressed with the way you pursued it. Relax, sweetie. You don't have to sell me on your abilities these days. You know I believe in you, and I didn't mean it to sound like I was challenging you."

She smiled at him, feeling redeemed. "Thanks. I have to tell you that I think we're getting closer to solving all this. I'm gonna sleep on it, and I suggest you do the same. And then Daddy will bring his unique perspective to it tomorrow when you tell him everything we've been tossing around."

"To a good night's sleep, then," Ross told her with a tired smile that quickly disappeared.

CHAPTER 19

Bax had slept in because of the exhausting day before, but when he finally arrived in his own good time at his office, Ross was waiting to bring him up to date quickly on Wendy's drug mule research and her new theory as a result. Bax listened patiently to it all and then pulled out Aurelia's autopsy report from the ME in Jackson, solemnly shaking his head.

"The woman just doesn't seem to fit the profile," he said. "She snorted herself to death, and that's that. I can't see her as both a phony psychic and a drug dealer. That's probably been done before somewhere on the face a' this planet, but I got the feeling it's not a staple among the scams that are out there."

"But your daughter doesn't think she was a dealer as much as she thinks Aurelia was a mule, carrying for somebody else," Ross said, suddenly feeling the urge to defend his wife. "And then she thinks that something went drastically wrong, and as a result, Aurelia paid with her life."

"I understand where you're coming from, but I still can't quite see it. But if it makes you and that daughter a' mine feel any better, we'll have Vance Quimby come in, and we'll run it past him for his reaction."

Ross sounded almost sheepish now. "Well . . . that's . . . what I told Wendy we would do."

Bax chuckled at some length, breaking the tension. "You married quite a woman, you know. She's always trying to figure out something with that brain a' hers, and I have to admit her track record is pretty good so far. So you go ahead and get Quimby in here, and we'll see what he has to say about all this."

"Thanks, Bax. She'd be after me big-time if I didn't follow through."

"She'd be after her dear old dad, too. She's like her mother in that respect. Both of 'em never let up until they got things done their way."

Bax then sat in his comfortable chair behind his desk and gestured to Ross. "Have a seat, son. There's something else I need to talk to you about."

Ross followed through quickly with an expectant expression. "What's up?"

Bax seemed ill at ease at first, not making direct eye contact, but he finally cleared his throat and caught his son-in-law's gaze. "I wanted you to be the first to know and get your reaction on this. Then, based on that, I guess, I'll go ahead and tell Wendy about it."

Ross perked up, leaning forward. "Let me take a wild guess. Can this possibly be about Miz Lyndell Slover?"

"Good wild guess," Bax said, conjuring up a wide grin. "Or maybe I'm an open book. But I never thought I'd feel about another woman the way I feel about her right now. Not after the wonderful life I had with my Valerie. But . . . it's happened to me big-time, son. I've fallen for Lyndell, and maybe I even want to take the next step with her."

"You mean marriage?"

"Yep. Do you think I'm crazy as a loon to consider taking that sorta plunge at my age?"

Ross stopped just short of rolling his eyes. "Whaddaya mean, *your* age? You're what—fifty-eight?"

"Fifty-nine."

"Big difference. So you're pushing sixty. They say sixty is the new fifty, fifty is the new forty, and on down 'til you get to puberty."

"Ah, puberty. That pretty much stays the same: acne, hormones, rebellion, and impatience. But do you believe the rest of that sequence? Now that you brought it all up, I gotta admit I don't think of myself as old. I work out at the gym, and I know I'm fit. So what I really need is just a tad bit of encouragement from someone I trust like you."

Ross leaned in as close as he could get from across the desk. "Well, then you got it. And I also believe that when I get to be your age, I wanna be as lean and healthy as you are. So I'll make this easy for you—if you love this woman like you say you do, go ahead and pop the question. You have nothing to lose but happiness for the rest of your life."

Bax settled back with a satisfied expression on his face. "I kinda thought that's what you'd say. Thanks."

"My take is that happily married men don't hesitate to recommend it to others, and your daughter has made me crazy happy from day one. And I think she'd be crazy happy for you, too. After all, she was the one who brought you two together with that little dinner party of hers."

Bax's tone grew somber. "She did do that, but I wanted to discuss Lyndell with you first. She'll never replace Valerie in my heart exactly, and I don't want Wendy to think I'm even trying to do that if Lyndell and I get married."

Ross's smile was warm and genuine. "Give your daughter credit. I live with her, and I know what a beautiful person she really is. I can't see her thinking that for a second. My personal opinion is that you're nearly home free. All you need now is a yes from Lyndell."

"Thanks for the listen," Bax said, giving his son-in-law a wink. "If you would, let me be the one to tell Wendy about my plans. Maybe I'll invite her to lunch at The Toast of Rosalie for some shrimp and grits or something like that. Maybe even today if her schedule at the paper'll allow it."

"Go for it. No better time and place for it than that, and I know it'll go well."

Wendy was amused at what clearly was a sigh of relief from her father. He was seated to her right at their The Toast of Rosalie table near the front window and reached out to grasp her hand warmly.

"The hard part is over," she continued. "Did you really think I wouldn't jump for joy that you and Lyndell feel that way about each other? Or that I didn't already know it without a doubt? I don't just investigate and solve. I observe carefully, thank you very much."

He gently withdrew his hand. "It was the marriage part I was worried about. Granted, I haven't asked her yet, and she hasn't said yes yet. But I would never take your feelings for granted in a situation like this."

Wendy took a sip of her lemon water and maintained her smile through the sour taste. "I know that. You and I went through losing the most wonderful woman in the world together, and we came out the other end of that ready to go on living. I've found Ross, and now you've found Lyndell. You already know I think she's the boss from Heaven above. I'd say we've both moved on in the right way. Have you told Ross about this, by the way?"

"Just this morning. He's on board, too."

Wendy sat back and scanned the chatting luncheon crowd surrounding them. They all appeared to be immersed in their conversations but happy—the perfect audience. "I feel like shouting out the good news to all these people right now in the middle of their salads and cocktails."

"Your plain ole approval will be more than enough," he told her, and they both enjoyed a quiet chuckle. He checked his watch and raised his eyebrows. "The service is a bit slow today, but they are pretty crowded. I've been hankering for those shrimp and grits all morning."

"I know," she added, after which she made a sweeping gesture. "You see people all around you digging into them, and your stomach practically goes into a major meltdown." Then she leaned toward her father. "If you don't mind my asking, Daddy, when did you realize you were so much in love with Lyndell that you wanted to marry her?"

Bax put a pat of butter on a slice of French bread and chewed thoughtfully for a short while. "Strangely enough— or even appropriately enough, whichever way you want to look at it—I'd have to say it was at your wedding, and then later at the reception inside that tent. It was that gardenia she'd put behind her ear. Something changed the moment I laid eyes on it. I'm not sure I can explain it."

"Did she give you a private Billie Holiday concert or something even better later on?"

Bax shot his daughter a wicked glance. "Or something even better later on." Then he shifted his weight and twitched his mouth. "There was something else some people might consider slightly crazy that I was considering doing, but . . ."

Wendy picked up on the hesitancy immediately. "But what?"

"Maybe it's not such a good idea?"

She drew back and narrowed her eyes. "This I have to hear. Second-guessing yourself before you even get the words out? That's not like you at all. Where's my take-charge Chief of Police daddy I've known all these years?"

"I'm right here. Maybe just a bit out of touch with what's appropriate in the world of romance these days. You see, I was considering sending Lyndell one a' those singing telegrams. Whaddaya think?"

Slightly confused, Wendy said, "You don't mean you're going to ask her to marry you by proxy, do you?"

"No, don't be ridiculous. I was thinking I'd ask her first in private and then if she says yes, I'd surprise her at some odd hour at the paper with that young man singing to her. Maybe you could even help me write the lyrics?"

Wendy's jaw dropped. "I have to admit, that is a surprise. I wonder if I'm even up to it."

"It shouldn't be that much more difficult than writing a Valentine poem, the way I figure."

The waiter arrived with the plates of shrimp and grits they had both ordered, temporarily shelving their conversation. Priorities were priorities. They each just had to blow on a forkful of the restaurant's specialty and get that first spicy, memorable taste out of the way: one full of the sweetness of bell pepper and translucent onions, the creaminess of cheese grits, and the delicate texture of briny, grilled shrimp. It took several satisfied bites before their conversation returned in earnest.

"So, whaddaya think? Could you come up with some lyrics for me if I buy Lyndell a singing telegram?"

Wendy did not want to disappoint her father, but she also didn't want to put herself in the position of creating something that backfired on them both because it turned out to be too cheesy. "I think they have some lyrics and poems that are already written. Maybe one of them will get the job done."

"You don't wanna try for an original?"

"Well . . . only if you can't find anything else you like, okay? Tell you what, why don't I drop by there on the way back to the paper and pick up some of their old standbys. You can take it from there. Believe me, they know what they're doing, and I'm betting you'll like something of theirs."

"Sounds like a plan," Bax said, anticipating the rest of his shrimp and grits by rubbing his hands together and then digging in. His heart and his stomach were in heaven, along with those of his daughter.

"To what do we owe the honor?" Merrie Boudreaux said from behind the counter just as Wendy walked through the front door of Party Palooza. "Another party in the works? Or maybe a singing telegram?"

"No party just yet," Wendy said, shaking Merrie's hand warmly. "But perhaps a singing telegram. I'm doing a bit of research for my daddy. He's thinking of sending one to his lady friend, Lyndell Slover. In fact, they could be getting married, so I may have misspoken. They could be in the market for a reception like mine, sooner rather than later."

"You know we can pull it off."

"I certainly do," Wendy said. "I still dream about how much fun my reception was—it was fit for a queen." Wendy picked up one of the tuxedoed rag dolls with their smiling faces lined up all in a row atop the counter. "And these are just so adorable. I'm sure Lyndell would love to have one."

"All of our customers do, you know. We have a few who have more than one, they're so thrilled."

"Well, what I need to look at right now are some of your standard telegram messages to take home to Daddy so he can make a decision."

Merrie reached over and tapped a laminated stack of messages to the right of the dolls. "Just browse through these, sweetie. We have all the holidays, national and religious— even the obscure ones—and all occasions for both genders, everything you could possibly want to send. Rex wrote some, his Aunt Mathilde wrote others, I wrote a couple, and even

our Milton Bagdad contributed. He's such a talented boy."
The enthusiasm level in Merrie's voice rose considerably for
the last couple of comments.

Wendy began sifting through the stack, mouthing words,
smiling and nodding along the way. She was clearly being en-
tertained. Finally, she lifted one out. "This one titled 'What
You Mean to Me' seems especially appropriate. It would
apply to just about anyone who's in love, I think."

"Yes, that one's particularly popular—as you say, sort of
an all-purpose sentiment for anyone who has a crush or anything more serious than that."

"Just give me a moment," Wendy said, taking the time to
hear Milton singing each line in his rich, baritone-tenor in her
head—and picturing him on bended knee, no less.

> *I'm telling you right now just what you mean to me,*
> *There's no one else on earth I'd rather love,*
> *I'd move the highest mountains, swim the deep-blue sea,*
> *To bring you down from Heaven up above.*
> *For when it comes to beauty, no one can compare,*
> *My lifelong search is coming to an end,*
> *To lose you for an instant I could never bear,*
> *On you my happiness will now depend.*
> *So let me take this moment to sing out with praise,*
> *I hope this tune will fill your heart with glee,*
> *I want no greater treasure than your lovely gaze,*
> *And now you know just what you mean to me.*

Wendy came out of her musical reverie and said, "I think
this is the one I'll recommend to Daddy."

"You can't go wrong, believe me."

"Can you make me a copy?"

"Of course. I'll just run back to the copier in the other
room. It'll only take me a second."

While Merrie was gone, Wendy browsed the colorful party posters on easels scattered around the lobby. Here was one for a pirate theme with Rex in costume, complete with eye patch, hat, earring, and a dialogue bubble that read in all caps: *ARRGGH, YE LANDLUBBERS!*

Over there was another for a Peter Pan theme, with Merrie doing the honors as the impish young immortal. Both husband and wife were unquestionably imaginative and talented when it came to delighting the little ones throughout the mileposts of their lives. No wonder they had been so successful ever since coming to Rosalie.

"Here you go," Merrie said, returning to the front with a gracious smile and handing over a copy of the lyrics.

Wendy thanked her, folded the copy once, and dropped it into her purse. "I'm sure Daddy will be getting back to you soon. By the way, who is that sweet lady smiling in that picture behind the counter? She looks like somebody's dear, devoted grandmother. Is she yours or Rex's?"

Merrie did a half turn and then gestured with her hand. "Oh, that's Rex's aunt Mathilde who lives down in New Orleans, where all this first started up. She's actually the one who invented this singing telegram business to go along with her party-planning talents. Rex and I are her first official Party Palooza franchise, so to speak, and I don't have to tell you how well it's worked out for us."

"Yes, it looks like she made a great decision," Wendy said. "And speaking of Rex, where is that handsome husband of yours today?"

Merrie pointed west, in the general direction of the Mississippi River. "Down on Water Street. One of the Viking Cruise Line ships is docking today, and Rex negotiated a gig with them, all dressed up as a riverboat gambler. He greets the passengers and tips his hat as they leave the ship and get on the shuttle up the hill to downtown. Maybe it's a little on the corny side—some of the things we do are, I'll admit—but the cruise line seemed to go for it, and the actor in Rex has a field day."

Wendy snapped her fingers. "I completely forgot about them coming in today. Maybe there's still time for me to go down to Bluff Park and watch them disembark. I always love doing that, especially when the paddle wheelers dock and their calliopes start playing. It's like an invitation to the whole town to come to the river where it all started and do a bit of gawking and daydreaming."

Merrie took her smartphone out of her pocket and glanced at the time. "They should be docking just about now if you wanna run down to Bluff Park and see them. I'd join you, but somebody has to stay here and mind the store, you know. But before you go, would you like to take one of the souvenir rag dolls with you? You're such a good customer, and you're here drumming up more business for us, so why don't you help yourself? Think of it this way—when you and Ross have your first child, you'll be one toy ahead of the game."

Wendy smiled at first, then cocked her head. "That's such a sweet thought. Are you sure? I know you don't do this for just anyone who walks in off the street."

"No, we don't, but you're not just anyone," Merrie said, taking one of the dolls off the counter and offering it up. "As we say in South Louisiana, just consider this your lagniappe."

Wendy took it with a grateful smile and glanced down before opening her purse and fitting it in—just barely. Its head and arms were still stubbornly hanging out. "Thanks. I love that cute little smiling face. I can see why they've become such a hit with everyone. Anyway, thanks for all the help. I think I can just make it to the river in time," she said, waving and then dashing out the front door.

Wendy stood in the middle of the favorite of all the

tourists on foot—the Bridge of Sighs, which straddled Roth Hill Road in Bluff Park, some two hundred feet above the Water Street dock below. There were a few other people to her right and left, breathing it all in. When any of the scores of tourist ships docked on either Silver Street or Water Street, it was still a big deal to Rosalieans, even after hundreds of years of the city being a wide-open river port that welcomed all comers.

From Wendy's distant vantage point, the sleek Viking Cruise ship fit between her thumb and forefinger held some six inches apart. The passengers walking down the ramp to spend the day touring mansions and town houses, sampling the cuisine, and buying souvenirs appeared even smaller—not like ants exactly, but not a great deal bigger. Amazing how such an enormous vessel and its human cargo could be reduced to such diminutive status. It was all essentially a matter of perspective, of course, and Wendy was playing that particular game with gusto.

She could also make out Rex in his costume, shaking hands and no doubt spouting period dialogue he had created himself to bring the part of riverboat gambler to life for those from Michigan, Connecticut, and other parts of the country not remotely connected to or familiar with the Deep South. Or at least a particular, romanticized version of it that had stood the test of time. Playing such a role, he perfectly symbolized what Rosalie had become since the preservation movement had begun in the '30s, saving many unique architectural and historical treasures that would have gone the way of the wrecking ball otherwise. It was also Wendy's perception that nothing was being built to last these days as they were in the eighteenth and nineteenth centuries. Would all these franchised businesses even be around in fifty years or so? She highly doubted it, and that caused her to wince.

Wendy headed back in her car to the paper when she'd

gotten her fill of what the river and its brawny current had brought to town today. Her mind started racing, and at first she thought it was because of the news her father had given her about proposing to Lyndell. After all, she had the telegram lyrics she thought he'd like best practically burning a hole in her purse. But the closer she got to work, the more unsettled she became. Something else was tantalizing her, and she finally realized that it was not about Bax and Lyndell; it had something to do with the murders that had taken place.

By the time she had settled into her cubicle and clicked on the saved draft of the article she was writing about possible embezzlement at one of the local banks, her mind was anywhere but on her work. She decided that she was a victim of a double whammy; part of her wanted to waltz into Lyndell's office and tell her what a romantic little interlude was likely coming her way shortly. But that part relented soon enough and mentally slapped her hand.

"Don't spoil things," she heard herself saying inside her head. "You can keep a secret with the best of them."

She could also hear her father fussing at her. "That was my moment, daughter a' mine. You had no business takin' it away from me."

The other part belonged to her relentless sleuthing instinct that simply would not leave her alone until she had figured out whatever was gnawing at her. She began to retrace her steps. When and where had it started on this particular day? She concentrated and pinpointed everything precisely. She had been standing in the middle of the breathtaking Bridge of Sighs not fifteen minutes ago, gazing down at the Water Street dock and observing what a difference perspective made. What a difference distance made. How size was relative, depending upon both distance and perspective. Somehow, she needed to integrate all that and apply it to what was truly motivating her these days—the murders of Aurelia Spangler and Earl Jay Doxey.

She could hardly stand it because she couldn't break through to connecting all of those things in the various lobes of her brain—at least for now. But she knew it was only a matter of time before she added it all up. Based on cases she had solved before, such as The Grand Slam Murders and the death of the obnoxious Brent Ogle at the Rosalie Country Club over the past couple of years, she recognized the signs. There was a geyser of resolution building up steam inside her and rising toward the surface, where her brain cells resided. It had started slowly enough, but now it was well on its way, and there was no stopping its eventual explosion into her aha! moment.

CHAPTER 20

Vance Quimby was nonplussed at Ross's surprising and complicated scenario. This was the last straw. "I'm telling you, my sister would never have been engaged in drug trafficking. If I'm not sure of anything else in this insane world, I'm sure of *that*. You're just wasting your breath suggesting such a thing. In fact, I'm downright insulted that you'd even go there."

Then he quickly scanned the interrogation room and ended up craning his neck at the camera high up in the corner, recording their conversation. "You can keep me here with that thing running twenty-four hours if you want, Detective, but I won't change my mind. This mule theory of yours that you keep talking about has to be a figment of your imagination, at least as far as my Relly is concerned. It seems to me you're more interested in blaming my poor sister, the victim, instead of trying to track down the monster who killed her."

Ross rested both of his hands on the table and cleared his throat with great authority. "I assure you, sir, that we don't operate that way here in Rosalie. We've pulled in every favor owed to us to try and find out who's responsible for this. But no one's talking—either that, or no one actually knows what's going on or what went on. It's like some mysterious force has put the kibosh on anything resembling a clue in this town. So that's why we have to follow every lead with everyone, no matter how unlikely it seems to be."

Vance offered up a sneer and raised his voice. "It's all well and good for you to sit there and say that to me as calm as you please, but it doesn't get us much closer to justice for my sister and me."

"We understand your frustration."

"Well, understand this, then," Vance continued, his anger level rising even further. "Stop calling me in here with these unproven, frivolous accusations, or I'll take you to court for police harassment. I've done everything humanly possible to cooperate with you since my poor sister's death, but I don't want to hear from you people again unless you have a confession from the murderer."

"You've made yourself perfectly clear," Ross told him. "We won't keep you any longer. And please know this much— the next time you do hear from us, we *will* have the case solved."

Vance rose from the table and gave Ross one last icy stare. "Believe me, I'll hold you to that."

Wendy had just slid into the front seat of her car after delivering the "What You Mean to Me" lyrics to her father at the police station. At least that particular issue had been put to bed satisfactorily.

"You thought right," Bax had said to his daughter after reading the poem and beaming at her. "This is the one I'd have chosen, too."

At that point, he had told her that he would be dropping by Party Palooza to order the telegram as soon as Lyndell accepted his offer of marriage.

"And when will you be proposing, Daddy?" she asked.

"Tonight at the bungalow," he told her. "It'll be just the

three of us—myself, Lyndell, and the engagement ring. I'd let you take a sneak peek, but I left it at home. Anyway, I trust you'll be seeing it soon enough when Lyndell shows it to you on her finger at work tomorrow."

"And I'm sure you've got this, Daddy," she had said, and then given him a kiss for luck.

Now it was back to her cubicle to put the finishing touches on the bank embezzlement piece that was due for tomorrow's edition. She had to buckle down hard to meet the deadline and stop allowing conjecture about the murders to distract her so easily. For once, she followed through, and shortly before five, walked into Lyndell's office and handed over what she considered to be her latest masterpiece.

After scanning it quickly, Lyndell looked up from her desk and nodded at Wendy seated on the other side. "Good work. Especially the nepotism angle. That was just begging to be explored."

"Putting pressure on family members did the trick," Wendy added. "It all came out quickly after that. Saving face is a powerful motivation."

But something about the peculiar smile on Wendy's face was getting the better of Lyndell's curiosity. "All of a sudden, I'm getting the impression you're holding something back."

"Not about my research, no."

"Something else, then?"

But foremost in Wendy's mind was her father's request that his upcoming proposal of marriage be his moment and his alone. "No, there's nothing. I'm just pleased with myself, that's all."

"As you should be. I don't think I could have a better investigative reporter on staff if I had conducted a national search." A second or two later, Lyndell gave out with a little gasp. "Why don't we celebrate your latest piece? Bax and I are having dinner together at the bungalow tonight. Why don't you and Ross join us? Of course, I guess I better check with your father first."

Thinking on her feet, Wendy came up with the perfect reply. "I'm sure we'd love to . . . but I've had something in the Crock-Pot all day. It's Ross's favorite—pot roast with new potatoes, onions, and carrots. I know some people rave about leftovers, but I don't think my pot roast is as good warmed up the next day."

"Sounds wonderful either day to me. Maybe Bax and I should come over to your place."

"Nah," Wendy said, waving her off. "Let's just do the private couples thing tonight, shall we?"

"You just talked me into it," Lyndell said, winking. "And again, very nice work on the article."

Wendy looked up from her plate of pot roast, carrots, and potatoes and glanced at the owl clock on her kitchen wall with a smile. "Right about now, Daddy should be proposing to Lyndell."

"He was so full of himself today down at the station," Ross said after a sip of his glass of merlot. "I thought he was gonna explode, he was so excited." There was a pause, and Ross's expression grew thoughtful. "I was thinking all day that your daddy expected that the only outcome was that she would say yes to him. You don't suppose there's any possibility that she'd turn him down, do you? For some reason, that thought just flashed into my head. Have we all gone psychic since Aurelia Spangler came to town—and then went?"

Wendy did not answer immediately. After all, she had taken her time accepting Ross's proposal, even turning him down when he'd first asked. She'd put her career as an investigative journalist ahead of marriage for a while. Luckily for Ross, he had understood her objective and been patient.

"You know, Lyndell and I have never had one of those

girlfriend-type talks about Daddy. She's just mentioned now and then how much fun they're having going out and doing things together. I guess I've never considered the possibility that she might say no, either." Wendy shifted her eyes to the side. "Now you've got me worried. The thought had never entered my mind."

"Didn't mean to throw cold water on everything, babe," he said. "We'll prob'ly be getting a phone call soon from either Lyndell or your father announcing that it's *on* anyway."

"I hope so. We've all had enough drama in our lives lately." She decided to change the subject. "Did anything come of your interrogation of Vance Quimby today?"

"I wish. He threatened to get a lawyer if we continued to bring him in and run our theories past him, and he might even have a case for harassment at that. The CID has been spinning its wheels for a while. With Earl Jay Doxey gone, we have no informant to go to anymore. Nothing from our undercover guys, either. It's entirely possible that whoever did this has skipped town, been paid off, or both. I have such a bad feeling that both cases will go cold. I have to tell you—that's the worst feeling in the world for a police officer."

"I feel exactly the opposite," Wendy said, dashing his pessimism immediately. Then she trotted out the strange insights she'd stumbled upon that afternoon on the Bridge of Sighs. "You know how I am about puzzle solving. Suddenly, it will all come together for me by some process I'll never be able to explain fully. Let's just be thankful it's there for the taking."

Ross repeated some of the more intriguing words she'd just emphasized to him more than once. "*Perspective . . . distance . . . size.* I'm not quite getting it."

"I'm not, either. Yet. But I know it's on the way. Trust me."

"So, are you gonna wake me up in the middle of the night with the detailed solution? Is that what I'm in for?"

Wendy laughed. "Don't put it past me."

"I would never underestimate anyone who can make pot roast like this and also solve puzzling crimes," he said, spearing another bite with gusto. "I believe I've married the most talented woman in the world."

"And I've married the Prince of Patience."

Bax sat stunned on the living room sofa in his full-dress uniform. Finally, he managed a weak, "I . . . don't understand, sweetheart."

Lyndell did not let go of his hand, which she had been holding tightly all through his eloquent proposal and presentation of the ring. "You have to know by now that I love you, Bax. That hasn't changed."

He hardly seemed convinced and even turned away from her for a few seconds. "But something has changed for you to turn me down the way you did just now. It didn't feel like your heart was really in your refusal, if you want my opinion. Whatever the reason, I have to say that I really didn't see this coming."

She straightened her posture a bit but still held on to him as she spoke. "Nothing has changed between the two of us. But I haven't told you certain things about myself in the time we've spent together. There's a reason I've reached the age of forty-seven without getting married. I've had other chances to, you know. But it all goes back to my parents and their messy divorce when I was eleven years old. It seems like they were never happy and fought all the time when I was growing up. Finally, they stopped making life miserable for each other and split up. I lived with Mom from then on. She didn't seem to be any happier, though, and I felt cheated out of what all my friends had when I visited them for sleepovers—both parents there for them and getting along with each other."

"That must have been rough on you," Bax said, his voice as soft as he could make it.

"It was. So by the time I got to college, I decided I was going to concentrate on a career and not put myself at the kind of risk my mother experienced. It's not that I don't care a lot about you, Bax, because you know I do. It's just that— well, I'll go ahead and admit it. I'm afraid of the institution of marriage. I'm afraid it will ruin what we have. Of course, I realize I could be completely out of touch with reality here. So, go ahead and set me straight if you can."

There was a look of something resembling relief on his face. Then smugness replaced it quickly. "Well, I think I'm up to the challenge. The deal is that you're just not gonna go there. A piece of paper and a ceremony can ruin what we have? No, no, no. I understand what you're saying and why you have your concerns, but we don't have to be your parents. We *aren't* your parents. You can just go ahead and be brave and make your own decisions not because of what happened to them, but in spite of them. If you and I love each other, then that's all that matters. You should give yourself credit for your insights on your parents, but they shouldn't dictate what you do now with what really matters in your life."

Bax continued to feel the tightness of her grip. He decided that it was a good and hopeful sign, that it meant she was trying her best to hold on, and he was not about to let her go without a fight. "I'll go ahead and tell you that I've had my reservations to work through, too. More than a dozen years ago, I lost my Valerie, as you know, and I threw myself into my work, just as you did in yours for different reasons. That, and helping my Wendy heal, if I possibly could. Now I find myself with feelings I haven't had since Valerie and I were so happily married all those years. It's like I've been reborn, and you're looking at the brand-new version of me."

There was an element of surprise in Lyndell's voice. "I didn't know you could be such an inspirational speaker. That was . . . lovely. I feel like I should be volunteering for something noble like the Peace Corps."

He was positively beaming at her remark. "Good for me, and good for you. But the truth is, I make that kind of speech all the time down at the station. It comes with the territory when you're the chief of police and have to make assignments for all your officers and keep them motivated to catch the bad guys. For some strange reason, we never run out of those, unfortunately."

Lyndell's laugh was bright and prolonged with a satisfying release to it. "It's the power of suggestion, then. You almost make me want to become a police officer."

"And you make me want to become a newspaper editor with some of those editorials you write. But I'll settle for the two of us becoming husband and wife."

Now she was pressing up against him even harder. It was impossible for her to get any closer. "I suppose you know you're making it very difficult for me to turn you down right now," she said.

"That was the plan. I intend to win you over."

"Do you?"

"I do." He paused and stared her down with great affection. "And those are the words I intend to get out of you, Lyndell Slover. So, upon further review, what do you say now?"

She gave him a peck on the cheek, but he did not settle for that, kissing her on the lips convincingly.

"Well?" he added, finally allowing her to come up for air and pulling back slightly. "What's the verdict?"

They kissed again, even longer this time, and she said, "If I can catch my breath again, what I'm going to tell you is that I've decided to take your advice and be brave. I accept your proposal, and here's what you were after: *I do.*"

He shifted his weight slightly to wrap her up in his arms and face her. Then he drew back and worked the ring down her finger. "This diamond becomes you, and it's been waiting all this time to dazzle you," he told her, and they kissed yet another time. "Come on, let's take a breather and call Wendy and Ross with the good news. It's certainly worth sharing."

Wendy awoke the next morning a good fifteen minutes before the alarm was set to go off. The room was filled with the gray light of early morning, struggling to establish itself and banish the darkness for good. She felt it was entirely conducive to her thought process. There was nothing bright to distract her yet the way a shaft of the sun would, bouncing off a spot of metal here or glass there as it angled through one of the bedroom windows.

She allowed all the people involved in the current cases to appear before her, not in any particular order, but as a review of suspects. They tumbled forth, sometimes smiling, sometimes frowning—here seeming to be suspicious, there to be beyond reproach, according to the context. But always as a framework, a proscenium for those faces, was Aurelia's frightening vision. Now, with the elements of perspective, distance, and size applied, the meaning of the cold reading she had given to Milton became clear at last.

Wendy shivered and sat up against her pillow at her epiphany, taking care not to wake Ross, who was facing in the other direction, breathing rhythmically but quietly. It was all out in the open now, and she felt the accompanying adrenaline rush as a reward. The rush continued as she worked all the angles until they fit neatly. Here, at long last, was her aha! moment, incredibly dark and evil as it was, now fully realized. She knew the first thing she had to do was to text Milton and get that much out of the way. But she would not do it in bed next to her darling, sleeping husband.

Slowly, she pulled back the covers and slid over the side into her slippers, grabbing her smartphone on the nightstand

and taking it with her into the living room. Yes, it was very early, and she might be waking Milton up, but she had to ask him that one question. His answer would confirm that she was correct about everything, even if he didn't realize what she was talking about. In fact, it would be far better for him if he didn't.

Once settled on the living room sofa, she thumbed her message to him and then waited patiently. If he were sound asleep, he might not respond. On the other hand, he might be up and about, fixing his coffee, and able to tell her what she needed to know within a reasonable length of time.

Five interminable minutes passed. Things were so quiet that she could hear the owl clock in the nearby kitchen ticking away methodically. She used the time to iron things out further in her head, making sure she wasn't missing anything. Logistically, she was certain her father and Ross would approve of her plan and the roles they would play, even if it all shocked them. Or maybe they would give themselves face palms for not coming up with it themselves. No matter. This was not a competition—it would be a cooperative effort to bring these investigations to a close.

Then Wendy's phone pinged. Milton had finally texted back.

Yes, now that you mention it. Why? came his reply.

I'll tell you on the Bridge of Sighs. Meet me there around 9 a.m. instead of going in to work right away

But I'll be late if I do

I'll write a note to your teacher to excuse you—LOL

Milton closed the exchange by sending her back a smiley face followed by a couple of question marks.

Good. That much of her plan was done.

Although she would rather have let him get those few extra minutes of sleep, she knew she had to awaken Ross and tell him what she'd figured out at last and what she thought he should do. She brought him coffee and a powdered donut from the kitchen to get him alert and focused, and he listened in utter fascination as she trotted out and justified everything down to the last detail.

"That's incredible. I never even thought of that," he said. "I won't ask how you came up with all of it, but my gut tells me you've prob'ly nailed it. I think you've done it again."

"Pretty insidious scheme, I'd say." But she took a second to flash a smile his way as she pointed at him playfully. "You've got some powdered sugar on your upper lip."

"You know how to lighten things up, too," he said, running his finger across it and then licking up what he'd accumulated.

Next, she had to talk to her father and tell him the same things she'd told Ross; after that, she envisioned that the three of them and perhaps some backup from the station would go in action. The end result would be that they would successfully prevent the murders from going cold. She did not let herself think for one second that either of them would not go along with her, and it was with a feeling of great accomplishment that both of them enthusiastically congratulated her on the superb detective work she had done. It was making as much sense to them as it had to her.

"Let's meet up at the station at eight," Bax said, winding up his session with Wendy over the phone. "We'll review everything again and make sure we've covered all the bases."

If Wendy was right about everything—and both men indicated to her that they thought she was—it could all go down very fast.

CHAPTER 21

Wendy stood in the middle of the Bridge of Sighs once again, gazing out at the river from the railing. The Viking Cruise ship that had docked the day before on Water Street was now pulling out to head upstream against the strong brown current to its next stop—Vicksburg. Eventually, it would make its way all the way up to Memphis from New Orleans. It was as good a way as any for her to pass the time until Milton arrived. It was already 9:05, making him five minutes late. Had he ignored her instructions to meet her here first instead of going into work? She fervently hoped that was not the case.

Her worries vanished, however, as she turned away from the river just in time to see him parking his car on Broad Street and then heading her way with a snap to his step and offering up a friendly wave. His utter obliviousness was the confirming sign she had expected to see.

"You're looking chipper this morning," she said as he neared, disguising the sense of relief she was feeling.

He continued to smile and then stopped briefly to take in the activity on the dock below, speaking without making eye contact as if she were far below him. "Thanks, but I'm slightly confused. Why did you want to meet me here? And why did you text me that strange question? What in the world's going on?"

"I was trying out an ambitious and rather chilling theory of mine," she told him, glancing down at her phone for the time.

9:07.

She took a breath and continued. "I needed confirmation from you before I went any further."

Milton turned away from the river and the departing ship and faced her at last, but by then his smile had turned into a frown. "And my answer to your text confirmed something for you?"

"Yes."

"That seems so weird to me. Your question didn't make any sense in the first place. I had never even given the matter any consideration, and I still haven't figured out what it means."

"I can see why you'd say that. In fact, I'm greatly relieved that you *don't* know what it means."

"Should I have known?"

"I doubt it. I doubt anyone else would have, either."

"Are you gonna explain it further to me, or are you just gonna keep me hanging like this?"

Wendy checked her phone again.

9:08.

"Why do you keep checking the time like that?" he said. "Is something gonna happen soon that I don't know about?"

"Yes, and it's my opinion there's a lot you don't know about. It's part of the explanation that I'll get to shortly. But the main reason you're here with me on the bridge right this minute is so I can keep an eye on you."

His frown lines grew deeper, and he almost looked hurt. "Keep an eye on me? You make it sound like I've been doing something wrong. Have you been spying on me? I know your husband is a detective. Has he been tailing me?"

"Don't get upset," she told him. "It's nothing like that. What I'm going to tell you is not going to be easy to hear, but I want you to listen to me very carefully and tell me the truth as you know it."

Wendy could not recall seeing the young man's handsome face so full of creases and doubt, and she kept recalling the descriptions of Milton from various sources as being "naïve" or "too trusting."

"Am I in some kinda danger?" he said, intensely surveying their surroundings for anything and anyone that looked suspicious.

"Just calm down and listen to me, because you're in the safest place you can be right now."

Bax sidled up to the counter at Party Palooza with the biggest smile he could manage. Both Rex and Merrie stood behind it with warm, expectant smiles of their own. It was always how they greeted their considerable batch of loyal customers they had earned with their hard work and creativity over the years.

"Bet I know why you're here this morning," Merrie said, her voice as welcoming as her smile. "You're gonna place that singing telegram, aren'tcha? Your pretty redheaded daughter was in here doing all the research for you. If you don't mind my saying, marriage appears to be agreeing with her. I think she's even more beautiful now than she was on her wedding day."

"Thank you for the compliment. I have to agree with you. My son-in-law is just as happy as she is, too. And she did a great job running interference for me on the telegram business, too," Bax said. "She picked out just the right lyrics for me, and that's the one I wanna pay for right now. I'll be sending it to my wonderful, brand-new fiancée, and I know it'll be the last thing she'd be expecting to get."

"Would that be one Miz Lyndell Slover?" Merrie said. "I still remember how pretty she looked at the reception with that gardenia behind her ear. I thought it was the perfect romantic touch."

"Yes, it was. And, of course, my fiancée is Miz Lyndell. Funny you should bring that up about the gardenia," Bax said, adding that treasured recollection to his smile. It went all the way up to his eyes. "I thought the same thing the second I saw it. In fact, it blew me away."

"My warmest congratulations to you both," Merrie added, while Rex seconded the sentiment. "We noticed how cozy the two of you were throughout Wendy's wedding. We figured it might not be long before there was another wedding in the works in your family, didn't we, Rex?"

"I have to admit we have an eye for these things," he said. "You Winchesters may end up being our best customers of all time. Or at least here in Rosalie."

Bax unfolded the copy of "What You Mean to Me" that Wendy had given him, placed it on the counter, and tapped it twice with his index finger. "This is the one I want, of course. I can almost hear that talented young man singing it right now."

"It's our most popular delivery," Merrie said. "You've certainly made an excellent choice."

"Milton really does a great job, too," Rex added. "It's such a straightforward, simple tune that everyone seems to relate to. We keep a record of customer comments, and we get the most compliments on it."

"You don't have to sell me," Bax said while reaching into his coat pocket. "Say no more. I'm assuming you'll take my check?"

"Of course. We did last time for your daughter's reception

and everything," Merrie said, reaching under the counter and producing a clipboard with forms. "You'll need to fill out all these details for us—you know, the date and time of day of the delivery, the address, and the rest of that stuff so Milton can get it all just right. There's a pen attached for your convenience."

"Thank you. I'm sure he'll do a great job. From all the reports I've gotten, he always does. After all, he's the face and voice of Party Palooza, right?" Bax said, putting his checkbook on the counter in front of him.

"He is, indeed," Rex said. "We couldn't do without him. For a brief period there, we thought we had lost him, but we upped the ante a bit to let him know we just couldn't do without him, and he came home to us."

"I can imagine. But before you tell me how much I owe you, I need to clarify something with you if you don't mind, Mr. Boudreaux."

"Of course. What's that?"

"How do I make sure Milton delivers one of those heavy rag dolls as a souvenir to my fiancée? I want to get my money's worth, you know. Do I need to pay extra for that? I'll be glad to, of course. Nothing flimsy for my Lyndell, you understand. I want only the very best."

While Merrie's face was the epitome of confusion, Rex narrowed his eyes and cleared his throat noisily. "What are you talking about, Mr. Winchester? Pay extra for what?" he said.

Bax quickly turned to Merrie and said, "Do you know what I'm talking about, Miz Boudreaux?"

"I'm afraid I don't have any idea," she said. "What do you mean—heavy? All our rag doll souvenirs are the same size and weigh the same."

"Yes," Rex added. "You can see for yourself from the ones lined up here on the counter. They're all the same. Go ahead and pick them all up if you want. There's no difference. We have no irregulars."

"Interesting word to use. Semantics is an underrated subject," Bax said.

"I'm afraid I'm not following you," Rex added.

Then Bax followed through with Rex's suggestion and picked the dolls up and set them down, one by one. "It seems you're absolutely right. These are all perfectly consistent. But I still want one that's heavier than these are." He finished with a wink.

Rex shook his head slowly. "I'm still not understanding you, sir, and I'm trying very hard."

"Don't you? Do you perhaps keep them somewhere else?" Bax continued. "I know you have that large costume and prop room in back from my previous visit when we planned my daughter's delightful reception. Maybe another grand tour would be in order. This time, to every nook and cranny. Perhaps an inspection of a closet or spare storeroom or two? Is that where you keep them? Or should I say—*it*?"

In a sudden and breathtaking sequence, Rex quickly pulled his hand back from the counter, trying to reach under it, but Bax preempted him by pulling out his gun like the professional he was. "Don't even think about it, Mr. Boudreaux. I want to see both your hands above your head right now." Then he turned to Merrie. "I'll need to ask you to do the same thing, Miz Boudreaux."

With a look of pure terror on her face, she complied, and the tone of her voice was panicky as well. "What's . . . going on?" Then she turned to her husband. "Rex? Why did you reach for the gun like that? We're not being robbed. What were you thinking?"

"You can't search these premises without a warrant. That's the law," Rex said, flashing on Bax. His tone had morphed into something loud and harsh, while his features were no longer handsome and benign. The complete transformation was on the order of startling.

"Detective Rierson has been waiting outside in his patrol car with one. We had sufficient probable cause for the judge. We have another car covering your back door just in case something went wrong in here and you got it into your head to try and escape or something equally foolish. We're onto your scheme, you know. Do you want to prolong this or come clean?" Bax told him.

Merrie continued her meltdown. "What is he talking about, Rex? What have you done?"

"For what it's worth, I don't believe that's an act you're putting on, Miz Boudreaux," Bax said. "If you really weren't a part of this, you need to make that perfectly clear to us."

"What are you talking about? A part of what? Party Palooza? Of course, I'm a part of it. Rex and I own it together. You're not making a bit of sense to me, and you're one of our best customers."

"Mr. Boudreaux," Bax began, ignoring Merrie, "on the chance that you might be working for somebody else and this isn't all of your own doing, now would be the time to tell me everything you know. It might make a difference in your sentencing down the road. But before we do or say anything else, I want both of you to come from behind the counter and leave that gun a' yours where it is. Keep your hands up while I call for Detective Rierson to come in with the warrant so we can start searching and can get the proof we need."

They both complied, but Merrie was in tears. "What have you done, Rex?" she said. "What in holy hell have you done?"

"Are we officially under arrest now?" Rex said. "If not, you need to leave my building."

"No, you're not under arrest right this second," Bax said. "But we're not going anywhere, either. Give us a little time, Mr. Boudreaux. We haven't searched the premises yet."

"Knock yourselves out," Rex added, trying to sound tough, but he came off much more like a punk who had just been cornered.

Some twenty minutes later, Bax and Ross together ushered Rex Boudreaux into the cavernous prop and costume room and directed him toward the locked closet in the far corner that one of the CID officers had just discovered.

"Unlock it for us, please," Bax said.

Rex exhaled noisily and selected a small key from his larger ring and then did as he was told. And there on several shelves were the "heavier" rag dolls that both Bax and Ross had expected to find. That Wendy had theorized they would find. That Wendy had predicted was at the heart of all this death and devious behavior. Although Aurelia Spangler had not seen completely beyond the veil with her undependable gifts, Wendy had done so with her remarkable brainpower.

"And there's the proof we needed, Mr. Boudreaux," Bax said. "We'll let you do the honors and slit open one a' these souvenirs for us. And you don't need to do it with a knife or whatever it was that Aurelia Spangler saw. A letter opener or anything handy will do nicely, I'm sure."

Rex looked around and took a pair of scissors from a nearby table, where repairs to costumes were routinely made. He made short work of cutting open one of the dolls right down the middle of its tuxedoed chest—Aurelia's vision now fully realized, though in truncated form. Begrudgingly, Rex reached in and pulled out the packet of cocaine and handed it over to Bax in resigned silence.

"You are now officially under arrest for possession. I will read you your rights, and then you can come down to the station and tell us everything you want to—with or without a lawyer." Bax turned to one of the other officers standing behind him. "Cuff him, please."

"What about his wife?" the officer asked.

"Bring her down, too," Bax added. "We'll have to sort it all out once Mr. Boudreaux has his say." Bax caught Rex's contemptuous gaze. "I assure you that you'll have your chance, sir. It all depends upon how far-reaching this all is. If you're a pawn, it might be wise for you to give up the king at this point."

Rex said nothing and sneered, but with cuffs around his wrists and a police escort guiding him none too gently toward the door, that was all he could do.

Over on the Bridge of Sighs, where an intermittent breeze was blowing in off the river below to mitigate the July heat only slightly, Wendy scanned the text from Ross that said she had been on point about everything, and that both Rex and Merrie were on their way to the station for further questioning. Then she continued to unspool things for Milton, whose eyes seemed about to pop out of his head over what she had already revealed to him.

"Whatever else it was in this town of ours, Party Palooza was also a cover for drug trafficking. The cocaine was dispensed in small packets to certain customers via your singing telegrams inside the rag dolls. The trouble with Aurelia's vision was that she and everyone else assumed that the knife to the tuxedoed shirt was to an actual man, a real person. But then I stood here on this bridge yesterday practically on this very spot and noticed what a difference that perspective and distance and size made regarding all the objects far below me—from the cruise ship to the people pouring out of it for their day ashore. That's when I realized that the knife to the shirt could well have been an image pertaining to the tuxedoed rag dolls. They were the mules, not a human being. That's why I asked you if you could remember if any of the souvenirs seemed heavier from time to time, and you said yes."

Milton grabbed the railing to steady himself and said, "It was so odd that the moment I read your text, it seemed to rush back into my head that I remembered a doll seeming heavier now and then. I even recall thinking to myself and laughing out loud once, 'This one hasn't been pushing away from the table much.'"

They both allowed themselves an awkward, fleeting chuckle, and Wendy said, "If you had said you didn't remember, we still would have proceeded with our plan to question Rex and Merrie. After all, you might have been all wrapped up in rehearsing on the way or listening to the radio to notice that something about that part of your deliveries was different."

"It's like you were riding along in the passenger seat beside me all those times, saying that just now," Milton added in amazed fashion. "That's pretty much what I did—rehearse or sing along with the radio. I admit it—I'm a show tune addict and a Broadway wannabe."

"Yes, I can easily picture you doing that and being one."

"But what I can't picture is Rex and Merrie being criminals," Milton said, sounding genuinely distressed. "They were always so nice to me—especially Merrie. Sometimes she was a little too touchy-feely for my tastes, but they bent over backward to get me to come work for them again after I skipped town in a panic like a fool over Aurelia's vision. Neither of us thought it might pertain to the dolls when it came out of Aurelia's mouth, but I can vouch for the fact that it did terrify us both when we were together in the reading room. Aurelia just couldn't quite see through the veil to what her vision really meant, but now I see why Rex and Merrie wanted me back so bad."

"That was by design, of course," Wendy told him. "With you as the face and voice of Party Palooza, no one could possibly suspect anything of a criminal nature was going on behind the scenes. It was important that you continue playing that role for them. I mean, face the facts, Milton. You are eye candy in every possible way. You were their goodwill ambassador."

Milton turned a bright pink and looked down at his sneakers. "You're embarrassing me now."

"That wasn't what I was trying to do, but it's the truth. You made everyone in Rosalie think you were the All-American boy."

"I really don't think I fit that description, if you want to know the truth," he said, looking up again as the color in his cheeks faded somewhat. "But I guess I shouldn't go into all that with you. Maybe I should leave things just as they are. Let me just be a voice in a tuxedo." There was a pause that implied further anxiety. "Do you think . . . I mean, is it possible that I could be in trouble because I delivered cocaine to customers?"

"Not in my opinion. I believe that you did so unknowingly. Isn't that the truth of the matter?"

"Yes, I never had an inkling."

"Then you were being used shamefully. All you need to do is to repeat everything you've told me down at the station and that there was no kickback to you. If necessary, you can make your bank records available to my father and my husband. I'm confident that you'll be in the clear, however."

Milton nevertheless looked horrified. "I swear to you there was never any kickback. I did get some good tips from certain people, but nothing from Rex and Merrie other than our agreed-upon commission for each delivery. So, what you're saying is that some of the deliveries were just ordinary singing telegrams with ordinary dolls—but there were others where I actually delivered cocaine to customers. No wonder there were a few instances where I delivered to the same customer more than once. Here all this time I thought they just couldn't get enough of me and my singing, but what they really couldn't get enough of was the cocaine. Do I have the complete picture now?"

"That's the way it lays out at the moment." She pointed in the direction of his car. "The next thing you need to do is head on down to the station. I'll text Ross that you're on the way. And please don't disappear like you did before. If nothing else, that'll prove guilt of some sort, and you'll be tracked down, I assure you."

"No," Milton said, trying to resist a smile that came upon him anyway. "I won't ever run away again like I did then. I want to do my part to clear all this mess up. It's been a nightmare to deal with since we found out about Aurelia."

Then, something seemed to jolt Milton, jerking his head back as if a land mine had exploded beneath his feet. "Wait . . . does that mean that Rex and Merrie were the ones who killed Aurelia Spangler? I really can't imagine them doing something like that. It gives me goose bumps all over."

"Well, you couldn't imagine them being engaged in drug trafficking, either, could you?"

"That's true enough," he said, the color again rising in his face. "But I'm feeling like I'm a damned fool, if you wanna know the truth."

"No, you shouldn't feel that way at all. You did the job you were paid to do very well. You were paid to use that beautiful voice of yours and be charming to strangers, and the rest you had no control over. Anyway, we expect to find out who really killed Aurelia Spangler very soon now," she told him as they both headed toward their cars. "We may not be through with surprises yet, either."

CHAPTER 22

Ross and Bax were sitting next to each other in the interrogation room, taking turns questioning Rex Boudreaux. At the moment, however, Rex had upset the ebb and flow of the exchanges with an unexpected but emphatic monologue of his own and would simply not relent.

"I mean it. I want it clearly understood that my wife, Merrie, is innocent in all of this. She's never known the truth. To her, Party Palooza was just that—a business meant to entertain adults and children alike. It was the same for her when we lived down in New Orleans and we worked for my aunt Mathilde. Merrie did have her periods of boredom and restlessness with it all, wanting something different now and then or thinking that we needed to move away, but she never knew what I was up to behind the scenes. She can tell you nothing because she knows nothing. I know she has to be practically jumping out of her skin waiting out there in the hallway for something to happen. Please don't punish her for what I did."

"Your concern is duly noted," Bax said. "As for your wife's involvement, we've already halfway reached that conclusion on our own, judging by her reactions to what took place earlier at Party Palooza. So, stop worrying about that for now. We want to know what you can tell us. Why don't you go back to the beginning? I assume there was one."

Rex did not look either of them in the face as he spoke to an imaginary person slightly to one side. "Yes, there was a start to it all. Mr. Winchester, I believe it was you who said back at Party Palooza that if I happened to be a pawn in all of this, it was time for me to turn in the king."

"You remember correctly. So, are you ready to do that for us? Are you ready to turn in the king?"

"Yes," he said. "But I believe you mentioned to me some sort of deal if I came clean with you?"

"You're not in a position to bargain with us very much," Bax said. "But, yes, you need to tell us everything you know about the deaths of Aurelia Spangler and Earl Jay Doxey if you expect anything at all to go your way. You're already in way over your head. So level with us—are the two murders related?"

"Yes, and I'm turning in the queen, not the king, as it happens."

"And she would be?"

"My so-called aunt Mathilde Boudreaux down in New Orleans. She's nothing of the kind. She's my stepmother from my late father's second marriage—an ill-advised one at that. She took what she inherited as seed money and became a drug dealer with it. Yeah, it surprised me when I first found out, but she's been doing it for a long time now, and then she made it too lucrative for me to refuse her offer to join her. She and I told Merrie that she was my aunt to muddy the waters and camouflage things a bit; but the two of us ran the whole racket down there behind the scenes, while Merrie seemed to be delighted with dressing up and planning the actual parties and doing most of the idea work—"

"I think you've already convinced us that your wife is innocent in all this," Ross interrupted. "You can move ahead, please."

Sounding chastised, Rex continued. "Well, it was Mathilde who came up with the idea of hiding the cocaine deliveries in plain sight with the singing telegrams and the rag dolls. No one ever caught on down there in a city as big as New Orleans. They still haven't. It's amazing what you can hide behind a smile, even if it's just the smile of a rag doll. I'd make a run every now and then to get more of the mules when I'd sell out up here. We certainly didn't want to trust things to the U.S. Postal Service and their prying eyes. No, we took a hands-on approach. So, I'd take Merrie with me on these trips, telling her it was a fun outing to eat at Commander's Palace or Galatoire's, or see a Broadway show at the Saenger or something like that. I never worried about being caught because who would suspect rag dolls of being anything other than rag dolls. The truth is, Mathilde is the very picture of a sweet, old matron with all the gray hair pinned atop her head and the quiet voice, but inside, she has the heart of a demon from Hell itself, believe me. In fact, I still have my doubts about the way my father passed away. He did have heart problems, but I wouldn't be at all surprised if Mathilde found a way to make them fatally worse."

"Was she officially suspected?"

"No, I'm just speculating."

"And you decided to go into business with such a woman. Well, I have to say you paint a charming picture," Bax said, wincing. "I believe I can live the rest of my life without meeting her."

"You have no idea how wickedly clever she is," Rex continued. "Anyway, when she found out that you guys up here in Rosalie had sent the only games in town to Parchman and left a void in the market, she decided that I should move up here and take the town by storm with her special telegram service. She said publicly that she was 'franchising' and branching out, but behind the scenes she knew there was a lot of money to be made up here in an old, moneyed town like Rosalie. For many long decades, Rosalie paid a black-market tax to the state to keep its twenty-four-hour bars open. That was before counties could vote for being wet legally. There were even slot machines if you knew where to find them. Rosalie's always been wide open and will use any excuse to party."

"Okay, forget the history lesson. I'm aware of all that," Bax said, clearly annoyed. "Get back to your aunt or whoever she was."

Rex contorted his features for a moment and then continued. "Yeah, well, Mathilde had already gotten hold of a list of existing customers who would pay and pay big. It's a tight-knit, territorial, nasty little universe of trade, believe me. She also told me it wouldn't hurt in the least that the only party planner doing business in Rosalie had conveniently moved away for health reasons. I can't remember her name—"

"Fayette Marie LaFonda," Bax interrupted.

"Whatever. The point is, Mathilde did her research thoroughly and had every angle covered before she made a move and sent us up here."

"So you're fingering this Mathilde Boudreaux for the drug trafficking. Are you also fingering her for the murders of Aurelia Spangler and Earl Jay Doxey?" Bax said, the anger in his voice and glint in his eyes clearly evident.

"She ordered up the hits, yes. When Milton Bagdad told us about Aurelia's vision of the knife to the tuxedo shirt, it hit too close to the bone. Milton was raving about the accuracy of the cold readings with all of the other bridge players, especially the reading that pulled Vance Quimby's novel plot out of thin air. That seemed to do the trick for everyone, including me."

"Which was a scam since Aurelia and Vance were brother

and sister," Ross said, getting a word in quickly. "They had it all planned out. But the sad part is the scam worked too well. There was an element of truth in it that they hadn't counted on—just enough to get two people killed."

"Yes, but I didn't know that at the time. I reported to Mathilde what Milton had said, and she was convinced that Aurelia might be a real psychic and that she had stumbled onto a vision of one of our cocaine customers opening up one of the tuxedoed dolls with a knife or whatever to get to the packet. Mathilde was also concerned that the entire truth behind Party Palooza might be revealed sooner or later if this psychic was allowed to hang around too long. Mathilde didn't want to take any chances, and I have no idea who she paid to do it, where they came from, or where they are now, but I was told that whoever it was would show up and force Aurelia to overdose on cocaine at gunpoint, and as you now know, that's what happened. It was supposed to look like a suicide with the note she was forced to write and all. Of course, these hit men are experts in covering their tracks. You may never track them down, but Mathilde will be easy enough to find down there in New Orleans."

"The suicide angle fooled us for a little while," Ross said. "But not that long. It didn't seem to add up when people like my wife and Aurelia's brother kept insisting that it just wasn't like the woman to take herself out like that. And they were both right. Human behavior doesn't change overnight."

Rex managed an indifferent shrug and then continued. "I didn't know Aurelia Spangler, so I have no further comment about that. She was just a name to me. As for Mr. Doxey, I can only guess that he had the misfortune to dig too deep until he'd made contact with someone here in Rosalie who got back to Mathilde, and she had him taken out, too. I have no further info for you on that, either, but maybe the FBI can get to the bottom of it here and down in New Orleans. This racket has as any many tentacles as a giant squid, and it's really good at sucking the life outta people."

Instead of taking all the revelations in stride, Bax's composure became increasingly hostile. "Yet you continued to stick with it for the money. And now you're ratting out your stepmother to save yourself. Aren't you the man of the hour?"

"But you said if I leveled with you—"

"Don't flatter yourself. I might say anything to get a confession from the likes a' you. I suppose you realize that you are still an accessory to murder both before and after the fact. I have no control over what a jury might decide, in any case. And I won't make light of the fact that your stepmother had a good friend of mine killed, not to mention Miz Aurelia. This is very personal to me because it hurts me where I live." He made a fist and thumped his chest twice, knowing full well how threatening the gesture appeared. "So take my advice and get yourself a good lawyer, because I can assure you this is going to trial."

There was a prolonged, awkward silence among the three men, but Bax finally broke it while flexing his fingers after the tight fists he had made. "Humor me, Mr. Boudreaux. I have a tough question for you, but something tells me you're up to answering it honestly."

"Why not? Do I have anything to lose at this point?"

"No comment. But I would like to know what you—or this Mathilde relative of yours—would have done if Milton Bagdad had somehow discovered what was going on with some of his deliveries. Hypothetically, let's say something happened to one of the dolls, and it got busted open somehow and the packet got exposed. Suppose Milton figured things out. What would you have done about it?"

Rex answered as if he were commenting on the weather. "First of all, I doubt anything would ever have happened to one of the dolls the way you're proposing. Mathilde sewed those suckers up like nobody's business, and she taught me how to sew, too, in case anything ever happened up here. But one of the reasons we hired Milton—in addition to his voice, of course—was the fact that he was pretty young and naïve and did exactly what he was told and nothing more."

Bax nodded but did not seem satisfied. "Okay then. I'll take this one step further because you can't seem to get past the world-class sewing aspect of all this. Pretend for one second that something *did* happen and Milton *did* catch on. What would have happened to him at that point?"

Rex continued his stoic approach. "Assuming he wouldn't have gone to the police first, Mathilde would have put out a hit out on him. Of course, it would have been made to look like an accident. Car crashes happen all the time, you know. But you have to understand that Milton handled the dolls only as long as it took to get to the delivery address. The risk was extremely small that something along the lines of an 'outing' would take place. The rest of the time, I guarded them jealously in the locked closet. Merrie wasn't allowed to handle them, either. At least not the mules—just the ones for the ordinary deliveries. It was just highly unlikely that any harm would have come to either type." Then there was a surge of emotion in Rex's voice. "But regarding Merrie, you have to believe her and me when we both say that she wasn't aware of any of this. Don't punish her, punish me. I'm just trying to protect her."

"You should have thought of that when you got her involved in all this in the first place—with or without her knowledge."

"No sanctimonious lectures, please. But I'm not lying to you. She'll be lost without me as it is."

"I suspect you're overestimating yourself, but if she had no knowledge of this, then she's as innocent as we believe Milton Bagdad is. You used them both to cover your dirty work,"

Bax said. "But don't think for a second they'll get off scot-free, either. They'll have to live for the rest of their lives with the parts you made them play. You and your stepmother have done some serious damage here and in New Orleans to both the living and the dead. And I'll expect you to provide us with a list of all your cocaine customers here in Rosalie, by the way."

Rex was shaking his head as he closed his eyes. "You won't like a couple of the names that show up, I can guarantee you that. I wonder if you'll just end up looking the other way, depending upon which side of town people live on. I'm sure you catch my drift."

Bax and Ross briefly exchanged glances, and Bax said, "We'll deal with that when we see the list. But here's a bulletin for you: There are already way too many people who buy their way into and out of what they want as far as the justice system in this country is concerned. It's time some people stopped getting free passes because they think the laws don't apply to them or they're above the law."

Wendy had been sitting on one of the benches in the hallway outside, then rose to her feet quickly when Merrie Boudreaux emerged in tears from the interrogation room, where her recent session with Bax and Ross had just taken place. At the moment, she seemed inconsolable.

"Here, come be with me for a few minutes," Wendy said, sitting back down and patting the spot beside her.

"What am I gonna do?" Merrie said, taking a handkerchief out of her purse and sniffling into it. "Here, all this time I've been involved in a murderous, criminal lie, and now it looks like Rex will be going to prison for who-knows-how-long. That's what your father and your husband just told me. What can I do with my life now?"

"I'm sure this is a shock to you. I know it wasn't easy to hear the things Daddy and Ross had to tell you about Rex and

Mathilde. Just know that they realize you were innocent in all of this and go from there. Your lawyer will help you navigate what's ahead of you."

"But where do I go after this is over? My whole world has disappeared just like that," Merrie said, snapping her fingers. "Everything I believed in and worked toward is completely gone. I was so naïve. I never asked Rex any questions about that closet he kept locked. He said it was where he kept extra cash and bullets for his gun inside a safe. And I believed him. I never thought anything about the trips we took now and then down to New Orleans to see Mathilde and pick up more of those rag dolls. We ate a lot and drank a lot, and I thought it was all because Rex knew how much I missed being down there. But it was all a lie—every single bit of it. So how on earth do I start over from all this death and deception?"

Wendy rubbed her arm gently and said, "I do have something that might work for you. I spent some time with Sarah Ann O'Rourke, one of my bridge pupils, when she was at the Rosalie Women's Shelter, and I got to know the place pretty well. They are always looking for help there. I could make an appointment and put in a good word for you with the director, if you'd like. Maybe something will work out to let you get your bearings. It's a thought anyway."

Merrie dabbed at her eyes and then stared straight ahead. "But what could I do there? I'm not a nurse or a cook, or a social worker or anything like that. Isn't that what those places need more than anything else? I'm sure I'd be unqualified."

"Yes, they do need all those professions represented, but I know for a fact that you can entertain. You've done it for both adults and children for a long time now. Many shelters and homes have an activities director who plans all sorts of fun things for the women to do. I could suggest it on your behalf. It couldn't possibly hurt."

Merrie turned to Wendy with a hopeful expression on her

face. "Do you think I could pull off something like that, that is, if they're even interested?"

"I know you could. You covered all the bases at my wedding reception, and I've heard people all over Rosalie rave about the parties you planned for them. Whatever else was going on with your husband behind the scenes, your role in the business was successful, legitimate work that you accomplished with a great deal of confidence. I wouldn't hesitate to recommend you to anyone I know. Plus, many of the women at the shelter bring their children to stay there with them. You'd already have a built-in audience, even if it's on a much smaller scale."

Now Merrie had made the journey from utter devastation to a tentative smile. "If you could get me an appointment to discuss something like that . . . I know I'd be very grateful."

"It's as good as done."

But it did not take long for Merrie to lapse into sorrow again. "I still can't believe what's happened. I don't think I'll ever get over it, no matter what I end up doing from here on out."

"It'll take some time for you to heal up from all this. But you have to start somewhere. And whether the shelter works out or not, I know of at least one wedding and reception coming up that you can plan—the one between my daddy and Lyndell Slover, my editor. I'm sure they wouldn't think of giving anyone else but you their business. Everything's not as bleak as it appears."

Merrie's sigh seemed to take the weight of the world off her shoulders. "I hadn't even thought of that. But you may be right. I really don't need Rex to plan these affairs anymore. I won't go into it with you or anyone else, but I . . . well, I'd fallen out of love with him for any number of reasons over the years. It's better left unspoken some of the thoughts I've had lately as a result of that. Let's just say that I didn't act on them, and I thank God I didn't."

Her pause was prolonged, as she seemed lost in thought. "I don't think Party Palooza as a brand will be viable anymore anywhere, certainly not once it gets around town what was really going on; but maybe I could offer up my party-planning services informally by word of mouth. Do you think that might work?"

"I think you have a plan and a backup plan now," Wendy said. "I'll be happy to help with the word-of-mouth part, too. Something tells me you'll be on solid footing once all the smoke has cleared."

CHAPTER 23

Exactly three weeks after Wendy had begun teaching her newbies the game of bridge, she decided that it was time to integrate those who had stuck with it into the Bridge Bunch at large who met out at the RCC. With Aurelia Spangler dead and her brother, Vance Quimby, having returned to Nebraska following the solution to her murder, only Charlotte Ruth, Sarah Ann O'Rourke, and Milton Bagdad remained.

Wendy had given an extensive amount of thought to the trio's partner assignments and had finally settled on the following: Charlotte would be paired with the patient RCC director, Deedah Hornesby, while Sarah Ann would be teamed with Hollis Hornesby, her son. As for Milton, she decided that she would be his partner, while the often-discombobulated Crystal Forrest and her favorite partner, Verna Kaye Carmichael, would round out their table.

In fact, Verna Kaye, who worshiped Crystal's restoration of Old Concord Manor, along with the resurrection of its gardens at the hands of the talented hipster, Arden Wilson, was practically the only player in the entire club who was willing to put up with her forgetful antics and poor play. Not only that, she dressed up for an ordinary game of bridge as weirdly as Crystal always did, and in all other meaningful ways functioned as her sycophant deluxe.

But Wendy had a method to her madness in that she figured if Crystal followed form, then she and Milton would have a much better chance of winning the day. She wanted nothing more than for Milton to enjoy his first outing as a full-fledged member of the Bridge Bunch, while she was certain that Deedah and Hollis would mentor Charlotte and Sarah Ann, respectively, at the other table.

The cards hadn't even been shuffled for the first deal, however, when Crystal, dressed in a sparkly formal gown, opera gloves, and her hair teased and swirled beyond normal salon practices as usual, took the stage.

"I just *cahn't* think of what to do," she began in that faux British accent of hers, which she exaggerated further by talking through her nose. "They've arrested my *godnuh*, Arden Wilson, for possession of cocaine. Everyone knows he's the best *godnuh* around. He did wonders first for Miz Liddie Langston Rose until her death, and then I hired him to come make a showplace of Old Concord Manor again. Now, tell me, where am I to find anyone like Arden here in Rosalie or anywhere else, for that matter?"

"I can't help you with that," Wendy said. "There were rumors that Arden might be on drugs back when he was working for Miz Liddie at Don José's Retreat. He was probably on the list that Rex Boudreaux turned over to the CID when they solved the murders of Aurelia Spangler and Earl Jay Doxey. As you already know, my husband and father and I all had a hand in solving those cases."

"I'm well aware of that accomplishment, and kudos to you all for putting all that dreadful druggery to bed," Crystal said. "Wait . . . is that a word? Druggery? Or do I mean thuggery?"

Wendy struggled mightily to keep a straight face. "Thuggery is a word. Druggery is not."

"But they do rhyme. Do I at least get any credit for that?"

"Only if you're writing a Dr. Seuss book," Wendy said, pleased with herself for finding just the right response. She could only take so much of Crystal's calculated obliviousness.

"What about drudgery? Is that what I could have meant?"

"I'm not a mind reader, Miz Crystal, but, yes, drudgery is definitely a word."

"Anyway, *cahn't* they make an exception in Arden's case?" Crystal continued, getting back on track. "Or put him on probation or something? He never bothered to teach me a thing about what all he did to keep my flowers and bushes and trees up to snuff, so other than watering with a hose, I know nothing about keeping greenery alive. I can see my beautiful *goddens* just going to rack and ruin."

Wendy sensed that she needed to take control of the situation immediately, or they would never get around to playing bridge. It would soon turn into a one-woman show starring Crystal Forrest doing an imitation of Hyacinth Bucket in *Keeping Up Appearances.* "Now just calm down. I'm sure there's someone who works for one of the nurseries here in town who can help you out in the interim."

"You mean while Arden serves some misbegotten sentence in prison somewhere, don't you?" Crystal continued, her voice approaching a nearly hysterical pitch.

"What you mentioned before is possible. He could get a suspended sentence or be put on probation for a first offense. I can ask Ross about it if you want, and then I'll get back to you."

"Oh, would you please do?" she said, clasping her hands together dramatically.

"I'll be happy to."

But it wasn't over, and they hadn't gotten any closer to playing bridge yet. "What if something dreadful happens to Arden in prison? He's a young lad, and they say that the young ones don't fare well behind *bahhz*. What if he's maimed or killed, or something even worse than that?"

"There's something worse than being killed?"

"You know what I mean."

"Let's don't go there."

Crystal shuddered. "Indeed not."

"In any case, you've been watching too many crime shows on TV."

Wendy caught Milton's gaze across the table and saw that he was smiling back. She was glad that he didn't seem fazed by Crystal's antics so far. "I've seen Mr. Wilson's work at your home, Miz Crystal," Milton began, "and I agree that he is one helluva gardener. Maybe they'll go easy on him since he has contributed substantially to tourism here in Rosalie. I believe your gardens at Old Concord Manor get raves from the tourists all the time."

But instead of soothing her, Milton's praise just seemed to inflame Crystal all the more. She was even fanning herself with her right hand, a gesture she frequently trotted out when she wanted to be the center of attention, which was always.

"Exactly. And that's why I *cahn't* afford to lose him at this point in time. You should've seen the *goddens* when I first started restoring the house. Nothing but weeds and dead bushes and twigs and just a ghost of what they once were. I researched what they looked like in their prime at the Historical Society's Photography Display of Old Rosalie at the First Presbyterian Church, you know. But Arden brought them back to life, and now they're the talk of the town. I *cahn't* afford to lose that *grahnd* honor, so I'm just beside myself."

Wendy decided to try another ploy, one she thought might just work. "Do you not want to play today? I can call up one of the subs if you'd like. Or someone from another table whose dummy can bid for us, and you can go home and lie down until your attack of the vapors lets up."

Happily, that seemed to put out the flame. "Oh, I didn't mean to imply that I'm not feeling up to snuff when I said I was beside myself. Of course I want to play. I always want to play. I do so want to get better at this game, you know."

"I'm sure we all want that for you," Wendy said, while giving Milton a sly wink. After all, she had taken him aside well before the game to try to explain Crystal Forrest to him, hoping against hope he would be somewhat prepared for whatever she threw at them.

"Well, then, let's draw for dealer and get this show on the road," Crystal said, sipping the mint julep Carlos Galbis had prepared for her.

As it happened, Crystal drew the highest of the four cards—the king of hearts—and therefore became the first dealer. It was no surprise to anyone, however, when two people ended up with thirteen cards, while the other two—Milton and Wendy—had twelve and fourteen, respectively.

"Have I misdealt again?" Crystal said. "Now, why does that always seem to happen to me?"

"A matter of concentration, I'd guess," Wendy said, as evenly as possible. "But don't worry about it. Milton can just take one of my extra cards, and then we'll be on our way."

"I just hope I get some faces and points. The kings, queens, and jacks all ran away and hid from me *lahst* time," Crystal added. "Do you think it's possible the gods of bridge don't like me?"

Wendy told Crystal politely that she was not to even consider such a possibility, but her own internal monologue kept on reviewing the question. For nearly three years running, her not unreasonable ambition to become a competent bridge player had been either delayed or obstructed by the far more serious subject of death—and not due to natural causes. It was a sobering fact of life for her, but she had dealt with all the challenges admirably and had become Rosalie's most famous amateur sleuth of record as a result.

Still, it was her fervent hope to be allowed to play bridge

in peace—with nothing more eventful to deal with than an underbid, an overbid, a renege, or a miscounted trump. If that was to be the case, she was off to a great start with Milton as her partner. After Crystal's misdeal was straightened out easily, Milton went on to bid his hand perfectly—one heart—which she was able to support with a two-heart bid. The partnership had gone on to bid game at four hearts, and Milton had played and made the contract, plus an overtrick.

Then, the first time she was dummy, Wendy wandered over to the nearby table where her other two protégés—Sarah Ann and Charlotte—were sitting, and she promptly did some kibitzing.

"Don't worry. They're both acquitting themselves beautifully," Deedah told her as she approached quietly.

"It's actually been very exciting," Sarah Ann said while following suit with a club during the current hand. "I've won a game, and so has Charlotte. We've kept everything in mind that you taught us."

"Absolutely correct. We haven't let you down, teacher dear," Charlotte added. "Though I have to admit, I was very nervous at first."

"Yes, I dearly wish now I'd had you for a bridge instructor from the beginning," Hollis said with a dramatic flourish. "I'm afraid I was flying by the seat of my pants when I first started out decades ago."

By the time Wendy had returned to her table, it was quite obvious that Crystal's play wasn't going to improve, principally because she'd ordered up and started on a second mint julep from the masterful Carlos. Oh, well—what else was new? They'd all just have to muddle through somehow.

Two hours later, the latest Saturday session of the Bridge Bunch had come to an end with enjoyable results for nearly everyone—including all three of Wendy's earnest pupils.

Even Crystal, herself, had managed to bid and make at least one contract without having to apologize to everyone for spilling drops of her julep on the cards or forgetting to write down the score properly. Perhaps the unthinkable was happening and she was evolving into a player who was actually paying attention. Only time would prove that, however.

But Wendy had some unfinished business to attend to and asked Milton to linger a bit, taking him aside as the others were saying their goodbyes and leaving. He had kept putting her off regarding his future plans, and she was becoming a bit concerned about him.

"You still haven't told me what you're going to do now that Party Palooza is closed down," she said. "There won't be any roles for you to play in children's parties or telegrams for you to deliver now. Even if you have a little saved up, you'll have to go back to work at something."

"Well, I do have a little in the bank, but I've been giving my future a lot of thought," he said. "I didn't want to say anything to you or anyone else until I was sure, but I've finally decided to go back to school and get a master's in theater at LSU. My wonderful parents have agreed to finance me, bless them—and what I'm leaning toward doing with my degree is to teach somewhere. I know myself like nobody else does, and I don't think I'm good enough to make it all the way to Broadway—at least not now. But maybe I can help someone else get there."

Wendy drew back in surprise. "But you have a beautiful voice, and that's not just my opinion. Everyone says so. You're still just starting out. Don't you think you owe it to yourself to see how far it takes you?"

"Don't get the wrong idea. Nothing is written in stone. I could change my mind," he added. "That is, after I get my degree. Nothing's to stop me from going to New York and waiting on tables while showing up for the cattle calls if I think I'm good enough by then. But in the meantime, what's taken place over the past month with what happened to Aurelia Spangler and Mr. Doxey has given me a much more realistic perspective on my life. As a matter of fact, on life in general. It can get brutally serious at times, as I've seen. It can scare you to death and send you running for the hills, too. So maybe I should think twice about driving around singing along with the radio and believing that I'm getting somewhere. Do I really have time to waste doing that?"

"Just please don't lose that spark and that boyish enthusiasm you have," Wendy said, not bothering to mute her pleading tone. "I know what it is to settle in life or just mark time. I was writing the society column at the *Citizen* for three thankless years until I was able to solve The Grand Slam Murders and show my curmudgeon of an editor that I was capable of being an investigative reporter. Just promise me that as you complete your courses down in Baton Rouge, you'll keep an open mind about yourself and where you're headed. Be your own strongest advocate, and I promise, you won't have any regrets later on."

"That was quite a stirring speech, Wendy. Seriously, thanks for all your confidence in me."

The two of them hugged with genuine affection, and Wendy said, "Next question: How much longer will we have the pleasure of your company at the bridge table? When will you be starting back to school?"

"Fall semester, so I have about six or seven weeks left to polish up what you've already taught me and even try for a grand slam. But don't worry. I'm sure I can find some students who play bridge down at LSU. It's a huge university, as I already know quite well."

"I'm excited for you, then," she said. "There's no doubt in my mind that you'll be a winner at whatever you end up doing."

CHAPTER 24

It was the most spectacular example of déjà vu ever, Wendy decided. Here she was over five months later in December, standing inside a wedding reception tent set up in her own yard; but this time it was heated, not air-conditioned, and the couple who had just exchanged their vows in her childhood home were her father and her editor. They were now Mr. and Mrs. Baxter Winchester, just as she and Ross had become Mr. and Mrs. Ross Rierson earlier in the year. Could it all have come full circle more neatly than that?

Back again to do the honors as the dance band of choice was Bishop Gunn, and they were no less full of their catchy rock rhythms as they had been before. At the moment, in fact, Bax and Lyndell were working out on the dance floor, along with nearly the same extensive guest list that had been invited to the Winchester family's June wedding.

Among those in attendance were the "graduates" of Wendy's somewhat compressed but effective course for bridge beginners who were still in town—namely, Sarah Ann O'Rourke and Charlotte Ruth—and they appeared to be blending in as well as when they had become permanent members of the Bridge Bunch. Milton Bagdad had also been issued an invitation but had been forced to decline with regrets because of his pressing upcoming exams at LSU. He had, however, sent along a beautiful spray of flowers and one of those "sincerest congratulations" cards.

"What will you be calling Lyndell now that's she's married to your father?" Charlotte said, standing next to Wendy as they both watched all the dancing from a certain distance.

"Not Mother, if that's what you're thinking," Wendy told her with a good-natured smile. "She and I have both agreed to just keep calling each other Wendy and Lyndell. I think we'll both be more comfortable that way. Besides, she's enough of an authority figure to me already as my editor. I don't need any sort of double whammy going for me."

"Makes sense to me."

Sarah Ann sidled up to them with a cup of punch in her hand. "When are you two gonna stop being wallflowers and find someone to dance with? I've just gone a couple of rounds with a hunk of a police officer who actually has a sense of rhythm, and I gave him my phone number when he asked."

Wendy could not help herself. "Do you mind telling me his name? I know just about every officer down at the station."

"It was Detective Ronald Pike, if you must know."

"I hope you're not kidding," Wendy said, unable to restrain her delight. "I love that man to pieces. He and Ross have been partners from time to time, so I trust him with Ross's life, not to mention my own. Let me give you some good advice, woman-to-woman: Give him a fair shot if you're the least bit interested. He's a terrific cop, of course, but underneath all that burly swagger of his is a sweetheart of a man looking for just the right woman to fall in love with. And who knows? You could end up being the one. I'm excited for you, I really am."

"I'm glad you approve so much, but it's a bit early yet," Sarah Ann said, slightly taken aback by Wendy's enthusiasm. "If we do start seeing each other regularly, it remains to be seen what my mother will think of us, though. I'll still have that holy hoop to jump through."

"I thought things were better between the two of you. At least, you haven't told me they've gone downhill."

Sarah Ann shrugged but did not seem upset by the remark. "They are better—off and on. Mother still has a slight tendency to pass judgment on everything I do, but she's gotten better. At least, she's trying to give me a little space. I think you made her realize that it wouldn't be all that long before I graduated and was out of the house and on my own. Being grateful for what she has now was something she could understand. At any rate, I'm glad you helped us talk things out."

Then, Sarah Ann turned to Charlotte. "Weddings seem to bring out these social questions for me. So, what about you? I never hear you mentioning anyone at our Bridge Bunch games."

"I've decided not to press things too much at my age," Charlotte said, striking a demure pose. "What happens, happens. But I have to say that I did enjoy playing last week with that widower who's recently joined us. We made a grand slam together at our table. When a man and a woman take all the tricks together, it does make me wonder if that's an omen of things to come."

Wendy chimed in with a big smile. "Of course, you're referring to Mr. Dawkins, the retired teacher. I agree that he's a charming addition to our growing group, and I've heard through the grapevine that he's quite a good player and earned tons of master points at duplicate as well."

"Yes, he did happen to mention that to me. So I have to thank you again for inviting him to your father's wedding. As I mentioned, I intend not to force things. I'll just try to play

my hands as best I can," Charlotte said. But she could not resist winking and added, "Meanwhile, I spy Mr. Dawkins lingering around the punch bowl, and I do believe I'm feeling
thirsty again. So off I go, and please excuse me if I can't seem
to get there fast enough."

Wendy waved playfully and said, "Bon voyage."

The romantic intrigue continued as seconds later, Ronald
Pike came over and asked Sarah Ann in gentlemanly fashion
for yet another dance, and she accepted without a moment's
hesitation. Wendy could see for herself quite clearly that
something might indeed be in the works.

No sooner had she left than Ross came up to join his wife.
"Sorry I haven't been paying proper attention to you for a
while," he said. "But I got involved in a powwow with a couple of my guys over at the carving table. Believe it or not, we
were having a debate on how rare prime rib should always be.
There was a 'well-done' faction that kept jawing about it like
they'd invented it, but we ended up taking a vote, and 'the
rarer, the better' guys won."

Wendy tried to conjure up a look of exasperation but
couldn't hold back a gentle laugh. "And you were among 'the
rarer, the better'?"

"Now, you know very well I was from serving it to me
and from the way I always order it when we eat out."

"Leave it to you men to have a prolonged discussion about
meat. On behalf of all women everywhere, I have to ask you
whatever happened to romance?"

He put his arm around her waist and drew her to him in
one smooth motion. "Are you by any chance ignoring our
fantastic October honeymoon in Hawaii? A whirlwind tour of
all four major islands?"

"Touché."

"We'll have to go back sometime. Especially to Kauai with
all those mountains and valleys. I don't think I've ever seen

such wild, beautiful scenery in one place. The memories of a lifetime."

"Why, thank you for such a nice compliment," Wendy said, enjoying their clever repartee.

"Matter a' fact, you *were* truly breathtaking. I'm still dreaming about all those walks we took on the beach in the evenings with the trade winds blowing around us. I loved the way they played with your hair and whipped it up in all different directions at once. I thought you might just be getting ready to fly away, but I didn't want you to leave without me."

It was at that moment that Bishop Gunn slowed down the frantic pace somewhat, and Ross took her by the hand and led her to the dance floor. "This seems like the right tempo, don'tcha think? Something where we can get up next to each other?"

"Yes, and I thought you were never going to break away from your buddies and ask me again."

"Not to worry. Here I am at your service."

On the floor, they found themselves not so much dancing as they were establishing an intimate choreography at close range. There was an almost palpable warmth between them that had nothing to do with the space heaters placed around the tent at regular intervals. To anyone observing from near or far, it was obvious that they were a couple who were very much in love.

"The year's almost over," Ross said at one point, his lips so close to hers that they should have been kissing.

His musky cologne was almost making her swoon, but she played it cool. "Your point being?"

"I was wondering what you thought about trying to make a baby for our New Year's resolution."

She drew back slightly, the better to gaze into his eyes and determine how serious he was. She could tell by now at a glance when he was joking. "Has Daddy been pressuring you, by any chance? We've both practically memorized his speech about how he just can't wait to start spoiling his grand-children—and the sooner, the better. He's nothing if not a broken record."

"I cannot tell a lie," Ross said, letting go of her just long enough to cross his heart. "He has mentioned it a time or two down at the station. As you know, he's a model of consistency in everything he does."

"He didn't mention it in the form of an official memo, I hope," she said, careful to maintain her sense of humor.

He gave her his sexiest smile by hitching up one side of his mouth, along with a raised eyebrow for devilish emphasis.

"That's a funny image, but no, nothing like that. I was thinking, however, that you and I might sit down and discuss the subject seriously now that you're good and settled into your job at the paper. You told me that Lyndell was more than satisfied with your work, and I've read for myself how spot-on you've become this past year. Your articles just flow effortlessly. Of course, I have to say that I expected nothing less."

"Thank you for the support. So you're hinting at some maternity leave for me, are you?"

"The thought had crossed my mind."

They continued to move slowly and comfortably to the music, but neither of them said anything for a while. When the song was finally over, Ross pointed to an empty table on the perimeter, and they moved to it quickly to take their seats.

"I definitely want to discuss it with you," Wendy told him. "But I do want to be sure we're both ready to become parents. I've seen couples rush into it because they think it's expected of them."

"That might be true of some people, but I think we'd be very good at it," he said, getting straight to it. "We both take our jobs seriously, and we're at a stable point in our lives. I don't see why there's any reason we wouldn't approach parenthood the exact same way."

"You are the sweetest man among men," she said, taking hold of his hand. "I doubt there are many others out there quite like you."

"Oh, I don't know about that. You might be surprised at how much of themselves the guys down at the station reveal over time—especially at the end of a shift in the locker room when they're whipped and dog-tired. They're about much more than guns and arrest warrants, you know. They put their lives on the line daily, but they want something gentle and reassuring to go home to when it's all said and done. The patrol cars aren't the only things that need refueling, if you ask me."

Wendy's expression was one of supreme amusement. "I don't know why, but that last comment seems strangely poetic, and service station pumps don't usually bring that out in me."

"Just call me Fill-'Er-Up Shakespeare."

Wendy continued smiling while pointing toward her father and Lyndell, still wrapped up in each other out on the dance floor. "For the record, I certainly believe what you're saying about your fellow officers. For a while, I thought Daddy would never find that kind of love again and would go without it for the rest of his life, but there he is with his arm around her waist. Not to sound too clichéd about it, but don't they make the loveliest couple?"

"They do. And we do, too. So, whaddaya think? Feel like mixing up some a' our genes soon?"

Her laugh had a subtle, teasing undertone that tailed off into a first-rate, come-hither look.

"Let's talk about it some more tonight when we snuggle under the covers. Something tells me we might just reach a definite decision."

ACKNOWLEDGMENTS

Cold Reading Murder, the third installment in my Bridge to Death mystery series, was so much fun to write since it combined certain elements of my life history. As usual, consultations with my agents, Christina Hogrebe and Meg Ruley, proved to be very fruitful and started me on my way. My editor at Kensington, John Scognamiglio, is always ready with helpful suggestions and is more than willing to do legal research for me on certain issues.

I would especially like to thank Dr. David Himelrick, lately retired at LSU in Baton Rouge, for his interesting and encouraging input regarding this novel from the mentalist standpoint. I am eagerly awaiting his reaction to the finished product in 2021. Also due nods are my publicist, Larissa Ackerman, for reaching out to an actual celebrity worked into the plot—Seth Rudetsky of the Broadway Channel on Sirius XM; and my therapist, the very capable Rebecca Avery, who shares with me a particular view of the universe that works for both of us.

Lastly, I would like to thank the younger me, who decided to accept a position one summer in New Orleans delivering singing telegrams all over the city for a company in New York City. From that unforgettable experience came part of the plot of *Cold Reading Murder*, including one particular character who reminds me of how freeform my life was back then.

Connect with Us

Visit us online at
KensingtonBooks.com
to read more from your favorite authors, see books
by series, view reading group guides, and more.

Join us on social media

for sneak peeks, chances to win books and prize packs,
and to share your thoughts with other readers.

facebook.com/kensingtonpublishing
twitter.com/kensingtonbooks

Tell us what you think!

To share your thoughts, submit a review,
or sign up for our eNewsletters, please visit:
KensingtonBooks.com/TellUs.